Copyrighted Material

Worlds Apart Copyright © 2020 by Variant Publications

Book design and layout copyright © 2020 by JN Chaney

This novel is a work of fiction. Names, characters, places, and incidents are either products of the author's imagination or used fictitiously. Any resemblance to actual events, locales, or persons, living, dead, or undead, is entirely coincidental.

All rights reserved

No part of this publication can be reproduced or transmitted in any form or by any means, electronic or mechanical, without permission in writing.

1st Edition

STAY UP TO DATE

Join the conversation and get updates on new and upcoming releases in the Facebook group called "JN Chaney's Renegade Readers." This is a hotspot where readers come together and share their lives and interests, discuss the series, and speak directly to J.N. Chaney and his co-authors.

https://www.facebook.com/groups/jnchaneyreaders/

He also post updates, official art, and other awesome stuff on his website and you can also follow him on Instagram, Facebook, and Twitter.

For email updates about new releases, as well as exclusive promotions, visit his website and sign up for the VIP mailing list. Head there now to receive a free copy of *The Other Side of Nowhere*.

Stay Up To Date

https://www.jnchaney.com/the-messenger-subscribe

Enjoying the series? Help others discover *The Messenger* series by leaving a review on Amazon.

WORLDS APART

BOOK 6 IN THE MESSENGER SERIES

J.N. CHANEY
TERRY MAGGERT

CONTENTS

The Messenger Universe Key Terms	ix
Previously on The Messenger…	xv
Chapter 1	1
Chapter 2	15
Chapter 3	33
Chapter 4	41
Chapter 5	55
Chapter 6	67
Chapter 7	85
Chapter 8	105
Chapter 9	131
Chapter 10	153
Chapter 11	171
Chapter 12	187
Chapter 13	203
Chapter 14	229
Chapter 15	243
Chapter 16	255
Chapter 17	267
Chapter 18	287
Chapter 19	295
Chapter 20	315
Chapter 21	327
Chapter 22	349
Stay Up To Date	355
About the Authors	357

THE MESSENGER UNIVERSE KEY TERMS

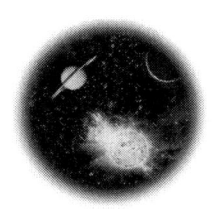

The Messenger: The chosen pilot of the Archetype.

Archetype: A massive weapon system designed for both space battle, close combat, and planetary defense. Humanoid in shape, the Archetype is controlled by a pilot and the Sentinel, an artificial intelligence designed to work with an organic humanoid nervous systems. The Archetype is equipped with offensive weaponry beyond anything known to current galactic standards, and has the ability to self-repair, travel in unSpace, and link with other weapons systems to fight in a combined arms operation.

Blobs: Amorphous alien race, famed for being traders. They manufacture nothing and are known as difficult employers.

Clan Shirna: A vicious, hierarchical tribe of reptilian beings whose territory is in and around the **Globe of Suns** and the **Pasture**. Clan Shirna is wired at the genetic level to defend and protect their territory. Originally under the control of Nathis, they are space-based, with a powerful navy and the collective will to fight to the last soldier if necessary.

Couriers: Independent starship pilots who deliver goods—legal, illegal, and everything in between—to customers. They find their jobs on a centralized posting system (See: **Needs Slate**) that is galaxy-wide, ranked by danger and pay, and constantly changing. Couriers supply their own craft, unless they're part of a Shipping Conglom. Couriers are often ex-military or a product of hard worlds.

Fade: A modification to the engine. It is a cutting edge shielding device that rotates through millions of subspace frequencies per second, rendering most scans ineffective. If the Fade is set to insertion, then the ship will translate into unSpace, where it can go faster than light. The Fade is rare, borderline illegal, and highly expensive. It works best on smaller masses, so Courier ships are optimal for installation of the Fade. One drawback is the echo left behind in regular space, an issue that other cloaking systems do not have. By using echoes as pathway markers, it is possible to track and destroy ships using the Fade.

Golden: A transhumanist race of beings who are attempting to scour the galaxy of intelligent life. The Golden were once engaged in warfare with the **Unseen**. They are said to return every 200,000 years to enact a cycle of galactic genocide, wiping out all technologically advanced civilizations before disappearing back from which they came. They destroyed their creators at some unknown point in the distant past and are remaking themselves with each revolution of their eternal, cyclical war.

Globe of Suns: A star cluster located in the far arm of the Milky Way Galaxy. It is an astronomical outlier. Dense with stars, it's a hotbed of Unseen tech, warfare, and Clan Shirna activity. Highly dangerous, both as an obstacle and combat area.

Kingsport: Located in the Dark Between, these are planetoid sized bases made of material that is resistant to detection, light-absorbing, and heavily armored. Oval in shape, the Kingsport is naval base and medical facility in one, intended as a deep space sleep/recovery facility for more than a thousand Unseen. The Kingsports maintain complete silence and do not communicate with other facilities, regardless of how dire the current military situation.

Lens: Unseen tech; a weapon capable of sending stars into premature collapse at considerable distance. The Lens is not unique—the Unseen left many of them behind in the Pasture, indicating that they were willing to destroy stars in their fight with the Golden.

Ribbon: Unseen tech that imparts a visual history of their engineering, left behind as a kind of beacon for spacefaring races.

Sentinel: A machine intelligence designed by the Unseen, the Sentinel is a specific intellect within the Archetype. It meshes with the human nervous system, indicating some anticipation of spaceborne humans on the part of the Unseen. Sentinel is both combat system and advisor, and it has the ability to impart historical data when necessary to the fight at hand.

Shadow Nebula: A massive nebula possibly resulting from simultaneous star explosions. The Shadow Nebula may be a lingering effect from the use of a Lens, but it is unknown at this time.

Unseen: An extinct and ancient race who were among the progenitors of all advanced technology in the Milky Way, and possibly beyond. In appearance, they were slender, canine, and bipedal, with the forward-facing eyes of a predator. Their history is long and murky, but their engineering skills are nothing short of godlike. They commanded gravity, materials, space, and the ability to use all of these sciences in tandem to hold the Golden at bay during the last great war. The Unseen knew about humans, although their plans for humanity have since been lost to time.

unSpace: Neither space nor an alternate reality, this is the mathematically generated location used to span massive distances between points in the galaxy. There are several ways to penetrate unSpace, but only two are known to humans.

Pasture: Unseen tech in the form of an artificial Oort Cloud; a comet field of enormous size and complexity. Held in place by Unseen engineering, the Pasture is a repository for hidden items left by the Unseen. The Pasture remains stable despite having thousands of objects, a feat which is a demonstration of Unseen technical skills. The Lens and Archetype are just two of the items left behind for the next chapter in galactic warfare.

Prelate: In Clan Shirna, the Prelate is both military commander and morale officer, imbued with religious authority over all events concerning defense of their holy territory.

PREVIOUSLY ON THE MESSENGER...

Expanding outward, battle by battle, Dash and his people decided that there was power in a name, and thus, the Cygnus Realm was born, with the Forge as its beating heart.

Using their advanced scanners, Dash discovered the first cache of Dark Metal left behind by the Golden—but finding it would not come without a cost. In the ensuing fight with Golden drones, a warning was sent to all who would listen.

The Aquarian Collective is a massive ring project under the command of a stalwart ally in the making. Al-Bijea is calm, commanding, and well aware of the Golden threat. Joining the Cyngus Realm, his people revealed many secrets, not the least of which was the missing ship *Wind of Heaven*. The Golden have been jarring ships out of unSpace and harvesting people as well as hardware.

Working together with Al-Bijea, Dash discovered that it was

not just humans that the Golden needed. In order to remain immortal, the Golden have been harvesting human nervous tissue to replenish their bodies in preparation for a return to power.

The Golden were not alone in their pursuit of immortality—so were the Bright, a race both vile and gifted, who are becoming less human with each passing generation. When the Realm found a Bright corpse, the second part of their plan was revealed. The Bright were stealing more than simple nervous tissue. They were harvesting memory, and by extension, the technology and achievements of an entire race.

Al-Bijea and the Aquarians added to the Realm knowledge when they shared a discovery from a comet they were harvesting. There, in the cold center was a machine designed to gather Dark Metal—the final piece of a puzzle that could give the Realm an overwhelming edge in the coming war. But there were obstacles to using this technology, not the least of which was the Verity, who were the next level of Golden allies. Their initial fleet was crushed in a massed battle that yielded victory—and even more secrets.

As Custodian begins to add capabilities after the victory, it is revealed that the Cygnus Realm will not be a static place. The Forge can move, and the first change of locations will be to take the fight to the Verity—at a place known as Point Vengeance.

1

Dash threw the Archetype through a wrenching turn, a combo of hard acceleration by the mech and a shot from the distortion cannon. He'd gotten damned good at using the weapon to help the mech maneuver, the sudden, sharp pulses of gravitation giving it an extra pull and accentuating his maneuvers. It threw off the Harbinger's firing solution enough that the massive blast of energy from its chest cannon missed him by at least a klick—close enough that it registered as a surge of heat and radiation against the Archetype's feet and legs.

The enemy mech spun, trying to track Dash as he maneuvered, but he knew the chest cannon had a long recharge cycle, at least five seconds. He began to count in his head—*one-one thousand, two-one thousand, three-one thousand*—

He somersaulted the Archetype and drove hard again in a random, lateral direction. Again, the Harbinger missed. If the enemy mech had had teeth, it would probably be gnashing them in raw frustration by now. Dash grinned and checked the range; each one of his unpredictable, random dodges was calculated to not just jink hard side-to-side, but to close slightly with each zig and zag. To improve its own aim, the Harbinger had slowed, letting Dash gain. He entered that sweet spot for the dark-lance, the range band where it fired with maximum effect—not far enough to attenuate its impact, and not so close that the beam hadn't stabilized fully and wasted power as radiant heat.

He fired and was grimly satisfied to land a solid hit on the Harbinger. It staggered and spun around as the mech was shaken down to its quantum bones.

Dash streaked in for the kill while he had the chance. As he did, he checked on the second Harbinger—the one he'd already damaged. It raced on, well ahead, trailing a vaporous wake of gases and shimmering globules of fluids. It seemed to be aimed at a big, icy planet orbiting the nearby star, one marked as uninhabited on the stellar charts.

Fine. It wasn't posing a threat, so Dash ignored it for the moment, concentrating on the Harbinger he'd just hit. Sentinel had tweaked the dark-lance to make it more effective against the enemy mech's Dark Metal-infused armor, but Dash still aimed carefully, selecting the legs as his target. The Archetype's fire-control system, now also upgraded, instantly turned his intent into a firing solution.

He fired the dark-lance, expecting another disabling hit, bringing the Harbinger incrementally closer to defeat.

Instead, it simply exploded.

Dash blinked. "Whoa. What the hell happened?"

"Uncertain," Sentinel said. "The first hit must have done more damage than it appeared."

"Yeah, no kidding." Dash veered the Archetype, avoiding the expanding cloud of debris that had been the Harbinger. "I mean, compared to the first time we fought one of these things, this has been—and I probably shouldn't even say this so I don't jinx it—this has been easy."

"Jinx it?"

Dash smiled. "Yeah. If you say something out loud about a situation that's good, you might cause it to turn bad."

"How is that possible? Is there some sort of telepathic influence involved, that can alter reality?"

Dash laughed. "Right on cue!"

"What do you mean?"

"I knew you were going to say something like that—wonder what the hell I was talking about and if I meant something literal."

"Ah, this was an idiom."

"More like a bit of superstition. It's along the lines of, if you manage to pay your bills and have some credits left over, don't mention it in front of the fusion drive, because it'll break down."

"That does not follow known human logic."

"Not one bit," Dash agreed, but his laughter faded as he took in the second Harbinger's trajectory. "Speaking of things that don't follow, what the hell is he up to? He looks like he intends to just fall right into that planet's atmosphere. Could there be a Golden outpost or something on the surface?"

"Very unlikely. There are no Dark Metal signatures—"

Sentinel cut off abruptly, a sign she'd noticed something else and was evaluating it. Dash just waited.

"There are, however, weak power emanations from the planet. They cycle at a constant frequency, suggesting they may not be natural."

"Huh. Well, I don't want to let that bastard get away anyway, so let's kill two birds here, shall we?"

"Kill two—?"

"I'll explain later," Dash said, chuckling and shaking his head.

DASH DECELERATED the Archetype but kept it on the track that would bring it into the planet's atmosphere. The loss of velocity meant the mech would steepen its angle of entry, which would have been a problem in the *Slipwing* or any other conventional ship. For the Archetype, though, it was barely an inconvenience.

"I'm seeing intermittent signals at best," Dash said, frowning at the heads-up. "He's down there, but whatever crap is in the atmosphere is getting the way, isn't it?"

"Yes. The planet is too cold to maintain water in liquid form, especially near the top of its atmosphere, so there is considerable wind-borne particulate ice attenuating the sensor returns."

"I wonder if he learned that from us," Dash said, thinking back, again, to his first battle against one of the enemy mechs called Harbingers. He'd used a brown dwarf in much the same way, exploiting its natural emissions of energy and radiation to conceal the Archetype while he recovered from a battle he was, at the time, losing.

"It is possible. Technologically, both of these Harbinger are identical to the one that you first fought near the Forge. However, their tactical behavior has varied from what we've seen them previously exhibit. It wouldn't be surprising if their respective AIs were sharing information in an attempt to adapt to your uniquely human approach to fighting—at least until their technology can be upgraded."

"Makes sense," Dash said. There had to be the Golden equivalent to the Forge out there somewhere, working hard to upgrade and improve their Harbingers and other military tech. It underscored why Dash and his cohorts of the Cygnus Realm had to stay on their toes and not take anything for granted; these two Harbingers might be older versions, less capable and easier to defeat, but the next ones might not be.

"Ten seconds to the upper atmosphere," Sentinel said. "I no longer see any sensor returns from the Harbinger."

"He must have dived even deeper," Dash replied. "I really don't want to lose this guy. I'd love to take one of these things more or less intact, because if there's any way to stay ahead of these bastards on the tech curve—"

The Archetype shuddered and rocked as it plowed into the first wisps of atmospheric gas. Dash shallowed out its trajectory slightly, at the same time slowing the mech. He wanted to reduce the friction of its passage through the atmosphere; too much superheated, ionized air around the mech would just further diminish the effect of its sensors.

Now muffled clicks and thumps rose as the Archetype raced through roiling clouds laden with ice chunks. The stratospheric winds of this planet were ferocious, racing along at hundreds of klicks per hour, fast enough to keep big pieces of ice aloft. It seemed counterintuitive, this high in the atmosphere, but Dash was no planetary scientist—this might be a treasure trove of research-worthy data, but to Dash it was just another battlefield. He kept his attention on the heads-up, hunting for any hint of the elusive Harbinger. Their last clear sensor return had been less than a hundred klicks from here—

Something slammed into the Archetype, hard, pitching it into a slewing skid. Dash recovered and frantically scanned the heads-up. Fragments of a missile spun off into the roaring sky. Sentinel tracked the trajectory to its source and tagged the Harbinger on the display, a flickering signal among the clouds several kilometers below them. As he dove, he did a quick check of the Archetype, concentrating on the left leg where he'd *felt* the impact through his Meld with the mech. Superficial damage, nothing more.

"Why didn't that missile detonate?" he asked Sentinel.

"Unknown. It is most likely it hadn't yet travelled far enough to arm itself, possibly because it was fired inside a planetary atmosphere."

"What, the Golden are worried about safety? I find that hard to—*dammit*."

He skidded the Archetype hard aside, narrowly missing a burst of fire from the Harbinger and darting among the thickening clouds below. It was just point defense fire, though, little threat to Dash's mech.

"Oh, okay—it's got weapon problems. We've probably disabled that damned chest cannon, so they're probably just trying to buy time to get it working again."

Dash knew from hard experience that the chest cannon, the Harbinger's most potent weapon, could disable the Archetype with a single, well-placed shot. That meant he had a window of opportunity here. Powering up the mech's drive, he raced after the Harbinger, accelerating hard. The clouds became a soft blur and ice pellets hammered on the Archetype hard enough to vaporize on impact, leaving the mech trailing a billowing contrail of water vapor.

The Harbinger powered on ahead of him, flickering as it passed through clouds. A sonic shockwave now built around both, abruptly parting and passing down the mech's length as it passed into supersonic flight. The Harbinger swung hard aside, friction making the air ploughing ahead of it suddenly glow. Dash veered to follow. The Golden mech tried frantically to break contact, but Dash stayed doggedly on its tail, closing the distance.

They punched through the eyewall of a massive storm. A vast column of clear air rose to the upper edge of the atmosphere, the cloudless sky a pale blue-grey. The Harbinger suddenly climbed, zooming straight up, apparently heading back for space. Dash grimly followed. He was determined to disable this Harbinger, not destroy it, and recover whatever tech he could. This wasn't just about Dark Metal, this was about getting a leg up on the AI that drove these Golden constructs. This chase was about *knowing*, instead of guessing at what made them tick.

Less than a klick away now, the Harbinger abruptly slid

aside and vanished back into the eyewall. At the last instant, Dash saw the wind shear warning and decelerated hard. The rushing river of air, a massive jet stream tearing along the top of the atmosphere, caught the Archetype and cartwheeled it sideways.

"Are you shi—"

"Is this your new combat methodology?" Sentinel cut in.

"What? Firing and sweating and being generally pissed off?" Dash asked while somersaulting toward the Harbinger.

"Yes to all of those things, but I refer specifically to what Leira calls your *potty mouth*, a term which makes little sense given that Freya says you can kill artificial plants," Sentinel said.

"What? She swears like a—well, a sailor, but then again she is one, technically—"

"As are you. Note, we have entered the top of a thermal updraft, which feeds a—"

A dazzling flash enveloped the Archetype. For an instant, Dash thought the Harbinger had reactivated its chest cannon. But there was no impact, no discharge of energy that engulfed the mech. It was just a pulsing flash and a spike in electromagnetic discharge.

"Oh, that's lightning," he said. "Hell, that's lightning like I've never seen before."

"Yes," Sentinel replied. "The upper portion of this storm is highly energetic atmospheric gases being strongly charged by static electric effects—"

Then came another searing flash; this time, Dash felt a deep bass boom through the Archetype's structure.

"—which is interfering with scanner operations. This planet is well suited to lightning on a grand scale."

Massive hail hammered the Archetype, lofted by hurricane-force updrafts that swirled around them in a tumult. Worse, though, ice was now accumulating on the mech, supercooled water droplets hitting its hull and instantly freezing. The musical pinging accelerated into a long, steady noise as the storm intensified.

"How is this thing rated for ice build-up?" he asked. "Had it happen in the *Slipwing* once, led to a pretty hairy minute where she didn't want to fly on thrusters alone."

"It should have little direct effect. However, it may further degrade sensor efficiency."

It was a terrible environment for even *trying* to pursue a wounded foe like the Harbinger. Dash's bubble of awareness had shrunk to about a klick, a claustrophobically tiny volume compared to the virtually infinite expanse of space through which he was used to flying and fighting. On instinct, he deployed the power-sword and charged it, then took the Archetype straight up.

"I really don't want to lose this guy, but this is getting too tight even for me. Remember, this, Sentinel—Dash is admitting that sometimes discretion really is the better part of valor."

A dark blur flashed past and shook the Archetype. Dash lashed out with the power-sword at the same instant and was rewarded with a shock of collision through it, the blade biting through—something.

The Archetype spun through another cartwheel. With both

left leg actuators abruptly offline, the Harbinger managing to get in a solid hit as it flashed by. Dash recovered and raced after it, chasing it straight up the core of the storm. Lightning flashed like detonations; thunder boomed as distant blasts. Once more, they punched through supersonic flight and, again friction began to heat the mech, quickly puffing away the accumulated ice as steam.

Any second now they should reach the top. *Should*, Dash thought. There were no guarantees in this atmosphere.

The Archetype erupted into clear air shot through with rippling crimson light, punctuated by fleeting, fountain-like jets of bright blue. A distant memory—such strange phenomena sometimes happened at the very tops of big storms, the curtains and jets and fountains given equally-strange names like elves and sprites. The effect was strikingly beautiful, but Dash didn't have time to admire it. The Harbinger was dead ahead, still rocketing straight up, apparently determined to return to space.

A poor tactic, Dash thought, but he could sense desperation in the alien mech, as its remaining weapons had scant chance of finishing the Archetype off. Maybe the Harbinger's AI was damaged, and this last effort was a failsafe built for escape, not victory.

Dash shrugged to himself. It didn't matter. If he could just catch up to this thing—and he would, sometime within the next minute or so—he could disable it with the power-sword then lug it back to the Forge for detailed study.

Or, it was up to something.

But Dash would never have the chance to find out. A few

seconds later, something slammed into the Harbinger, shoving it hard aside and ripping chunks of it free. Its left arm simply spun away. A collision warning crashed across the Meld and Dash flung the Archetype into a hard, lateral acceleration that yanked it away from the trajectory of whatever had just struck his opponent.

The crippled Harbinger decelerated then began to fall back into the atmosphere.

"You have got to be shi—"

"Again with the potty mouth? It truly is your default setting," Sentinel chided as Dash decelerated the Archetype in turn, then reversed course and plunged back after the Harbinger. Before it dropped back into the clouds, he saw that its emissions had dropped to nearly zero, its power levels flat. It was falling, and would continue to fall until aerodynamic forces ripped it apart and the debris struck the planet's surface like a shower of meteorites.

"Sometimes, you need words with a bit more *oomph*," Dash ground out.

"But the sound you made sounded nothing like *oomph*. In fact, it was likely the beginning of your third favorite curse, invoking an archaic terminology for excrement. In case you were wondering, I have no experience with excreta, or any other body functions for that matter. You may be interested to know that—"

"Sentinel," Dash said, as the mech streaked down at maximum thrust.

"Yes?"

"This isn't the time for a lecture on bodily functions," Dash growled, making a desperate lunge for the dying Golden mech—but the Archetype couldn't gain velocity fast enough. The Harbinger plummeted into the clouds and vanished. Dash raced back in behind it, trying to follow, but was again immersed in howling, lightning-charged gloom that squelched any signal he might have followed.

"Shit!"

"Now *that* seems appropriate," Sentinel said.

The Harbinger could have been blown by the spiraling winds in any direction. Desperate, he picked an arbitrary heading and burned that way, emerging back into clearer air. There was no sign of the Harbinger, though—just a few flickers of sensor return, then it was gone, lost in the vast layers of cloud below.

"I can offer an estimate of where the Harbinger is likely to impact," Sentinel said. "So it should at least be possible to find and recover the remaining debris."

"Yeah, well, just put a pin in that for now and add it to the list of Dark Metal recovery sites." He shook his head. "So close to having an intact Harbinger, too. Damn it all, and *damn* these winds."

Dash sighed and took the Archetype back into a steep climb, racing up the flank of the storm and back toward space. "So what the hell happened to it? What hit it up there? I didn't see any threat alert for weapons fire or a missile track."

"It was neither. The Harbinger had the great misfortune of intersecting the orbital track of a damaged satellite," Sentinel replied.

"A satellite—wait. I thought this planet was uninhabited," Dash said.

"That is how it is recorded in the available stores of data, yes."

"So why would there be a satellite orbiting it?"

"Unknown. Perhaps it was a survey satellite deployed by some party as a means of examining the planet for future colonization," Sentinel said.

"Okay, I can buy that. And that Harbinger just happened to collide with it? What were the odds of that?"

"Fifty-fifty," Sentinel replied.

Dash gaped. "Fifty-fifty. How do you figure *that*?"

"It either collides with the satellite, or it doesn't."

"I really don't think that's how statistics work." Dash narrowed his eyes. "Wait. Are you making a *joke*, Sentinel?"

"Did you find it humorous?"

"I—yeah, actually I did." He laughed and shook his head. "Good one, Sentinel!"

"I am glad you found it agreeable."

As he set course to return to the Forge, Dash was still pissed at losing the Harbinger like that—but Sentinel's genuine, and actually pretty *good* attempt at a joke left him smiling anyway.

2

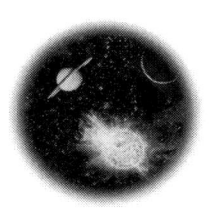

Dash kind of missed the War Room—a crew lounge in one of the habitat sections of the Forge that they'd repurposed into a command center. They'd made big decisions there—and hard ones, too. But it had also been familiar, and almost cozy. By comparison, this new Command Center was a vast, echoing space. Dash found it far more sterile and unwelcoming. However, it was far better equipped, being designed not just as a place to have conferences and make decisions, but to also put them into play.

"Custodian," Dash asked as he entered the new facility. "Is this the main command center for the Forge, or is there something even bigger somewhere aboard that we haven't seen yet?"

"This is the main strategic command, control, communications, and planning facility for the Forge. It can also be used to oversee the operations of the Forge itself, but that is intended as a redundancy and is not its primary purpose."

Dash nodded. He was glad that there wasn't something even bigger and grander aboard. This Command Center, which would easily accommodate a couple hundred people, seemed to swallow his little group that made up the "Inner Circle" of the Cygnus Realm's leadership. It was also festooned with screens and consoles, including a massive holographic chart that hovered nearly from wall-to-wall, as big as a cargo door on a large freighter.

Dash stopped at the top of a flight of steps leading down into the depressed area that made up the bulk of the Command Center. To his left and right, a raised gallery extended, wrapping completely around the big room. It offered a good vantage point for anyone not actually involved in operating the Command Center, as well as a quick and easy way of circumnavigating it. Below sprawled enough command, control, and communications systems to allow for the oversight of multiple fleets conducting far-flung, simultaneous campaigns. It was gross overkill for the relatively few ships they possessed—but Dash expected that would change as the war intensified and they gathered new allies to their cause.

Hopefully gathered new allies, anyway, because they needed them badly.

Dash descended the steps. As he did, everyone assembled fell silent and turned to face him.

It struck Dash with that sheer, bemused feeling of wonder—

all of these people, waiting to hear what he had to say. Once again, the question thundered through his mind—

How the hell did this happen? How did I, Newton Sawyer, space courier, end up here?

To one side stood the original gang who'd been with Dash since the start of all this—Leira, Viktor, Conover, and Amy. Nearby, Ragsdale stood with Freya, representing Port Hannah on the planet Gulch, where a crashed Golden starship lay. Close to them were Kai and several monks of the Order of the Unseen, and beside them were Harolyn de Bruce, geologist and engineer, and Benzel and Wei-Ping, once privateers—really pirates—but now two of their most skilled tactical commanders.

Apart from the rest, still not entirely comfortable as members of the group, stood their delegation from the comet miners of the Aquarian Collective, led by Al'Bijea, their chief executive and overall leader. The Aquarians had offered some military aid to the effort against the Golden—aid that had proved pivotal in their last big battle against the Golden minions known as the Verity—but still kept themselves short of a formal alliance. Dash got it; they were a proud, independent group who balked at subordinating themselves to anyone. He hoped he could change that, and inviting Al'Bijea here to participate in their planning was intended as a show of trust to hopefully move things that way.

So now Dash was engaged in diplomacy and politics, on top of trying to run a war.

Again, exactly how *the hell did I end up here?*

He reached the bottom of the stairs. "Custodian, run that clip we discussed, the one showing the last part of the fight against the Harbinger."

The giant screen lit up as the lights dimmed. Everyone watched from Dash's point-of-view as the Archetype broke out of the top of the thunderstorm, swept through the elves and sprites and other strange, luminescent phenomena emanating from its upper reaches, and raced after the Harbinger. A few seconds later, the Golden mech was struck by the debris from the unexpected satellite then plunged back into the atmosphere and, eventually, the clouds, before Dash could intercept it.

The recording ended and the lights came back up. Dash turned to those closest to him, Amy and Conover, and asked, "What did you see?"

He saw Conover starting to formulate an answer, but it was actually Harolyn who answered. "A missed opportunity."

"What do you mean?" Viktor asked her.

"That mech was clearly already badly damaged. If Dash had been able to catch it and take it intact, it would have been a major intelligence score, right?"

Dash nodded. "Correct. And I don't want it to happen again. That's why our next project is going to be a little different. So far, we've been all about scavenging and salvage to feed the Forge. We still need to do that, but we also need to go beyond just salvaging stuff. We need more and better insight into our enemies. So we're going into outright capture."

Ragsdale leaned against a console. "What do you have in mind?"

"I want to steal an idea from the Verity. I want to start knocking enemy ships out of unSpace in a way that would let us capture them intact. Conover, you did a bang-up job with the stealth mines and the Dark Metal detector, and you were a huge help with the scrambler mines. So I'd like you to take the lead in figuring out how we can adapt the scrambler mines into something like a buoy. Something reusable, over and over. Besides just pulling a ship out of translation, though, I also want to disable it, shut its critical systems down, especially drive and weapons."

Conover frowned. "Maybe a really strong EMP—"

But Dash shook his head. "No. Or at least not unless you can figure out how to generate an EMP that will temporarily shut those systems down and not just fry them. The point of this is to take enemy ships intact, in working order, so we can study them. Take them apart. Reverse engineer them and see what we can steal, and even improve. That's especially true for their AI."

"Okay, so you want permanent buoys—probably stealthy ones—that can knock selected enemy ships only out of unSpace with a temporary system interruption. Then, we can capture them without any permanent damage," Conover said, ticking the points off on his fingers as he talked.

"That's right," Dash replied.

"Anything else while we're at it, Dash?" Amy asked. "Maybe have them make coffee, too?"

Laughter buzzed through the room—except for Conover, who just stared into space. Dash could already see his mind chewing on the admittedly difficult problem. "Anyway, Conover,

I'll leave you with that. Get anyone here who's available to help you—besides Custodian, Sentinel, and Tybalt, of course."

Conover looked at him, stared for a second, then nodded. It reminded Dash of the somewhat disconnected kid who'd come aboard the *Slipwing* as a prepaid "tourist" so long ago. Like Dash himself, he'd come a long way.

Dash turned to the rest. "Okay, as for everyone else, I want to talk about the Forge. While it was stationary, just orbiting that gas giant where we originally found it, it was easy to think of it as home base, and a factory to produce weapons. But now that it's mobile and we're starting to move it around, I think we need to talk about the role it's going to play."

"Been wondering the same thing myself," Leira said. "Like, are we going to attack with it? Take it into battle?"

"It would *definitely* kick some ass," Benzel said. "It's pretty much a whole fleet all on its own."

Viktor frowned and crossed his arms. "That's taking a terrible chance, though, with what's basically the whole center of our war effort. We lose the Forge—"

"Yeah, that happens, we're screwed beyond recovery," Dash said. "So the answer to that, Leira, is no—at least, not soon. Someday, when it's truly decisive, then we might, sure. But for now the Forge has other purposes. And I see three main ones. First is gathering resources. That includes capturing things, like we just discussed, but also all the scavenging and salvaging we do, and things like mining that we might take up as our war effort grows." He looked specifically at Harolyn and Al'Bijea when he said that, and both nodded.

"Second is saving refugees." He immediately turned to Ragsdale, who was already opening his mouth to speak, and held up a hand. "I know, there's a cargo hold full of security issues that comes with that. However, we're supposed to be about preserving life, unlike the Enemies of all Life, right, Kai?"

The monk gave a grave, but firm nod.

"Saving refugees, people displaced from the war, is part of that. The Forge can accommodate thousands, and we've got, what, not even a few hundred aboard right now? We also have to remember that refugees are potential allies and can help bolster our war effort. But, all that said, the security issues are a genuine worry. Ragsdale, I'm going to let you develop all the protocols and procedures you think we need to protect the Forge from spying and sabotage."

Ragsdale nodded. "We don't need any more incidents like Temo."

Dash nodded back. Temo had been a supposed refugee who was actually a spy for the Verity. If he hadn't provoked Ragsdale's natural suspicions, prompting the Security Chief to keep an eye on him, he might have done serious, maybe even catastrophic damage to their war effort.

"The third main focus of the Forge is advancing our tech," Dash said. "I don't mean just getting the Forge and the mechs fully powered up, although that's part of it, sure. I mean improving our tech, refining the tech of the Unseen, back-engineering and incorporating Golden tech, whatever it takes. The more new technology we can bring to the battlefield, the better."

Discussion ensued, but no one particularly objected to the

points Dash had raised. He let the conversation hum on for a while, then raised a hand and turned to Leira. "While all of *this* is going on, Leira, Benzel, Wei-Ping, and I are going back to that planet where the Harbinger crashed. I'm hoping there's something useful we can salvage from it, other than Dark Metal. I also want to check out that satellite. Custodian can't find any records of anyone ever settling in that system, so whose satellite that was, and what it was doing there, is a loose end. I don't like loose ends."

After a little more discussion, they began to disperse, heading off to carry out whatever tasks they'd been assigned or simply needed to do. Dash gestured for Leira, Benzel, and Wei-Ping to join him, but Ragsdale stepped forward as well.

"Before you get buried in preparing for your excursion back to that planet, we have a problem."

"*A* problem? Only one?" Dash said, waving for Ragsdale to continue.

"This one we need to attend to right away," Ragsdale said. "We have a—a disciplinary matter, for lack of a better word."

"Sturdivan," Benzel said, scowling and crossing his arms.

Ragsdale nodded. "Sturdivan indeed."

Dash looked from Ragsdale to Benzel. He'd heard the name Sturdivan and recalled he was one of the Gentle Friends. "What about him?"

"Remember the incident from a week or so back? Our airlock fatality?"

"I do." It had been a rare instance of Unseen tech failing, an airlock suddenly opening and venting, killing a refugee who'd come aboard among those fleeing from the Verity. Sturdivan had, Dash recalled, been involved in dealing with the aftermath. Custodian couldn't find any reason for the failure and couldn't replicate it. They'd chalked it up to an unfortunate tragedy and had Custodian run thorough tests on all of the Forge's airlocks.

"Well, it seems Sturdivan was responsible for it."

Dash blinked at that. "He was? How? I mean, I thought he helped out when the airlock failed."

"He made it fail," Ragsdale said. "We caught him hotwiring an airlock last night, trying to bypass the Forge systems so he could work it manually without triggering any security alerts."

"He's a ship's systems engineer aboard the *Snow Leopard*," Wei-Ping said. "So he'd certainly have the know-how to do something like this."

"Okay, but how did he manage to rewire an Unseen airlock?" Dash asked. "How could he manage to rewire an Unseen, well, *anything*? It's not like there are tech manuals for it lying around." Dash frowned. "Are there?"

"Technical schematics and other specifications for the Forge are only available to those with authorized access," Custodian put in. "However, upgrades to the *Snow Leopard*, using the Creator's technology, were accompanied by uploads of relevant technical data for use by the ship's crew."

Now Benzel frowned. "Well, sure, but we didn't upgrade her airlocks. There was no reason to."

"Nonetheless, the airlocks *were* upgraded, at the request of the Chief Engineer."

Benzel looked at Wei-Ping, and they exchanged a nod that managed to convey both understanding—and anger.

"What?" Dash asked.

Benzel sighed. "The *Snow Leopard*'s Chief Engineer was injured when the Verity attacked our Fleet and the Forge, right before we went and kicked their asses at that blue-dwarf system. Sturdivan took over as acting CE until she got back on her feet."

"So he requested the upgrades to the airlocks and got the technical specs that went with them," Leira said, nodding. "That was all he needed."

"What the hell was he up to?" Wei-Ping asked.

Ragsdale looked grim. "I think we have to assume he's a spy." He looked at Dash. "We need to re-vet everybody. In the meantime, we need to restrict access—"

Dash held up a hand. He'd been watching the conversation bounce around and knew it would end up here: Sturdivan being labelled a spy and potential saboteur. But Dash didn't think he was.

"I have a sneaking suspicion this isn't about spying, sabotage, or anything like that at all."

"What do you think it's about, then?" Leira asked.

"Same thing I could see myself doing if I was in his place," Dash replied. "Have Sturdivan brought to my quarters and we'll find out for sure."

Dash had been given a suite of three rooms for his own use,

located on one of the upper hab decks. It seemed like an extravagant amount of space, especially to someone used to living in the cramped confines of a ship where every square centimeter was at a premium. Dash consoled himself with the fact that Custodian could have given him six rooms, or nine—hell, probably a dozen—without making an appreciable dent in the available living space on the Forge. The only downside was that they were buried deep in the station's interior, well away from the hull.

"It is protocol that commanders and other senior personnel are located in quarters deep inside the Forge, in order to ensure their safety and security in the event of a hull breach," Custodian had said, and that had been that—no arguing with two-hundred-thousand year-old bureaucracy, it seemed.

Dash had Sturdivan brought to the room he used as a lounge. The holo-image system allowed him to project a starfield if he wanted the illusion of having a view outside, but once he realized he could see the stars, he didn't want to. He'd had it project a variety of other landscapes and things. Now, though, it just showed a stark grey backdrop behind Dash, who sat on a chair.

As Ragsdale led Sturdivan in, accompanied by Benzel, Wei-Ping, and Leira, Dash studied him closely. The first thing he noticed was how Sturdivan tried to study him right back, but obliquely, as though just scanning his surroundings in curiosity. Right away, it began to fall into place for Dash—the way Sturdivan moved, his body language, expressions, the way he sat down and held himself when he did. It was like ticking off the boxes on a bunch of behaviors Dash knew intimately well, because he'd practiced them all himself at one time or another.

The door closed as Freya entered. She'd been brought in because she was the one who had found the dead woman in the airlock.

"Kai joining us?" Dash asked, just as the door opened again. The monk stepped into the room, his face an inscrutable mask. "Excellent. Freya, if you would. What did you see?"

Freya and Kai took their time, describing what they'd seen in clinical detail, their voices clear but echoing with disgust and horror. When they were done, Dash turned to Sturdivan and said —nothing.

The man curled his lip. "I gather this is the part where you stare at me silently until I can't take it anymore and crack." Sturdivan suddenly looked stricken. "You got me, Mister Dash, I did it all—I started this war, too, and I stole candy from some orphans on Penumbra, and—"

A loud thunk cut him off as Benzel cuffed him across the back of the head.

Dash held up a hand to Benzel. "That won't be necessary, thanks." He looked at Sturdivan and shrugged. "Anyway, nope, that's not it. I'm just trying to figure out if everyone else here is right, and you're a Golden spy. Because if you are, well, then we're going to have to kill you, and that just rubs me the wrong way."

Dash had long ago perfected the art of looking at one part of a room while actually seeing another, a skill that had proven handy in a multitude of seedy bars and grubby docking bays. He saw Sturdivan react to the term *Golden spy*, but with a hint of alarm, not guilt. It only crystallized Dash's suspicions.

So he shook his head and went on, "But I don't think you are a Golden spy. Tell me, how much did you expect to get?"

Again, there was a flicker of reaction from Sturdivan. The man was good at this, keeping himself closed up and his thoughts concealed, but Dash was a master at it. That was the only reason, in fact, he'd hadn't long ago been tossed out an airlock himself by some criminal or creditor. The flicker confirmed Dash's belief.

"What do you mean?" Sturdivan said.

"You wired that airlock to give yourself a private little cargo bay where you could load some Unseen tech and send it off to sell. You'd have made—hell, a *fortune*, am I right?"

"I don't know what you're talking about."

"Of course you do," Dash said, laughing. "I'm not sure how you expected to get any ships to or away from the Forge without being detected, but you're a smart guy, I'm sure you had something in mind." Dash narrowed his eyes. "Probably something like using a regular cargo shuttle, carrying it out to—I'm going to guess the *Snow Leopard*. That's your ship, so you know where you could stash stuff so it would never be found, as long as it was small enough. And there's lots of stuff around here that's small enough but would still make you that fortune."

Sturdivan said nothing, but he didn't have to, because Dash knew he was right.

Benzel scowled, hard. Wei-Ping fixed a glare on Sturdivan that would have vaporized ablative armor.

"Is this true?" Benzel snapped. "You're just a bloody *thief?*"

"A thief *and* a black marketeer," Dash said. "Don't forget that part. He was going to sell this tech to whoever would buy it." He glanced at Leira. "Imagine some of the things we've encountered since all this began, in the hands of some of the people you know."

Leira's face was stone. "Only if I want to start having nightmares."

Benzel leaned in, looming over Sturdivan, his fists clenched. "This makes all the Gentle Friends look suspect, you bastard."

"Oh, like I care," Sturdivan snapped back. "You really expect me to worry about a war between a couple of ancient alien races? I didn't sign up with the Gentle Friends for that, I did it to make money."

"And to kill an innocent woman, apparently," Freya said.

Sturdivan looked at the floor. "That was an accident. No one was supposed to get hurt."

Dash stomped across the room and stopped a pace in front of the man.

"I'm sorry, but you put some of this tech into the hands of the sorts of scumbags you're no doubt hooked up with, and *lots* of people are going to get hurt," Dash said, dropping the casual air and letting his anger come through. "But you never thought about that, did you? You just wanted to make a few credits, and hey, it's not your fault if an inhabited star system gets destroyed, right?"

Sturdivan stared at the floor.

"It gets worse," Dash went on. "I have no doubt you arranged at least one buy already, probably through some contacts you made when the *Snow Leopard* was off on a mission. You sent out some encrypted traffic—I'll bet you buried it in the carrier wave noise, made it sound like environmental static—and arranged a meetup. So that means there are people out there who you've told about this tech, and who are expecting to get their hands on it. Did you give away the location of the Forge, too?"

Sturdivan said nothing.

"*Damn* you," Dash snapped. "You've risked compromising our whole operation here, you son of a bitch."

Wei-Ping grabbed her sidearm. "I've heard enough. You know how we deal with backstabbers in the Friends."

Sturdivan looked up. "Go ahead, then! Except I don't think you will." He looked at Benzel. "You used to be about doing what was best for the Friends. Now you're all, oh, we have to save *everybody*. So I don't think you've got the guts to just space me. Not anymore." He barked out a laugh. "You want to preserve all life, remember? Well, killing me isn't going to bring that refugee back—and I really am sorry about that—but it'll make you a whole lot like these Golden, won't it? Killing someone to get them out of the way?"

"Works for me," Wei-Ping snapped, drawing her slug-pistol and aiming it a Sturdivan's head.

Dash put a hand over the gun's muzzle. "He's right, actually. We won't execute this man. He's what I used to be—completely self-serving. That's not the way either of us started out in life, but it's how we ended up." He nudged the weapon aside and stared hard into Sturdivan's face. "Trouble is, that's as far as you got. It's as far as you're ever going to get. Your *life* is as good as it's ever going to get. You could've done something bigger, something with real meaning to it—but, nope, you're just a petty thief who happened to kill someone through sheer negligence." Dash shook his head. "Hell, I wish you were a Golden spy, because then I'd happily blow your head off myself."

Dash gestured for Kai to join him and they walked to the other side of the room, speaking in whispered tones. After a moment, Dash turned back.

"You're banished," Dash said. "We're going to drop you on some remote place—liveable and inhabited, but really remote. I mean, it'll take you months, maybe years, to figure out how to get anywhere else. Meantime, you'll be on your own, not a credit to your name. You have fun with that." He looked at Ragsdale. "Keep him locked up in the brig for now, under guard and constantly watched. I'll make an announcement to everyone about what's going on shortly."

His face caught somewhere between *venomous glare* and *apprehensive as hell*, Sturdivan was led away. When he was gone, Dash looked at Benzel and Wei-Ping.

"We should have spaced him," Benzel said. "This way, he might come back to haunt us someday."

"Yeah, yeah, I know," Dash replied. "Believe me, I'm not any happier than you are to have these morals and ideals and the like. But Sturdivan was right. We can't let ourselves start down the road of killing anyone who gets in our way. We're liberators, not oppressors. Its life against machines and, well, he was right about that, too—we have to preserve life as much as we can." He shrugged. "But I know. It sucks to be the good guys."

"Sucks even more that you're right," Wei-Ping said, sighing and holstering her slug-pistol.

"That said, we don't have room for anyone who can't value what we're trying to do here," Dash said. "When we get back, we need to talk about Sturdivan's network and what to do about it. Meantime, though, we've got a mission to fly. Let's suit up and go do something useful."

3

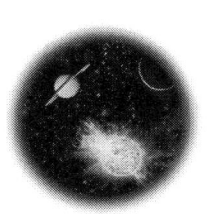

Now that Dash had a chance to study the frozen planet and wasn't chasing a Harbinger among its prodigious storm clouds, he had to admit it was one of the prettier worlds he'd seen.

It was mostly water, with two middling continents, several island archipelagos, and the peaks of mostly dormant volcanoes. It orbited just on the outer fringe of the habitable zone around its white dwarf star, getting enough heat to avoid turning into a giant snowball. Still, it was damned cold overall, with the radiance of the star pumping enough energy into the atmosphere to drive the fearsome storms that lashed its vast oceans and scant, rocky landmasses. The sprawling cloud cover made it gleam a pearlescent white on the side facing its sun, while almost constant pulses of lightning flickered across its night side.

"What did Kai say this place was called?" Benzel asked. "Tunnel, or something like that?"

"Burrow," Leira said. "That's not its official name on the charts, just what it was called in the only reference to it he and his monks could find."

The name had been given to the planet by a small group of water miners, a splinter group, apparently, of a larger resource consortium that had operated nearly a hundred and thirty years ago. A sub-faction had apparently decided to break off from the consortium and pursue their own fortune. Water was still precious, and therefore an extremely valuable commodity for outposts, stations, and even some worlds. What these hardy entrepreneurs hadn't counted on was that the rise of comet miners, like the Aquarian Collective, would make laboriously hauling water out of planetary gravity wells obsolete. There was no record of what happened to the splinter group after arriving here and staking a water claim to the world, beyond calling it Burrow.

"The satellite that took out the Harbinger probably belonged to those water miners," Dash said, studying the planet called Burrow on the Archetype's heads-up. He could also see the Swift hanging in space nearby. The *Herald* and the *Snow Leopard* kept station further back. More to the point, the threat indicator remained dark. Hopefully it would remain that way, so they could concentrate on recovering whatever they could from Burrow, and not end up in a fight while doing it.

"Wasn't it already debris, more or less?" Wei-Ping asked.

"Yeah, it was," Dash replied. "It had broken up at some point, meaning it was a debris cloud, which is probably why it managed to smack that Harbinger—it was like it got hit by a shotgun—if the pellets were travelling twelve kilometers per second, that is."

"You know, that raises a point," Benzel said. "A few years back, we looked at the idea of installing some projectile weapons—rail-guns—on our ships. We couldn't deal with the power distribution, so we dropped the idea. But you accelerate a hunk of something to a high enough velocity, there's not much that's going to be able to stop it."

"All that kinetic energy has to go somewhere," Wei-Ping added. "Ain't no energy shield or armor that can take too many hits from a rail-gun. Maybe with this Unseen tech we could make it work."

Dash nodded. "Good point. Sentinel, did the Unseen ever develop something like that?"

"Mass drivers, such as rail-guns, were part of the Creators' arsenal, but only for the defense of static points, such as installations and other defensive works."

"Okay, this is definitely a conversation we need to have back at the Forge, because I'm always looking for new and exciting ways to make things go boom," Dash said. "Meantime, how about we do what we came here to do."

"You got it, boss," Benzel said. "So how do you want to do this?"

"Well, Sentinel and Tybalt have narrowed the crash site of the Harbinger down to a few square kilometers. So, Leira and I are going to go down there, find it, and see if we can lift the wreckage back into orbit. You guys will cover us up here. Whatever we manage to recover, we take back to the Forge."

Dash waited for acknowledgements then powered up the drive and took the Archetype toward the planet, Leira following in the Swift.

Dash circled the jagged peak, eyeing the crash site. The Harbinger had impacted the side of the mountain, just below the summit, square into a glacier, burying itself in ice. The crater, a good sixty meters across, was already refilling—first with meltwater from the heat of the impact, which had frozen back over most of the wreckage, and now with new, drifting snow. Inside the Archetype, he felt none of what must be bone chilling cold, of course, but he shivered anyway just looking at the desolate, wind-scoured expanse of ice, snow, and rock.

Leira must have felt it, too. "I kind of wish I'd have worn my thick socks," she said.

"A toasty scarf might do nicely," Dash replied.

"Did you say *toasty*?"

Dash sniffed indignantly. "Sometimes I prefer creature comforts. I'm a man of culture. Did you notice I stopped burping in command meetings?"

"True," Leira said. "You're practically a diplomat."

Dash gave a satisfied nod. "Exactly. Now let's dig in—so we can dig out."

Dash eased the Archetype toward the mountainside. The mechs used graviters—gravity polarizers—for low-speed, atmospheric maneuvers, essentially much larger and more efficient forms of the tech that gave ships like the *Slipwing* or *Snow Leopard* their artificial gravity. Dash knew that human engineers had long wanted to upgrade them into actual drives, with some success, but nothing like the versions produced by the Unseen. It was just another piece of tech that might no longer seem especially remarkable to Dash but would be of almost unimaginable value to anyone in "normal" space.

He understood Sturdivan's motivations. He profoundly, fundamentally disagreed with the man's greed, but he understood it.

Dash settled the Archetype down beside the crater. The Swift landed on the far side of it. Gravity was about two-thirds standard, so Sentinel and Tybalt had to use the graviters to anchor the mechs securely to the mountainside, giving them the leverage to dig. Dash studied the wreckage for a moment, then said, "Okay, Leira, easiest way to do this is to just start scooping out the ice and snow right in front of us. We'll keep digging all around, then break it free and lift it. Should be easy in this lower gravity."

"Got it. I think we'll probably have to take some ice up to orbit with us, though. These mechs are great, but I don't think fine motor work is one of their strengths."

Dash looked at the Archetype's massive hands. Some of the fingers did end in fine manipulators, but they weren't meant for digging. "Even if we have to pull a block of ice up to orbit, that's fine. In fact, it's probably better that way—the ice'll hold things together."

They began to dig. Even taking time for care, it went fast, the mechs making short work of the ice, snow, and even rock, pulverizing it, then heaving aside the spoil. In a half hour, the two mechs stood in a shallow pit, a large, raised block of ice rising from the center of it. The wreckage of the Harbinger stood out as dark shapes inside of it, with parts protruding there and there.

"Okay, we break this free then lift it up to orbit," Dash said.

"Uh—we are sure it's dead, right?" Leira asked. "I mean, we've encountered Golden tech in the past that seemed dead, but wasn't."

Dash checked the heads-up. It showed no power emissions at all—not even heat, which meant the wreckage had cooled to the ambient temperature of the ice. Still, he asked Sentinel for confirmation.

"While it is not possible to entirely rule the possibility out, there is no evidence that this Harbinger remains operative to any degree," the AI replied.

"Not to mention, it took combat damage and was struck by fragments of a satellite before hitting a mountain at terminal velocity. Not exactly a recipe for keeping *any* kind of tech in working order—even a Harbinger," Tybalt said. "In the meantime, both the Archetype and Swift remain fully operational."

"I think Tybalt's telling us we're being nervous for no reason," Leira said.

"I prefer the term cautious," Dash said. "Anyway, I think we can assume it's dead, yeah. And it looks like we've got a storm coming in, so let's break it out of this pit and get out of here."

The clouds thickened, mist and snow driving against the mountain as a storm rolled in from the nearby ocean. The worst of it hit as they finally worked the ice-locked Harbinger free and started lifting it to orbit, the mechs shuddering as they were hammered by the howling wind.

DASH WATCHED as the *Snow Leopard* translated, followed by the *Herald*. They were on their way back to the Forge, the ice-encrusted Harbinger slung against the *Herald*'s hull. Hopefully, enough of it remained intact that they could extract more from it than just its Dark Metal. Benzel would hand that problem over to Custodian, while he and Wei-Ping started trying to run down Sturdivan's network, and especially whatever contacts he planned to sell Unseen tech to.

Dash and Leira remained orbiting Burrow because Sentinel had found something interesting.

"There's a signal emanating from a body of water, a lake, on the more northerly of the two continents," Sentinel had said. "It is weak, but distinct."

"Remnants of the water miners?" Dash asked.

"Unknown. I am analyzing the signal now."

As soon as Benzel and Wei-Ping had departed, Sentinel gave an update. "Tybalt and I have concluded our analysis. The signal is transmitting Golden machine language. Notably, it is neither Verity nor Bright in origin. It is being transmitted by a source at the bottom of a frozen lake between two large mountain peaks."

"So underwater, then."

"That is correct."

"Hey, Leira, feel like taking a dip?" Dash asked.

"In freezing cold alien water? Sure, I could use a swim. How deep?"

Tybalt broke in. "Three hundred seventy-one meters to the source, but the lake is considerably deeper. The beacon, or device, is on a narrow ledge. Any contact may dislodge it, sending it into a crevasse that is too narrow for pursuit."

"Huh. So love taps only, Leira," Dash said.

"Got it. Following you."

Together, they dove back into the raging storms.

4

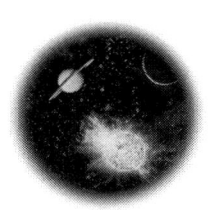

Dash swung the Archetype through a lazy turn, studying the frozen lake. Whatever was down there lay beneath not just almost four hundred meters of water, but also almost five meters of black ice, hard as rock.

"We can probably just dive right through it," Leira said.

"We *can*, but I don't want to risk disturbing things too much," Dash replied. "Remember, whatever's down there, it's sitting on the brink of plunging into oblivion."

"So what do you want to do?"

Dash deployed and charged up the Archetype's power-sword. "*This* is what I want to do."

He descended until the graviters held the Archetype just a few meters above the lake's surface. Powerful winds, roaring across the bleak landscape and funneled between the two towering peaks, buffeted the mech. Dash gingerly lowered the crackling sword and touched its point to the surface, which immediately puffed to wind-whipped vapor. He pushed, shoving the sword through the ice, then worked it around, drawing it through a circle thirty meters across. The power-sword had been designed to cut apart armor and alloy structural components, so the old ice, even as hard and dense as it was, simply parted around the massive blade. Dash then cut the circle into quarters and, together with Leira, lifted and threw aside the pieces, leaving a gaping hole into dark water.

"Okay, let's take a dip," Dash said, and stepped into the water. He used the graviters to arrest the mech's drop so it didn't just sink under its own weight. The Swift followed him in and then down. Visibility immediately dropped to nothing as the shimmering circle of light making the hole was swallowed by darkness. They activated powerful floodlights mounted in the mechs' hulls, something they had only rare occasion to use; the beams punched through the gloom, throwing their illumination surprisingly far.

"This water clarity is astounding," Dash remarked.

"Indeed, it is," Sentinel replied. "This lake apparently sees little current action or other movement of its water, so there are relatively few suspended particulates."

The Archetype's status was unchanged, all of its systems functioning normally. Dash had a question anyway. "How's the Archetype doing? Any problems being submerged?"

"Water is just a denser medium than air or space. The force required to operate the actuators is slightly increased, but that's all."

Dash nodded, smiling as he did. Sentinel's use of contractions in her speech was becoming more common. He assumed she'd just been picking up his own speech mannerisms but couldn't help wondering if her underlying psychology was changing through exposure to him as well. It wasn't anything he could ask her, so he resolved to watch.

And listen.

Something darted out of the gloom, turned, and shot back into the darkness. Dash had a vague impression of something big and wormlike, with many teeth. He was glad to have the Archetype's armor between it and him, but still, it was remarkable that there were living things in this cold, isolated lake at all.

"Life, even here," he said, his voice filled with wonder.

"Especially here," Leira said. "No war."

They continued sinking. Using radar, Sentinel could portray the rugged bottom of the lake rising up to meet them. The signal source seemed to be resting on the edge of a deep, narrow canyon. The submerged feature showed up as a long, jagged scar in the bedrock, the result of some ancient earthquake or other cataclysm.

Dash halted the Archetype about a hundred meters short of their goal. The Swift slowly dropped into view, then stopped just a few meters away.

"Sentinel, any chance in the signal from whatever that is below us?"

"None," the AI replied. "It continues to broadcast a repeating transmission in machine language. Tybalt and I have been attempting to determine its purpose, but we can find no translation key in the available stores of data."

"Can you block it? Jam it?"

"Yes, but are you sure that would be wise?"

"Well, since you're asking the question, you obviously aren't."

"If this message is simply a recurring status update, and it is suddenly cut off, then the suspicion of any party receiving it may be roused."

"Good point." Dash narrowed his eyes in thought for a moment. "Could we replace it with something? Something that would generate a similar signal?"

"I could configure one of the Archetype's missiles to do so, essentially by copying the message in its entirety to the missile's guidance computer, then instructing it to broadcast it using its telemetry transmitter. The missile's power supply should allow it to continue doing so for several years."

"Sounds like a plan. Let's do that."

Dash resumed sinking as Sentinel prepared the missile. The Swift followed. He kept his eyes locked on the threat indicator, ready for any hint of what might be a fire control signal, a weapon powering up—anything. But there was nothing, and now the bottom of the lake appeared in their lights, the illumination splashing across flat patches of sediment punctuated by jagged rock.

"I see it," Leira said. "It looks like a probe, about ten meters to your right."

Dash nodded as his light hit something metallic. "Yup, I've

got it." He could also see the yawning chasm right alongside it, a vast and distant drop into blackness.

"Okay, it looks firmly stuck in that mud," he went on. "We're going to need to brace against it for leverage, and the Swift's lighter than the Archetype. I think this is your show, Leira."

"Got it. How about you get ready to catch it in case something goes wrong?"

"Will do. Before we do any of this, though—Sentinel, is this potentially ordnance? You know, something that might blow up in our faces?"

"There is no indication of any sort of demolition or other payload. In fact, the probe seems to have at one time carried a missile or other projectile in a launch tube, which is now empty. Whatever ordnance it may have carried seems to have been expended."

"Alrighty, then," Dash said, and moved the Archetype to the far side of the abyss.

The chasm was about thirty meters wide, but it narrowed fast as it plunged into the bedrock. Once in place, Leira positioned herself over the probe then gingerly lowered the Swift's feet to the lake bottom on either side of it. Mud squelched from under them as the mech sank into the muck, raising billowing clouds of sediment that shimmered in their lights. The Swift bent forward and Leira worked the mech's fingers around the probe.

"Okay, here goes," she said, and straightened the mech, pulling on the probe.

It didn't budge.

"Wow, that's really stuck," she said, backing off. "Maybe we should do some digging—"

Her words cut off as the ground beneath her disintegrated, fragmenting into a slide of falling rock, and both the probe and the Swift plunged out of view.

"Shit!" Dash snapped. Then he dove into the swirling cloud of sediment. It was all instinct; there really was little danger to the Swift, but his brain registered *Leira in danger* and he reacted.

"I'm fine!" Leira called. "But I lost my grip on the damned probe."

"I've got you on scan—clear left, coming through!" Dash shouted back and kept the Archetype plunging straight down, headfirst. He swept past the Swift, missing it by maybe three or four meters, and continued dropping, hands reaching, desperately clutching for the falling probe.

It flared into view, lit brightly by the mech's lights amid the clouds of billowing mud. It fell a little more slowly than the sudden landslide itself, so it trailed the plunging rock; Dash lunged and managed to grab it maybe twenty meters short of where the crevasse simply became too narrow for the Archetype to have gone any further. The graviters whined as the Archetype stopped, holding the probe. Ahead of him, the last rocks plunged from view, vanishing into utter darkness—

No. Not *quite* utter darkness. The Archetype's lights brushed over something resting on a ledge sticking out precariously from the wall of the canyon. With a curious grunt, Dash back off the graviters a little, letting the Archetype slowly fall a few meters, until his light resolved the ledge and what was upon it.

"Leira, Sentinel's going to share some imagery with you that you *really* need to see."

THE WRECKAGE SPRAWLED across the ledge, clearly the remains of a ship resting on its side. The design, though, was old; the best match Sentinel could find was an entry in the data copied from the *Slipwing* of a *Hercules*-class shuttle—a type that hadn't been used in over two hundred years. The accumulated muck suggested it had been resting here at least that long—probably longer, by about a century, according to Tybalt and based on the rate of sediment build-up in the lake. The exposed portions of the ship were badly damaged, the hull plating buckled to expose twisted structural members in a chaotic tangle.

"This lake is very cold, with an extremely low oxygen content, so there has been negligible corrosion. This also explains why there are still biological remains."

Dash's eyes widened. "Wait, what?"

The heads-up zoomed in on a patch of sediment visible among some torn hull plates. A skull leered back, its eye sockets black holes. The sudden appearance of a pale, eel-like creature slithering among the wreckage only enhanced the creepiness.

"Human," Leira said. "Tybalt's found a few other bones scattered around, too."

"Is there any record of an expedition here, say, about three hundred years ago?" Dash asked.

"Not in the available stores of data," Sentinel replied. "However, there is an insignia that may prove useful."

The image switched to show a torso protruding from the mud, partly concealed beneath a loose hull plate. A grey uniform that included a mission patch of some sort hung across skeletal remains, which included a gleaming white stack of vertebrae; there was no skull. Moving the Golden probe so it was cradled in one arm, Dash reached down with the other, gently slid the hull plate aside, then used the fine manipulators on one of the mech's fingertips to tug the remains free. Most of the bones simply spilled out of the uniform, which mostly disintegrated, but he was able to retrieve the mission patch. Spooling up the graviters, he reversed the Archetype and backed straight up and out of the crevasse.

"So who do you think they were?" Leira asked.

"Well, that patch seemed to be a corporate logo," Dash replied. "I'm thinking this was some corporate-sponsored expedition, intended to look for—oh, I don't know, resources, valuable minerals, maybe even just habitable land. In any case, whoever they were, they long predate our supposed water haulers, the ones who apparently named this planet Burrow."

"Well, whatever it was they were looking for, they apparently never found it," Leira said.

"Or they did but never got to do anything about it."

"I wonder why they crashed," Leira mused. "Tybalt didn't see any sign of battle damage."

"We may never know. I don't really feel like taking the time and effort to go back down there and dig them out."

"In any case, that would be counterproductive," Tybalt put in. "Neither you nor Leira have any background in archeology, and the Archetype and Swift aren't optimal platforms for such work, anyway."

Dash wondered if Tybalt even could say anything without coming across as somewhat condescending, even vaguely insulting. Not for the first time, he wondered just what it was in Leira's personality that had prompted these AIs to decide that the snooty Tybalt was the best possible match for her.

Even so, Tybalt was right. They didn't have the expertise, and Dash didn't want to spend the time. "We'll record this and, who knows, maybe someday we can send someone back here to study this."

"When we're not fighting a war," Leira said.

Dash nodded. "Yeah. When we're not fighting a war."

As they headed back for the surface, it struck Dash that he could say it—*when we're not fighting a war*—but really it just sounded like wishful thinking.

A NEAR BLIZZARD raged when they surfaced, cracking through new ice that had formed across the hole Dash had cut, already several centimeters thick. They took the two mechs up into clear air, an empty space among towering stacks of storm clouds. Dash took the opportunity to more closely examine the Golden probe.

"Is our substitute for the probe transmitting?" Dash asked.

"It is. I suppressed the genuine signal in an erratic manner, as though it resulted from interference. Then, I configured the missile to begin generating a spotty false signal, as though the issue had abated."

"Clever."

"The probe is continuing to transmit, but I am continuing to fully jam it."

"So it seems to be a one-shot missile launcher," Dash said.

"It does. Nearly half of its internal volume is the launch tube. It incorporates a small amount of Dark Metal in its construction—less than a kilogram in total."

Dash narrowed his eyes at it. Something about it being designed to launch a single missile plucked at him. It seemed like a very specific purpose for the probe, and it made him wonder exactly what sort of missile it had carried.

"I don't think we'll be harvesting the Dark Metal out of this," he finally said. "At least, not right away. I'd really like to know what this thing was for—especially since we might end up running into versions of it that are loaded with whatever type of missile that was." He scowled at it. "It's a mystery, and mysteries make me nervous, especially when they're mysteries about the Golden. Anyway, we did what we came here to do, plus some, so let's head back to the Forge—"

"Dash," Leira cut in. "We're detecting another signal. This one's from a conventional radio, a high frequency band."

Dash looked at the heads-up, which was now portraying the incoming signal, and sighed. He really wanted to leave this planet and head back to the Forge, but it kept serving up new and intriguing things. "Do we know where it's coming from?"

"No, we don't know the radio signal's precise origin. It's bouncing off the planet's ionosphere, which means it could originate anywhere on the surface."

Dash powered up the Archetype's drive and lifted it back toward orbit. "Okay, let's gain some altitude, see if we can pin this down."

The mechs shuddered and bucked as they passed through varying layers of wind, which occasionally howled at hurricane strength. Some of the resulting wind shear was strong enough it might have made him worry if he was piloting the *Slipwing*. For the Archetype and Swift, though, it was only just noticeable. They punched through one final layer of thick cloud, ice pellets rattling against the mech's hull like machine gun fire, then burst into clear air.

"The source of the HF radio signal has now risen over the horizon," Sentinel reported. "It originates on a large island, part of an archipelago in the southern hemisphere. It is being modulated and is carrying information—what appears to be data about atmospheric conditions."

"In other words, weather reports," Dash said.

"Yes. There are other emissions from that island as well—weak radio broadcasts, thermal emissions, and radiation suggestive of an operating fission reactor."

"There are also traces of industrial pollutants in the volume of atmosphere surrounding the island," Tybalt put in.

"Huh. People down there," Leira said.

"So it would seem," Dash replied. "The question is, are they related to our old, crashed corporate spaceship in the lake, or to the water haulers, or are they something else entirely?"

"Only one way to find out," Leira said. "Shall we go pay them a visit?"

Dash pondered that as the two mechs made stable orbit. "I don't think so," he finally said. "They've got advanced enough tech for nuclear power, so we want to talk to them, but I don't think the Archetype and the Swift are the best ambassadors. Besides, I really want to get this missile probe, or whatever it is, back to the Forge."

"We could send Harolyn back to meet with them," Leira suggested. "She's a miner, and if they are water haulers they might see her as a sort of kindred spirit."

"I would suggest, Dash, that there is another compelling reason to meet with these people," Sentinel said. "The winter this planet is experiencing is only partly the result of its orbital period around its star. The system is also passing through a region of dust and gas that has significantly diminished the amount of the star's infrared emissions impinging on the planet. The effect will peak in approximately twelve years; the winter at that time will be so severe as to make the planet essentially uninhabitable."

"Indeed," Tybalt added. "Much of its atmosphere will freeze. What remains will be insufficient to support human life."

"So, whoever they are, they've got about ten years left—and then, what, they all die?" Dash asked.

"Essentially correct," Sentinel replied. "Unless they take extraordinary measures to prevent it."

"Okay, then. Let's head back and send Harolyn back here. Maybe she can convince these people to come to the Forge."

"More allies?" Leira asked.

"Maybe. More to point, though, some people who won't face either asphyxiating or freezing to death—whichever might come first."

5

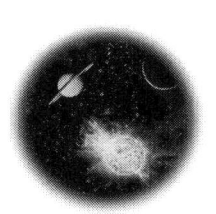

Dash watched, bemused, as Viktor, Conover, and Amy pored over the Golden probe they'd retrieved from Burrow. It squatted on a grav palette on the fabrication level, ready for detailed study by Custodian, but Viktor and the others had insisted on examining it first.

"They're like kids with a new toy," Dash said sidelong to Leira, and she nodded, smiling.

"A new toy that fires some mysterious sort of missile," Leira replied. "I'd be thrilled if they can figure out what it does, so more power to them."

"Whatever the missile did, we can't tell," Viktor said, apparently able to overhear them. "What we do know is that the targeting system for it"—he pointed at a bulge in the probe's hull—"isn't like any that we've seen before."

"It goes way beyond simple spatial targeting," Conover said.

"It seems to have something to do with unSpace—all the Dark Metal present in this thing is right here, tied into the targeting system."

"So it was meant to shoot things into unSpace?" Dash asked.

Conover gave an *I don't know* shrug. "Possibly?"

"More to the point, it doesn't have a translation drive of its own," Amy said. "So it was apparently meant to be carried by another ship, launched, and then fire whatever came out of there." She pointed at the gaping muzzle of the launch tube.

"So the bottom line is that we don't know what, exactly, it launched," Dash said.

Viktor put his hands on his hips. "Just based on this drone?" He shook his head. "No. But once Custodian has a chance to go over it in detail, we may be able to figure out more about it."

"Well then let him get to it," Dash said, a gently chiding tone to his voice. "I know you guys love your new and wonderful tech, but let the artificial man do his job."

"Yes, dad," Amy said, giving Dash a hurt look.

"Chin up, kid. We have giant death robots, after all," Dash said.

Amy brightened. "Okay. I'll take two. With extra lasers, please."

Once the laughter subsided, Conover spoke up. "I do have good news. Turns out it wasn't all that difficult to combine the scrambler mines with an EM pulse generator, like you asked. We call them surge mines, and we have—uh—Custodian, how many do we have now?"

"We have ten surge mines completed and loaded aboard the *Horse Nebula*."

Dash stared. "The *Horse Nebula*?"

"It's our new minelayer," Conover said. "Benzel wanted to free up the *Snow Leopard* from minelaying tasks, so he asked Custodian to take one of our drone minelayers and scale it up, give it a basic crew hab, cockpit, that sort of thing. He's picked the crew for it."

"Apparently, the Gentle Friends did some minelaying of their own, back in their, uh, privateering days," Viktor said. "He's got some people experienced in doing it, so they're the crew."

Dash gave an impressed nod. "Okay, then. Sounds like great initiative to me." He crossed his arms. "We're just sure these surge mines aren't going to permanently fry whatever they catch, right? Otherwise, it kind of defeats the purpose of doing it in the first place."

"You were pretty clear about that, Dash," Conover said. "Custodian and I ran a bunch of simulations, changing the strength of the EM pulse, the shape of the waveform, frequency—anyway, we fiddled around with it until we got something that seems to consistently overload circuits and systems aboard ships within range, but just enough to make them reboot."

"We test fired one with some systems scavenged from some of the Verity wrecks we've recovered," Viktor added. "Custodian stashed some, more or less intact, for the very purpose of testing things against them. In both simulations and field tests, we could force the systems to overload, then reboot and reset about ninety percent of the time."

"Ninety-two-point-five," Custodian said.

"Sorry, ninety-two-point-five. Anyway, the other seven-and-a-half percent of the time, we either weren't able to surge the system enough, or we fried it completely, depending on how well it was shielded."

"Huh. Ninety-odd percent isn't bad at all," Dash said. "And you guys did all of this in the time Leira and I were away?"

"We don't screw around, Dash," Conover said.

"Actually, we do, but we just don't let it get in the way of real work," Amy said.

"Okay then, that's good news all around," Dash said, nodding. "Good work, guys. Now we just need a target to use these mines on. Meet me in the Command Center in, say, an hour, and we'll figure out what to do next. Show up in fifty minutes, and I'll bring cake."

"Cake? We have cake? Like *real*—" Conover said, but Dash put a hand on his shoulder, shaking his head.

"There is no cake. Sorry."

"Why would you—" Conover said, then narrowed his eyes in suspicion. "Is this one of those life lessons, but also toying with my love of food?"

"Afraid so. You see, a good commander *never* works harder. Just smarter," Dash said.

"And meaner," Conover mumbled.

"I prefer the term efficient," Dash said, a winning smile on his face. He could get used to being a leader.

THE COMMAND CENTER really was overkill, Dash thought—especially with only seven of them there. He, along with Leira, Viktor, Conover, Amy, Benzel, and Wei-Ping vanished into the sprawling expanse of command and control systems, consoles and screens.

"Have to admit, I kind of miss the War Room. It was a lot cozier," Dash said.

"We can still use it if we want, you know," Leira replied. "I doubt we'll hurt Custodian's feelings if we do, occasionally."

"I will be devastated," Custodian said.

After a moment of exchanged stares, Dash finally spoke. "Really?"

"No, of course not. I am incapable of such an emotional state. However, I have observed, and both Sentinel and Tybalt have noted, that engaging in such empty banter seems to put you at ease and facilitate subsequent, substantive discussion."

Dash opened his mouth but paused. "Really?" he asked again.

"Am I incorrect?"

Dash grinned. "No, not at all. I love it, actually. Banter away, Custodian, whenever you want."

Actually, it did seem to put them all at ease, and it wiped away Dash's fussing over the looming expanse of the Command Center. "Anyway, we need to plan our way forward, so that's why I've brought you guys here. But before we do that, there's something else I want to talk about."

"Uh oh, I think we're in deep shit," Amy said in a stage whisper.

"Not this time," Dash replied. "I want to talk about our chain of command."

"What about it?" Benzel asked.

"We don't have one beyond me, and while I've got the archetype, my good looks, and completely reasonable confidence—"

"Um. Okay," Viktor said, carefully looking away.

"But I'm going to initiate a more tangible structure for the realm, starting now."

"Tangible is good," Viktor said.

"So I think. With that in mind, I've been doing some reading on how military forces do this, and here's what I propose. I'm the boss—somehow, and don't get me started on how the hell that happened. In any case, I'll be the High Commander. Leira is my second in command, my—uh, Deputy Commander. Benzel, I'd like you to be Commander of all of our offensive forces, and in charge of planning all of our offensive operations."

"I like that," Benzel said.

"Me too," Wei-Ping said. "After all, you *are* pretty offensive."

Benzel punched her arm and she grinned. Dash looked at her.

"Wei-Ping, you'll do the same for all our defensive operations. So you two guys will have to work pretty closely together to coordinate things."

"Got it," Wei-Ping said.

"Amy, I'd like you to take charge of our operational readiness. That means you'll be a Captain, one level below our two Commanders. You'll oversee our pilots, their readiness, and the readiness of our ships. You'll also keep flying the *Slipwing*." He smiled at her. "Makes me feel a lot better, knowing she's in such good hands."

For once, Amy wasn't flippant, she just nodded. "Thank you, Dash. I won't let you down."

"I know you won't. Viktor, Conover, you guys will have the rank of Captain, too. I want both of you to concentrate on our research, development, and production. Conover, you focus on evaluating new enemy tech as we capture it and bring it in, figure out what we can use and what we can improve. Viktor, you'll concentrate on the production and installation of our new tech. Both of you are going to be working close with Custodian, obviously."

Dash turned to Conover. "I'm also tagging you to keep flying the *Mako*, as a secondary duty. If we think we need to deploy her, we'll come to you."

Conover nodded. The nimble little atmospheric fighter known as the *Mako* held enormous potential, as it was designed to interface directly with its pilots' thoughts. It also mounted a variant of the most potent weapon they currently possessed, the blast-cannon. Unfortunately, the *Mako* was also giving them no end of trouble, its interface with Conover's optical implants still not working properly. Sometimes Conover lost the interface completely; other times, it overloaded his implants and locked them in safe mode until they reset their own interface with Conover's nervous system. They'd kept plugging away at it and seemed to be on their way to a solution. For now, though, the *Mako* was only deployed when they really thought they'd need it.

"Finally, Ragsdale is Captain in charge of our security—that's a no-brainer—and Freya is Captain in charge of our logistics, specifically food production and medical services. Harolyn is going to take charge of our civilian contingent, with the equivalent rank of Captain, too. So there we go—we have a chain of command."

"So what's this new chain of command going to do? What's our next move?" Wei-Ping asked.

"Good question. Custodian, show us all known and suspected locations of Golden activity to date," Dash said.

The big screen lit up with a star chart, depicting a multitude of icons scattered across the galactic arm.

"Holy shit," Amy said. "I mean—holy shit."

"There must be at least two hundred locations shown there," Viktor said.

"Two hundred and eleven," Custodian said.

"There are really that many?" Benzel asked. "I'm with Amy. Holy shit. How can there be so many?"

"Custodian," Dash said. "Remove all of these that are just suspected activity, inferred, unconfirmed, that sort of thing. Let's just see the ones that we know are real, or we're confident probably are."

"That's still got to be almost a hundred," Leira said. "There's an awful damned lot of Golden activity in the arm."

"What's this based on?" Viktor asked.

"Known activity, and extrapolations based on particular trigger events," Custodian said. "This would include Golden and Verity attacks and raids, our encounters with them, information that suggests they have attempted to recruit allies, and similar such criteria."

"There are a lot more Golden out there than I ever thought," Leira said. "Golden, and their minions."

"Okay, Custodian," Dash said. "Based on this, let's plot a course that starts at the coordinates of the Forge and passes through the confirmed locations, or the ones where our confidence is high—say, better than eighty percent. Make sure it passes through them in an optimum way, and move the Forge if you have to."

A trajectory appeared on the star chart, weaving and wobbling its way roughly along the long axis of the galactic arm.

"Okay, so there we go," Dash said. "That's our first cut at the progress of a campaign to wipe these bastards out." He turned to the others. "And I do mean wipe them out. We'll seize their tech and resources, but the Golden and all their lackeys—Verity, Bright, Clan Shirna, whoever—*they* are going to die, every single one of them."

Benzel gave a fierce nod. "Like eradicating a germ—you can't leave even one alive, in case it eventually respawns and you have to deal with it all over again."

Dash looked at those assembled, the Cygnus Realm's senior leaders. "Does anyone have a problem with that?"

After a moment of silence, Leira pointed at the map. "When do we get started?"

Dash powered the Archetype past the flotilla they'd organized to test the surge mines. He paid particular attention to the *Horse Nebula*, a squat, boxy thing that was essentially a square hull bolted onto a minelaying drone. It wasn't pretty and would never do an atmospheric entry—not in one piece, anyway—but she wasn't designed for any of that. She was functional, good at what she did, which was laying mines. And that was good enough.

Dash had instructed Custodian to manufacture more of the *Horse Nebula*-class minelayers. They could be used, of course, to lay any sorts of mines, but the surge-variant were proving to be a powerful and efficient component of the Cygnus arsenal—easy to make with minimal resources, and deadly for what they cost in time and materials.

He put the Archetype at the head of the flotilla. In company were the Swift, the *Herald*, and the Aquarian ship, the *Comet*, as their combat force, with the *Snow Leopard* and *Horse Nebula* as their auxiliaries. Amy flew the *Slipwing* as their reserve, sharing control with the *Snow Leopard* of a half dozen combat drones and a quartet of tug drones—essentially just grapples and thrusters strapped onto a translation drive, with a basic AI control unit. If their campaign to disable and capture enemy tech worked out, they needed a way to get it back to the Forge, and tying up ships like the *Herald* or the *Snow Leopard* didn't make sense.

"Okay, everyone, report green if you're ready to launch," Dash said.

Dash waited as everyone checked in, then gave the *go* signal and translated into unSpace, the rest of the flotilla following.

It didn't take long to get to their destination, thanks to having moved the Forge from its remote location and closer to inhabited space. Two hours into unSpace, Sentinel gave a five-minute warning for their return to the normal galactic plane.

"Okay, Benzel," Dash said. "This is your show as our new Offensive Ops Commander."

"Right. Dash, you and I will pop in and take a look at what's what in this target system. Everyone else stays in translation, in a holding pattern, until we're ready to commit."

Acknowledgements came in. Dash had Sentinel handshake with the AI aboard the *Herald*, Benzel's flagship, letting the Silent Fleet vessel take them both out of unSpace at the same time, using a lonely gas giant enclosed in a vast debris cloud of ice and rock, a so-called halo, as cover. Its primary, an enormous red giant, still filled much of the starfield with a dull, crimson glare, even this far out.

Dash saw the comm laser link with the *Herald*, giving them secure comms with no leakage the Golden or their allies might detect.

"Looks like the jackpot we were looking for," Benzel said.

Dash grunted his assent while studying what they'd found. There were two more rocky planets closer in, with a pair of asteroid belts between them. About seven hundred million klicks out from the primary, four ships were orbiting, their signatures matching Verity light cruisers. Something else orbited between the two asteroid belts, but between interference, and a design and composition not matched by anything in their databases, they couldn't identify just what it was.

"Looks like—I don't know, rings? Maybe it's something like what the Aquarians built?" Benzel said.

"Maybe," Dash replied. "Whatever it is, it doesn't seem very mobile. Okay, how do you want to do this?"

"The *Horse Nebula*'s going to sow the new surge mines along the most likely route for Verity ships entering or leaving the system," Benzel said. "I asked Leira to get Tybalt to work that out. Meantime, the rest of the fleet's going to translate in on the far side of the primary. That big red giant ought to give us enough cover to do a pincer move, with you and the *Comet* coming at the Verity over the star's north pole, and the Swift and the *Herald* over the south. That way, we catch from the top and bottom of the ecliptic plane. The *Slipwing's* going to take over the gun and missile drones and hang back as our reserve. Then—this is critical—the *Snow Leopard* will take over the tug-drones and wait until the shooting's done, all while ready to start towing whatever prizes we take back to the Forge."

Dash smiled. "Sounds like a good plan—almost like you've done this capturing ships thing before."

Benzel laughed. "Once or twice."

As they prepared to translate back into unSpace, Dash narrowed his eyes at the distant, unsuspecting Verity ships. In a short while, everyone aboard them would be dead.

To his surprise, Dash felt—nothing.

"And soon enough, you won't feel anything either," Dash said, but only the stars heard him, and they didn't care at all.

6

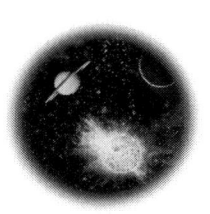

They tried to time it so the two pincers of their attack would race around the red giant and start their attack runs at the same time the *Horse Nebula* began laying her mines. But no plan survives contact with the enemy, as Ragsdale was fond of saying, so the minelayer dropped out of unSpace a little too early. As the Archetype, in formation with the *Comet*, rose over the star's north pole, Dash saw that two of the Verity ships had already accelerated hard to pursue the *Horse Nebula*. The other two kept station, apparently intent on covering whatever the Verity had orbiting between the two asteroid belts.

That thing—whatever it was—worried Dash. Things that were mysterious often turned out to also be dangerous, so he'd had Benzel build an escape hatch into their plan, which was two words—scatter and translate at receipt of a coded command, but that was nice and simple, which was always good.

Now, Dash's attention was pulled away from the *Horse Nebula*—which would have no difficulty escaping the Verity ships—and onto the enigmatic rings.

Dash dialed up the zoom on the heads-up to study it. And he *did* study it, intently, for a good minute. The effort left him grimacing, and even more unhappy.

"Sentinel, what the hell is that?"

"A large ship of unknown design."

"Well, thank you, awesome super-AI made by an unimaginably powerful alien civilization. I'm glad I have you and your keen insights."

"Your sarcasm doesn't change the fact that I do not know. There is nothing in the available data that matches it. That suggests it was designed and built by the Verity, although it is possible, albeit less likely, that is of Golden origin."

"Still doesn't tell me very much. What *can* you say about it?"

"For its size, it contains surprisingly little Dark Metal. That immediately suggests it lacks significant installations of advanced weaponry. Moreover, its power emanations are unusual, with most of it being in the infrared."

"It's hot."

"Relative to the surrounding space, yes. Assuming its outer structure is in thermal equilibrium with its interior, then you would likely consider it somewhat warm."

"It sure doesn't sound like a fighting ship."

"I doubt that it is. It likely has another purpose entirely."

Dash narrowed his eyes at it, still deeply suspicious. "Okay, keep an eye on it, and sound the alarm if it starts doing anything but just sitting there."

Dash focused back on the Verity cruisers. The two that had kept station were now burning hard to intercept them; the other two were decelerating just as hard, obviously giving up on the *Horse Nebula* and anxious to get back to rejoin the other half of their flotilla. The *Horse Nebula*'s timing error had actually worked in their favor, pulling the enemy squadron apart.

The two remaining Verity cruisers didn't slow their rush, though. They launched a swarm of missiles then opened fire with pulse cannons at maximum range. The Cygnus ships weathered the fitful barrage of energy pulses handily, then the Archetype, the Swift, and the *Herald* began swatting missiles into debris.

A trio of detonations rippled through the system, originating near the *Horse Nebula*. They threw off noticeable gravitational wave effects, which meant surge mines. Dash snapped his attention back that way and saw both of the Verity cruisers, having taken off after the minelayer, now drifting in space, their systems dead from the surge mine effects.

"Well, those worked really damned well. Remind me to buy Conover a drink back at the Forge."

"You mean alcohol," Sentinel said.

"Yeah, why?"

"You want to congratulate Conover for successful completion of the task you gave him, by providing him with a metabolic toxin to consume."

"Here's something else you can remind me to do, Sentinel—

make sure you monitor our next party. I need to teach you how to have a little fun."

Dash broke off as the threat indicator showed that the approaching Verity ships were now in range. He waited for Benzel to give the order to fire, since this was his show and he knew the former leader of the Gentle Friends liked fighting in close. Dash also saw the *Horse Nebula* closing on the Verity cruisers stricken by the surge mines. They must be intending to board their helpless foes. Dash opened his mouth to urge caution—but closed it again. If those Verity ships were eventually going to come back online, then they had a relatively limited window to deal with them. And dealing with them was just what the crew of the *Horse Nebula* was about to do.

"Weapons free!" Benzel announced, and Dash fired the darklance, snapping out shots as the Verity ships closed head-on. Fire erupted from the Swift, *Herald*, and *Comet* as well. The Verity ships raced through the onslaught, their tactics a dramatic change from their usual stand-off, fight-at-a-distance style. As they closed, Dash saw why. About ten seconds before they crossed the trajectories of the Archetype and the *Comet*, they opened up with salvoes of fast, short-ranged missiles.

The mech's point-defense systems joined those of the Aquarian ship in responding, taking down most of them; still, the Archetype was hit three times, and the *Comet* twice. Dash registered minor damage from the hits, but the *Comet* staggered under an impact on her port side that blasted a gaping hole in her hull. Venting atmosphere, she accelerated away, wisely opening the distance from Verity ships that were intended to fight in close.

So the Verity had changed their strategy pretty much a hundred-and-eighty degrees. If Dash and his people preferred turning space battles into knife fights, then they'd decided to try and bring bigger knives.

"Nice try, guys," he said, wheeling the Archetype around. "But you aren't the only ones who can try something different."

For an instant, the Archetype faced *away* from the onrushing Verity ships. Another missile slammed into the mech's backside, making Dash grunt against the shock of the hit—then smile at the idea he'd just managed to be shot in the ass during a space battle, and how many people could say *that*? But it left him facing the enemy ships as they flashed past. He opened up with the dark-lance, firing a continuous beam into the stern of one of them as it receded toward the red giant.

"Let's see how you like spanking, asshole," he muttered, and was rewarded with a powerful explosion that left the Verity ship crippled and falling sunward. Ships with fusion drives, like the *Slipwing*, actually had heavily armored and reinforced sterns to protect them from the fierce heat and radiation of their own exhaust. The Verity ships, powered by more advanced drives, didn't need the extra protection and weight, so the dark-lance penetrated the open exhaust ports and ripped deep into the engineering section.

The Verity still had some things to learn about knife fighting.

The remaining enemy ship pivoted and accelerated hard, intent on coming back, it seemed, for another pass. But now Leira and the *Herald* had closed and threw their weight of fire against it. Even the *Comet*, still struggling away from the battle, fired a barrage of missiles. The Verity had reinforced the ship's forward shields and armor, so it actually managed another attack run—but Leira got a clear shot at its stern and replicated Dash's attack, gutting its engineering section and leaving it suddenly dark and dead.

"Dash, reports in from the *Horse Nebula*. They've taken both those Verity ships," Benzel said.

His voice rang with pride, and understandably so. His people must have been outnumbered, but they'd made short work of any Verity defenders. Still, Dash held off a moment with the congratulations.

"Any casualties?"

"Two. One wounded, one dead. As for the Verity, nothing but casualties—all dead, just the way we want them."

"*Shit*. I mean, no, that's great. I just hate losing anyone."

"Me too."

Dash looked at the heads-up and the threat indicator. No opposition remained, aside from the mysterious ring ship.

"Anything left for me?" Amy's voice cut in. She'd kept the *Slipwing* disengaged as their reserve, but now she eased her, and her accompanying drones, around the limb of the red giant.

"Sorry, Amy," Dash said. "Battle's over."

"Already? Well, damn, that's no fun."

"Well, you can help Benzel recover our prizes. Benzel, I'm going to leave it to you to organize that."

"Will do. I've already ordered the *Snow Leopard* to bring the tug drones forward."

"Perfect. Leira, what say you and I check out that ring ship thing?"

"I've got nothing better to do."

Dash powered up the Archetype and shot off toward the mysterious Verity construct, the Swift falling into formation at his side.

AS THEY CAUTIOUSLY SIDLED UP TO the ringed whatever, Dash and Leira kept Sentinel and Tybalt analyzing the incoming data, trying to make sense of what they were seeing. Neither of the AIs had been able to offer much useful insight, though. They could only speak to what was already evident—it consisted of three rings, each almost a kilometer across, lined up along a central hub that bulged in the middle. Spokes connected the rings to the hub. One end of the hub flared into a drive module, while the other seemed to be tipped by a sensor cluster. There were point-defense batteries, which opened fire on the two mechs as they closed; several carefully aimed dark-lance shots took care of those.

Now, Dash and Leira hung outside an airlock in vac suits, waiting to see if Tybalt and Sentinel could hack into the strange ship's systems and open the lock up. Both kept pulse-guns ready. Both also sported new, prototype body armor Custodian had developed at the Forge—tactical breastplates, forearm- and lower-leg protection, all made from a layered carbon nanotube-honeycombed ceramic composite. It weighed almost nothing but, according to the AI, should be able to stop a pulse-gun shot or a projectile from a slug-rifle, even at point blank range.

The downside was that any given part of the armor could likely only stop one direct hit, so it would degrade with use. Still, it was far better than absolutely nothing but fragile vac suits or tactical coveralls; both of those contained some ballistic weave, but it wasn't enough to deal with anything more than fragments or ricochets. Dash wished they'd had it during the fierce, close-quarters fighting in the crashed Golden ship on Gulch.

The airlock slid open.

"I guess they managed to get in," Leira said.

"We did," Tybalt replied. "However, security protocols have engaged to prevent us from accessing helm, nav, and drive functions. It is unclear how long it will take to circumvent them."

"One step at a time," Dash said, and pushed himself into the airlock. Gravity immediately pulled him down to the deck. Leira followed, the outer airlock door slid closed, and the lock began to pressurize.

"This might have been a candidate for that knock-out gas weapon on the Archetype," Leira said. "Last time we did this, everyone was asleep, thanks to that." She hefted her pulse gun. "I kind of miss that, all the bad guys snoozing away."

"Sentinel said it was too compartmentalized," Dash replied. "And I'd rather not go punching holes in the hull until we know what this is all about."

"Okay, but it's just the two of us, and this is a big ship."

Dash frowned. She *was* right. Sentinel had detected only a few signals that indicated life-forms aboard, but there could be any number of bots and other non-living things that might hurt them.

"Sentinel, call up the *Horse Nebula*. They should still be close by. Let's get them aboard this thing, too."

"Actually, Benzel seems to have anticipated this. The *Horse Nebula* is ten minutes out and closing to assist. He further recommends you hold your position until they arrive."

Dash glanced at Leira. "I do *not* regret making that man our offensive commander, even if he is a pirate—yeah, I know, *privateer*."

Dash and Leira waited for the *Horse Nebula* to coast to a halt and disgorge two squads of Gentle Friends. Once they were aboard, they began making their careful way through the massive Verity ship.

THE PULSE-GUN FIRE died as the last Verity fell, hit by a shot from one of the Gentle Friends. He peered back around the bulkhead, saw no other opposition, then looked back.

"Okay, looks like we're in the clear again," he said. "Let's keep moving."

They resumed their way, Dash leading one squad of the Gentle Friends, Leira the other. Over the course of an hour, they'd cleared the hub, taking control of the bridge and engineering against spirited resistance. The Verity crewing this ship weren't numerous, though, and didn't even seem to be soldiers. They shot wildly, without fire discipline, and quickly fell to the accurate, sustained fire of their Cygnus attackers.

Dash stopped at the sight of a massive blast door just ahead. Based on how far they'd come along the spoke, this must be the entrance to the ring. "Sentinel, doors ahead. Can you—"

The doors parted and slid back. "Okay, I guess you can," Dash muttered, then started forward. He reached the doors, stopped, and peeked inside.

A forest?

That's certainly what it seemed to be. Dash saw trees, shrubs, smaller plants, some flowering, and beyond those, what looked like rows of crops. He knew some of the plants, but others were entirely unfamiliar—possibly alien, but Dash was no botanist, so they might be perfectly common plants he just didn't recognize.

"It's a farming ship," Leira said.

Dash nodded. "That it is. And that might make it the best prize we've taken so far."

"Uh, the Forge is producing way more food than we need now, as it is."

"It is. But I want to change that. I want to keep bringing more people into our cause, while still keeping us as self-sufficient as possible." He nodded. "And this is an excellent start."

For a moment, a vision flashed through Dash's mind. He saw the Forge, surrounded by farming and hab ships—the Cygnus Realm, but entirely space-born, dependent on no planets, and free to move where it needed or wanted to. He nodded again, this time at the mental image.

We're going to make that happen, he thought. *And it begins right here.*

CLEARING THE RINGS, which were full of vegetation and, therefore, had no shortage of places to hide, was going to take time. But it didn't really matter, because Sentinel and Tybalt had determined that breaking the encryption on the helm, nav, and drive was going to take many more hours, possibly days. So Dash decided on a different approach.

"Muller here," the voice rang across the comm. "What can I do for you, Dash?"

Muller, the Aquarian captain commanding the *Comet*, had gotten his damaged ship under control, and now kept station as cover for the *Herald* and *Snow Leopard* as they rigged up the captured Verity ships for towing back to the Forge.

"I think it's safe to say you Aquarians have a lot of experience with big engineering projects, especially ones involving rings," Dash said, running a gloved hand along the bark of a tree laden with some reddish-yellow fruit.

"Well, it's not my particular area of expertise, but yeah, I think you could definitely say that. Why?"

"Because I'd like you folks to take charge of recovering this Verity farming ship and getting it back to the Forge. I think it's a job beyond the rest of us."

"I'll talk to Al'Bijea about it, sure, and get back to you."

"Excellent. Dash out."

"Actually, the Aquarians might be even more at home with this than you think," Leira said, walking up beside Dash.

"How so?"

She made a *follow me* gesture. Bemused, Dash did just that, walking with her to the opening to the spoke that led to the bulged portion of the hub. She pointed at something enclosed in what looked like reflective foil, with hoses and conduits extending from it.

"That's a comet, or what's left of one, anyway. According to Tybalt, the Verity are extracting water, oxygen, nitrogen, carbon, all sorts of things from it. And apparently they're doing it with about twice the efficiency of whatever methods the Aquarians are using to harvest comets."

"Oh, Al'Bijea is going to like that—"

Something slammed into Dash's back, knocking the breath from him. He gasped and dropped to his knees; Leira tackled him into some bushes.

"Shit—Dash, are you okay?"

"Yeah." He winced. "Holy crap, what was that?"

"Pulse-gun shot. Came from that way." She pointed. "Looks like Custodian's new armor works—thankfully."

Dash nodded and pulled himself around to a prone firing position. Thankfully indeed. Without that armor, the pulse-gun hit probably would have been fatal.

"Do you see anyone?" he asked.

Leira shook her head. "No."

"Dash, Blue One here. Did we just hear shooting?"

It was the leader of the Gentle Friend's squad accompanying him. He told her where he was, and to hold firm wherever they were, because they seemed to have a sniper on their hands.

"Got him," Leira said, her faceplate lowered back in place. "On thermal. Fifty meters, just to the right of that big tree."

"I have him," Dash said, his own thermal imaging active. He aimed the pulse-gun at the glowing shape and fired. Shots came snapping back, but they passed well overhead.

"There's another one, five meters to the right of the first," he said.

"Got him." Leira took careful aim and fired, then she saw one of the thermal signatures stagger and drop.

"Good shooting," Dash said, firing again then crawling to a new location. He saw a third Verity, this time in the open, trying to move to a new firing position of its own. He aimed, tracking the slender, pale figure, then fired. He hit, the Verity went down to its knees, and a second shot finished it off. By then, Leira had taken out the first one.

"I see some more, further back," she said. "If you move right, I can—"

"Hang on," Dash said. "Hold your fire."

He could see the other figures without thermal imaging because they were moving into the open—with their hands up.

All Verity must die, no exceptions. He aimed—

"Dash, those aren't Verity."

He lowered the muzzle and sighted over the top of the weapon.

No, they definitely weren't.

DASH WATCHED as the Gentle Friends made sure their captives were unarmed. He hadn't expected they would be—grubby and dishevelled, with the haunted hope of those who were only just beginning to realize they were no longer in danger, they'd hardly come across as a threat. But he could almost hear Ragsdale making some flat statement to the effect that everyone was a possible threat, until it was certain they weren't.

The Gentle Friends' squad leader turned to Dash and nodded. "They're clean."

"Well, not really," Leira said, lifting a brow at the filthy captives.

"Uh, you know what I mean."

She just smiled, then turned to Dash. "Okay, so they're clean then—and human. Tybalt confirms it. They scan as fully human."

Dash studied them. "Okay, we're not going to treat you as outright captives," he said to the small throng of grimy figures. "But we've had enough experience with the Golden and the Verity to know that they have agents who could be—well, anyone."

"Who are you?" a woman asked.

"We're from the Cygnus Realm," Dash replied. "We're devoted to the destruction of the Verity and their masters, the Golden."

"Never heard of these Golden," a man said. "The Verity though—yeah, if you're planning to destroy them, then we are *definitely* on your side."

Dash walked up to the man. He, like his fellows, had a heavy collar clamped around his neck. Dash pointed at it. "I take it those collars are meant to keep you in line."

The man nodded but kept his eyes on the ground. "I got a plasma burn once on my arm—a leak from a conduit. I never thought there could be worse pain than that. But there is, and it comes from these damned collars."

"Sentinel, do you and Tybalt have access to anything that might help us get the damned collars off these people?" Dash asked.

In answer, the collars suddenly uttered a shrill tone—then popped open. Their bearers stared for a moment, then ripped them free and threw them away like live explosives.

"Thank you," the man said, his voice choking.

"Look at me," Dash said.

The man reluctantly raised his eyes. "You don't need to avert your eyes, or whatever it is you're doing."

"The Verity—"

"Are dead. And you're free. Got it?"

The man nodded. Tears rolled down his face.

"Who are you? And where are you from?"

The man wiped his eyes and face. "I'm Donner. Donner Alban. We're from a planet called Burrow."

Dash stared. "Really? We were…just there." He glanced at Leira. "I mean, what are the odds?"

Fifty-fifty, they were either from Burrow or they weren't, he heard Sentinel say. The thought made him smile, which made Leira narrow her eyes at him.

"What?"

He shook his head. "I'll tell you another time."

"Who are *you* people?" Donner asked. "And how did you defeat these bloody Verity? They've got tech like we've never seen before."

"We've got tech like you've never seen before, too," Dash said. "But we also have something they don't."

"What?"

"People. Damned good people, motivated and smart." Dash looked at Donner and his companions. "And we could use more of them. Can I assume you're not exactly fans of the Verity?"

Donner answered by turning and spitting in the direction of the nearest Verity corpse. "I only hope it died slow and in pain, because that's what they do to the people they take."

"Are there others like you aboard?" Leira asked.

"We don't know. We've seen others come and go. We've seen a few after the Verity have—done things to them."

Dash put a hand on Donner's shoulder. "That's behind you. You're under the protection of the Cygnus Realm now."

"You said you need people?"

Dash nodded.

"How can we help?"

Dash watched on the Archetype's heads-up as the *Comet* took station beside the Verity farming ship, which they'd named the *Greenbelt*. The *Comet's* crew had finished securing the big farming platform, and had contacted Al'Bijea, who'd dispatched a team to work out how best to get the massive construct back to the Forge.

They still couldn't light the drive or access the helm functions; the AIs said that the Verity had protected the *Greenbelt's* systems with encryption that *was* an AI, one that constantly morphed and changed, making it theoretically impossible to decrypt. It seemed the Verity had upped their cybersecurity game, which gave them another good reason to get the *Greenbelt* back to the Forge intact, besides taking advantage of its prodigious food output. They had to study and figure out how to circumvent this elusive, new cyber-protection. The Aquarians, therefore, would leverage their mega-engineering expertise and take on the task of hauling the big farming ship back to the Forge.

"Dash," Benzel said. "The *Snow Leopard* and the tug drones are away, heading back to the Forge. Meantime, we've finished working out a defensive plan to protect the *Greenbelt* and the Aquarians while they work on her. It's based mostly on mines and drones, like you asked. Custodian figures we can have it all set up in about two days, so I'd like to keep the *Herald*, the *Comet*, and the *Slipwing* on station here until then."

"You're going to live with Amy for two days. Good luck with that."

"I heard that," Amy said. "And you can bet I'm sticking my tongue out at you."

Dash chuckled, but it quickly faded. "What about Donner and the other ex-slaves?"

"They've all decided to stay and help out. They want to do

whatever they can to hit back at the Verity." Benzel paused. "There's some serious hatred there."

"Do you blame them?"

"Not one damned bit."

"Still, keep an eye on them. Just pretend Ragsdale's looking over your shoulder."

"Now there's a scary thought."

Dash chuckled again then prepared to head back to the Forge with Leira. But his good humor immediately faded again as he thought about Benzel's words.

There's some serious hatred there.

There was some serious hatred here, too—more, it seemed, every time Dash encountered the Verity. It made him wonder just how much capacity for hatred he had.

Something told him the Bright, the Verity, and all the rest of them would answer that question for him.

7

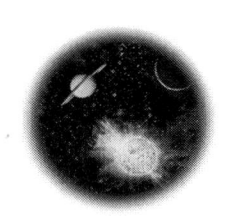

The *Greenbelt* had seemed so huge—until the Aquarians managed to get it back to the Forge. Now, in comparison to the massive station, it looked tiny. Still, Freya had, after about two minutes aboard, announced that it could provide as much food output as the Forge could, at least at the station's current power levels. It just confirmed to Dash that the idea of an independent, space-borne civilization might not be so far-fetched after all. One thing the universe did not have in short supply was comets, and the *Greenbelt* was, it seemed, supremely efficient at extracting resources from them.

"My people are almost bouncing with excitement," Al'Bijea had said. "Personally, I find it rather humbling. I thought we had mastered the engineering needed to exploit cometary resources. Now, it turns out we're far from having mastered it. The system the Verity uses is almost one hundred percent efficient, compared to our sixty percent or so."

"Well, you're welcome," Dash had replied. "Feel free to steal as much of it as you want."

"At this point, I think you'd have trouble getting my people away from it at gunpoint."

Dash had laughed and come away from the holo-meeting in a genuinely buoyant mood. Al'Bijea had, so far, walked up to the edge of entering a formal alliance with the Cygnus Realm, but hadn't yet stepped across. Dash got the sense the man was hedging his bets a bit—he was a cagey businessman, after all, and probably wanted to get something more of an alliance than just an opportunity to fight the Bright—but simply offering over the Verity comet-harvesting tech gratis had definitely nudged Al'Bijea's attitude in a favorable way. The fact that they could use liberated Verity tech to do it was just a delicious benefit.

Now, he walked along a path through the *Greenbelt*, Viktor at his side. Freya, who was as excited as Al'Bijea had been about the farming ship, had just briefed them on her latest finds. After a first, cursory pass through the plants and crops on board, she'd said she recognized about eighty percent of them, and none of them were unsafe for human consumption. The other twenty percent were new to her and would require more study.

"We need to keep a strict quarantine in place in the meantime," she'd said. "I have no idea how safe those unknown plants are. And even if we keep them off the Forge, there might have been some genetic hybridization with the other species on board. We'll just have to rely on the Forge to feed us until then."

Which wasn't going to be a problem. They could all easily eat their body weight in food every day, and still not make an appreciable dent in what the Forge was producing now.

Dash nodded to one of the liberated Verity captives from Burrow, a woman named Mila. She returned an enthusiastic smile. It reminded Dash that Al'Bijea and Freya might have their own reasons to be excited at the possibilities offered by the *Greenbelt*, but they paled in comparison to what these people had gained from them taking it from the Verity.

Viktor had been talking about moving the *Greenbelt*, despite the nav and drive functions being locked down. He'd described how Custodian had determined the Forge could simply tow it for now, using a tractor field to tug it along as the station moved. Dash opened his mouth on a question, but Viktor went on, his voice lowered.

"Do you really think we can trust these people, Dash?"

"Who? The former Verity slaves?"

"Yes. And I know they've been through some unimaginably terrible stuff, and we need the allies—but we really don't much about them, besides what they told us. It's not like the Verity kept detailed records on their lives and backgrounds."

"You've been talking to Ragsdale."

Viktor nodded. "I have. And the man makes sense. Besides, you once told me to be your devil's advocate, question what we do, look for flaws in it."

"I did, and I want you to keep doing that. I also absolutely value Ragsdale's position on all this." Dash stopped and looked back along the path they'd been following among a stand of what seemed to be ordinary apple trees. "Mila," he called back. "Is Donner with you?"

"He's right here," she said, pointing. Donner's head popped around a tree.

"Just working on an irrigation pump," he said. "The Verity might know super-advanced tech, but when it comes to water pumps, they suck."

Dash laughed and walked back, Viktor falling in beside him, obviously bemused. "So, I haven't had much of a chance to talk to you guys since we first met. How are you doing?"

A cloud passed over Donner's face, but he brightened—with effort. "About as well as can be expected. Still, far better than we were, thanks to you folks."

"Have to be honest," Mila said. "I fully expected this was it. I'd even kind of made peace with it. Seems weird now to realize that *wasn't* the end…at all."

"Well, we're almost as glad that we could help," Dash said. "So did the Verity raid Burrow? Is that where they—sorry, got you?"

Donner nodded. "We were already hanging on by a thread there. We figured we had another ten years, maybe, before the ice drove us off the planet, made us refugees."

"Yeah, according to our AI, Sentinel, that's about right."

"Until we met you folks, we assumed the Verity were only taking people for—other purposes, which I won't bother going into," Viktor said. "We didn't know they also took people for labor."

"I don't think that's why they first came to Burrow," Donner replied.

Dash lifted his brow. "Oh? And what makes you say that?"

"They seemed to be looking for something. They didn't even pay much attention to us at all, in fact. When we saw their ship entered orbit, and then sent down drones, we just assumed they were some planetary survey, and that someone was going to eventually come along looking for taxes."

Mila nodded. "It was a few days before they even attacked us. It felt almost like an afterthought."

Dash glanced at Viktor. "They were looking for something, and not someone? Or someones?"

"That's sure what it seemed like," Donner replied. "They kept at it for quite a while, too. They actually brought us back to Burrow a few weeks after they took us. Still had drones there, and they recovered them, then left again."

"I'm surprised they left any of your people—well, left them alone, once they'd found you on Burrow," Viktor said. "But there still seem to be some there. In fact, we were about to send a diplomatic mission to go meet with them right before we met you folks."

"Which is why I was surprised to find out you were from Burrow," Dash put in. "Small universe and all that. Anyway, what do you think the Verity were looking for?"

Donner shrugged. "Not sure. We did detect some anomalous power emissions from time to time but could never pin them down. And they were erratic, sometimes there, sometimes not. Maybe it had something to do with that."

"Not much else on Burrow otherwise," Mila said. "Besides water, more water, frozen water, and rock."

Dash glanced at Viktor again, then tapped his comm. "Custodian, I've got some people here I'd like you to talk to. They're from Burrow, and they say there are some strange power emissions on the planet that might have attracted the Verity. How about you pick their brains, get as much info from them as you can, and see if we can figure out what's going on."

"Very well. However, we are still unable to access many of the *Greenbelt's* systems, and that includes the comm."

"No problem," Dash said, pulling his comm off his belt and handing it to Donner. "Here you go. Custodian will debrief you."

Donner took the comm and looked at it. "He's—it's—an AI, right? That belongs to that alien race, the Unseen?"

"He's an AI, but he doesn't belong to anyone. That's not how we do things here."

Donner nodded. "Good to hear. Yeah, okay, um—Custodian, right? What would you like to know?"

Dash and Viktor left them answering Custodian's questions and headed back to the Forge.

DASH STARED at the image Custodian had put up on the big holo display in the Command Center. It showed—lines. Wavy lines, on a graph. Dash recognized them as some sort of waveform, but that's about as far as he went before his knowledge of physics became limited.

"What am I looking at?" he asked.

Conover answered. "They're waveforms."

Dash gave him a wry look. "Well, gee, thanks for that. I guess we're done here."

"These are waveform comparisons between various power signatures," Custodian said. "The five green wave functions are from various sources among our forces, such as the reactors aboard the *Herald*. The three orange ones are from power cores gathered and installed in the Archetype, the Swift, and the Forge. The green one is the power emission signature of the source on Burrow, as recorded by the Archetype."

Dash narrowed his eyes at that. "Sentinel recorded that while we were there but didn't say anything?"

"It was deeply buried in environmental background EM noise," Sentinel said. "And I had no reason to apply the various transformations and data synthesis that were needed to extract it."

"Sorry, Sentinel, didn't mean it to sound like a criticism," Dash said, holding up a hand.

"But it did," Leira said, with playful accusation.

Dash gave her an airy wave. "I was just surprised you'd missed it," he said. "I consider you more or less infallible. Unlike…well, humans."

"Again, it required a complex series of—"

"To clarify, that was both compliment *and* apology. We good now?"

"We are, yes."

"Anyway, that green waveform doesn't fit any of the orange

ones at all," Dash went on. "It's pretty close to the green ones, though. So it's—another power core? There's a power core on Burrow?"

"So it seems," Viktor said. "But it's also different. Custodian, get rid of the orange lines and rescale the graph." He glanced at Dash. "The power output signature from the *Herald* is so high it distorts the graph, makes it look like the rest of the lines are very close together." He looked back at the display. "See?"

Dash did and nodded. "That power core on Burrow has a higher output than the others, and it's noisier? The line is more jagged, while the others are smoother?"

"That's right," Conover said. "Sentinel says it's hard to tell how much of that jaggedness might really just be interference from the EM background on Burrow—there must be a lot of storms there or something."

Dash thought about the vast, towering thunderstorms he'd powered the Archetype through, the searing bolts of lightning, the strange, luminous phenomena like sprites and elves and fountains of charged particles erupting from their stratospheric tops. "Yeah, you might say that." He crossed his arms. "So this core is similar to the ones we've collected so far, but also different."

"That is correct," Custodian said. "However, with nothing to otherwise use for comparison with it, that is the only conclusion we can draw from these data alone."

"Looks like we're going back to Burrow," Leira said.

Dash nodded. "Yeah, except we're going to have to assume we're going back there to fight. The Verity have already raided Burrow, and—" Dash broke off, a sudden, horrified wrench tightening his gut. "Oh, shit. Harolyn hasn't set out for there yet on our diplomatic mission, has she?"

"No, not yet," Viktor said. "She's planning on leaving in a few hours. I guess we can turn that particular plan off, though."

Dash sighed. "Damned right we can." He looked around. "Where's Benzel?"

A moment later, the door slid open and Benzel strode through. Wei Ping followed him in.

[...] "The floor is yours."

[...] switched to the image of a star map, the [...] matic Dash thought he was soon going to start seeing in his sleep. The location of the Forge was clearly marked, as were a number of other systems. In all, a dozen stars were highlighted.

"Okay, I'll say it again," Dash said. "What am I looking at, exactly?"

"These are what Custodian and I believe are the systems controlled by the Verity. There are sixteen of them. This is based on every data source we had available, including data we were able to extract from those two Verity ships we took as prizes," Benzel said.

"Our measure of confidence in the results is therefore high," Custodian put in.

Dash stared for a moment. "You're saying that these are all the systems the Verity control? Like, this is all of them?"

"Well, we can't rule out some that might have slipped under the scanners," Benzel replied. "We're not sure every last outpost and installation is on here. But these are the main ones, what you could call their—I don't know, *empire*, or whatever. At least within our capability to scan. For now."

"Not all of these are settled planets," Wei-Ping said. "Some of them are orbital platforms, stations, and the like."

"What's that one icon there," Leira asked, pointing. "The one that's different than the rest?"

"Was just going to get to that one," Wei-Ping went on. "That, it seems, is a big mobile station. It's nowhere near as big as the Forge, but it carries a slew of long-range missiles, as well as the capability to launch and retrieve things like fighters. We're calling it a carrier."

Dash nodded. There were a few of the big ships called carriers in the fleets of various powers in the arm. They were powerful, he knew, but also had a reputation for being expensive to build, and even more costly to maintain.

"This carrier is sufficiently powerful that it could control a wide region of space," Custodian said. "It could extend its influence across several systems."

"Okay, well, that is definitely a priority target," Dash said. "I mean, damn—if we could capture that intact, still operational, and put it to use ourselves…"

He trailed off, thinking about the possibilities. But Leira's voice echoed in his head, speaking just behind his ambitious thoughts—saying that attacking this carrier with the intent of taking it as a prize would be a monumental, not to mention *extremely* dangerous, thing to take on.

"Okay, let's call that carrier—uh, Citadel. Yeah, Citadel works. Benzel, I'd like you to draw up an initial plan at how we might be able to go about attacking and capturing it."

Benzel scratched an ear. "Will do. That's going to be a tall order, though." He frowned in a thought for a moment. "I think, if we want to do this, we need to move the Forge in even closer so we're closer to our support, supplies, repairs, and such when we try this."

"Agreed," Dash said. "And while we're at it, we'll mine each system we pass through." He walked up to the big display and pointed at star systems. "Like this one, and this one." He pointed at the gleaming icons as he spoke. "These—and this one. Mine them, make sure they're clear of Golden stuff, and declare them *green*, meaning we can look at them for our own future use."

"Sounds like you're planning to carve out an empire of your own, Dash," Viktor said.

Dash shook his head. "Empires are run by emperors—and, before anyone who even hints at it, the *last* thing I want is to be an emperor. Let's face it, emperors are generally assholes." He shrugged. "I'm just trying to think of the time after this war is over, and we've won it, and—"

A shrill alarm sounded, cutting him off. Custodian immediately spoke over it.

"This is a security alert for the primary fabrication level. Intruders detected. Security protocols being initiated."

Dash and the others exchanged a momentary, stunned look. Leira mouthed the word, *intruders?*

In the next breath, they were all running for the exit to grab weapons.

"Arm up!" Dash bellowed, and as one, they raced to the fight, and the unknown invaders breaching the Forge.

DASH STOPPED, knelt, and looked around a bulkhead. He saw a sealed blast door at the end of the corridor; it normally stood open, giving access to the main fabrication plant. But he also saw Ragsdale crouching beside the entrance to a cross corridor, one that led to the various peripheral fabricating systems fed by the main plant. Two others—a woman Dash recognized as one of the Gentle Friends, and a young man he knew to be a former refugee, now very much a dedicated member of the Forge's growing crew—crouched on the other side of the corridor. Ragsdale leaned around the corner, fired a quick pulse-gun shot, then ducked back at a volley of return fire that struck the other side of the corridor behind him.

Dash ran to Ragsdale's side. Leira, Benzel, and Wei-Ping

followed, with another dozen of the Gentle Friends and a few more of the ex refugees following.

"What the hell's going on?" Dash asked.

"Verity," Ragsdale said. "Seems they were sealed into a compartment, part of one of those wrecked Verity ships scavenged from the last battle. Custodian brought it on board to disassemble it, and these assholes popped out."

More pulse-gun fire ripped out of the corridor, followed by a plasma-blast that howled right down the opposite corridor and slammed into something further down it with a rolling boom. Dash winced. This was just—wrong. The Forge was their safe haven. To have intruders, and Verity, no less, infiltrated into it, armed and shooting—

It just wasn't *right*. And, more than that, it pissed him off.

"Custodian," Dash snapped. "How did you not detect these bastards?"

"Unknown. At this point, I can only speculate that they somehow suppressed their characteristic biotech signals until they were somehow awake—"

The last bit was cut off by another fusillade of fire. Ragsdale swore. "Here they come again!"

The fire intensified. Ragsdale and the two with him snapped shots back down the corridor; Dash leaned in and fired over the Security Chief's head, while Benzel went prone and fired around them both. Leira and Wei-Ping organized the Gentle Friends and others following them, readying them to either take up fire positions, or to prepare for attack.

The added weight of fire from Dash and Benzel sent the

Verity—Dash saw at least a half dozen of them, pale and nearly skeletal—scrambling back into cover. He also saw the one with the plasma-gun—although it looked more like a plasma-cannon, big enough to probably warrant a tripod—line up another shot.

He snapped one shot back, then shouted, "Take cover!" A second later, the plasma bolt exploded against the corner of the corridor, sending both the Gentle Friend and the ex-refugee who'd been helping Ragsdale staggering backward, groaning from painful flash burns.

"They keep trying to rush us!" Ragsdale said. "If you guys hadn't showed up—"

"But we did, here we are, so let's deal with these assholes," Dash said. "Custodian, can they get out of that compartment they're in?"

"Only through the corridor you are now guarding. They have jammed the blast door that would secure it into the open position."

Dash thought fast. Trying to charge the Verity would be suicide, unless they took time-consuming measures to protect themselves. That was time during which the Verity could potentially cause any number of problems. But they were otherwise trapped.

"Custodian, can you just depressurize that compartment—oh, for—wait, you can't, not with the blast door jammed open. Shit!"

Leira appeared beside him. "Dash, they're cornered, and they know it. Why not give them another way out? We can try to move them somewhere where they'll be more vulnerable."

"Two of the Verity are attempting to open the blast door leading into the main fabrication plant," Custodian said. "I have enacted countermeasures, but there is a growing possibility they will succeed in overriding the Forge systems and open the door—"

"Let them," Dash said.

Ragsdale gave him an incredulous look. "Let them into the main plant? Isn't that exactly what we *don't* want?"

Dash glanced at the big blast door leading into the main fabrication facility. "We don't want to let them in there on their terms, no. But on our terms?" He nodded. "Yeah, we do. Once they're in there, there's a lot less cover, and they'll be out in the open."

"What if they don't fall for it?" Wei-Ping asked. "I mean, I've never—"

She broke off as the Verity opened fire again, loosing another plasma blast that erupted against the opposite wall with a concussive blast.

"I've never found it a good idea to count on my enemy making a mistake!" Wei-Ping shouted, probably over the same ringing that sang in Dash's ears.

"Then they'll be where they are now, but we'll have *two* ways of getting at them instead of one," Dash replied.

The rest of them nodded at that, who snapped out instructions, and the others hurried to carry them out.

"Okay, Custodian," Dash said. "*Now.*"

He watched from behind a big mold, currently configured for the casting of casings for their mines—a fabrication job still going on, despite the ongoing firefight. Dash was here with Benzel and a dozen of the Gentle Friends. Ragsdale, Leira, Wei-Ping, and another half dozen held the original corridor against the Verity.

The blast door leading into the Verity-held compartment slid open. Two Verity stood in full view, looking surprised; no one fired, though. Dash had been explicit about that—no one fired until he did. He wanted the Verity to exit that compartment and move into the cavernous main plant, where they'd be much easier targets.

The two Verity ducked back under cover. A moment passed, then a full squad of them dashed back into view, pulse-guns raised. Behind them came the plasma-gunner, lumbering a little under the weight of the big weapon.

It would take them about three seconds to cross from the open blast door to cover behind the fabrication machinery.

That was three seconds too long.

Dash waited until the leader was about halfway, then fired, blowing apart the side of its head and dropping it in a lifeless heap. His companions now opened, gunning down most of the Verity who appeared. Another group emerged, hugging the wall and trying to work their way around the outside of the main plant; the plasma-gunner covered them, pumping out searing blasts that slammed into the fabrication machinery around them. A pipe carrying liquid metal burst open, spilling its scorching contents and sending the Gentle Friends scrambling away from the spreading, glowing pool. Custodian immediately cut the flow.

Dash swore viciously as the situation changed yet again. The plasma-gunner had bought the other group some time, and now they snapped shots out from behind cover, at the same time working their way in short dashes further along the wall. The plasma-gunner went down, hit by a pulse-gun shot that spun it around to fall stone dead. A few seconds later, Ragsdale and Leira appeared in the doorway.

"This compartment's secure," Ragsdale said over the comm.

"Good. We've still got about a dozen of them out here worming their way along the outside of the main plant," Dash said. He looked around, trying to decide how to run these Verity intruders down before they did more serious damage.

"Custodian," he said. "Are they looking for another way out?"

"They are. Again, they are attempting to use a portable device to hack open the blast door leading to one of the salvage bays."

Dash gave Benzel a puzzled look. "Where the hell do they think they're going? They can't really believe they're going to escape."

Benzel narrowed his eyes. "Do you think they actually know *where* they're going, or are they just making it up as they go along?"

Dash could tell the man was going somewhere with this. "What do you mean?"

"When we bust into a ship, we don't exactly have the schematics handy. But all ships are laid out pretty much the same

—engineering to the rear, the bridge somewhere forward, but well-protected, weapons along the outer hull, that sort of thing. This station isn't laid out like that. Those Verity are probably just looking for somewhere secure to hole up—ideally, with some hostages, if they can take them, so they can negotiate." He shrugged. "We got that occasionally, some of the crew hunkered down in their ship, trying to make a deal with us."

"And did you?"

"Sometimes, sure, if it meant fewer people getting hurt." He scowled. "That doesn't apply to these assholes, though. They don't deserve anything but death. That's still our policy about them, right?"

"Damned right it is."

"Well, they want to get into that salvage bay. Let them." Benzel's scowl hardened even more. "It opens out on space, right?"

Dash gave a grim nod back. "Yeah. It does. Custodian, let them into the bay. Then close it back up and space them."

"Understood."

Dash could hear the distant roar of venting air through the blast door as the bay's outer ports opened. If there were screams from the Verity now trapped inside, he didn't hear them.

"WELL, THAT WAS FUN," Benzel said. "Not anxious to repeat it, though."

He stood with Dash, Leira, Wei-Ping, and Ragsdale, all of

them surveying the damage to the Forge. The Verity had managed to inflict serious, but not crippling harm, and Custodian said the systems should be operating normally again in a couple of days. It could have been much worse.

"Custodian and I are going to spend some time talking about how to prevent something like this from happening again," Ragsdale said. Dash could tell the man was taking it personally, as though the Verity sneaking aboard had been his failure. So Dash just nodded.

"I know you've got this," he said. "Just brief us on whatever new protocols you're putting in place."

"Will do."

"Meantime, we're going to do a thorough sweep of the wrecked ships we brought back before Custodian brings any more of their components aboard," Wei-Ping said. "We'll also sweep those two intact prize ships and the *Greenbelt*. We'll make sure no more of these assholes are lurking and waiting to come back to life."

"Yeah, that's something else Custodian needs to work on," Benzel said. "How'd they do that?"

Dash nodded. "This all sounds good, and I'm happy to leave it in your capable hands. For now, we've still got a war to fight. Benzel, let's get everyone assembled in the Command Center in two hours so we can plan our return to Burrow."

"What do you want to do with these dead Verity?" Ragsdale asked. "We've got a bunch of their bodies in storage now for study—do we really need more?"

"Custodian," Dash asked. "Do any of these Verity scan any differently from the ones we've encountered previously?"

"I can detect no significant variances."

"Fine. Then toss them into space. They can go join their friends in the big black."

"Damned right," Wei-Ping said. Benzel just gave a fiercely satisfied nod.

8

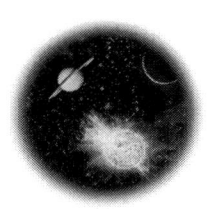

"Dash," Benzel said over the comm. "Striking the Verity from orbit is still an option. Do you really want to land and fight them up close?"

Dash looked at the imagery displayed on the Archetype's heads-up, the sprawling swirl of cloud, water, rock, and ice that was Burrow. They'd found no Verity ships in orbit, or in the system generally; it seemed those on the surface were relying on stealth and subterfuge to avoid detection while they tried to run down the power core apparently hidden somewhere on the planet. That explained why there'd been no sign of them registering with Sentinel or Tybalt when they'd been here before. The EM racket from the planet—and there was a *lot* of it, from the multitude of raging storms—had concealed whatever signals had been leaking out of their operation, including that of the mysterious power core. Now that they knew to look for it, though, it was pretty plain to see.

"Oh, like I said in our planning meeting, I'd love to just sit up here and pummel them from orbit," Dash said. "But there might still be some of the water haulers down there, and we don't know where, exactly, that power core is. So I'm afraid it's down we go."

"You're the boss. Okay, we've got landing sites identified around the settlement. But we're having trouble getting solid scans otherwise because storms keep passing over the place."

Dash nodded. "Since when have we ever had a complete picture of what we're heading into?"

"At least we know there aren't any other major forces around," Leira said. "Aside from some Dark Metal inside the settlement, Tybalt doesn't detect anything on the surface or elsewhere in the system."

Dash nodded again, but with a bit of a frown. Now that was a little strange—the Verity had some sort of force on the ground, but nothing in space to support them? Even stranger, they must have had designs on this system in the first place to have four cruisers and the *Greenbelt* here. But, again, now they had nothing because their losses had hit them worse than even Custodian and the other AI's assumed, and they'd just given up on Burrow entirely. For that matter, maybe there were no Verity left down there, only automated systems left behind, either abandoned or still active and dangerous as a final *screw you* to Dash and the Cygnus Realm.

"Well," Dash replied. "*Whatever's* here is down there. So let's proceed per the plan, and deal with whatever comes up when it does—you know, the way we usually do."

"The way we usually do?" Leira said. "You mean with enthusiastic violence?"

"Exactly," Dash said, starting the Archetype plunging into the atmosphere, followed by the Swift and the shuttles from the *Herald*, which were loaded with the rest of their assault force. "Come along, friends. It's time to deliver some *boom*."

DASH POWERED the Archetype through the base of a storm, buffeted by wind shear and driving ice. One instant, he was immersed in featureless grey shot through with occasional pulses of lighting; the next, the mech burst into open air, the settlement a klick ahead.

Sentinel had already calculated a firing pattern for the dark-lance, based on what they'd been able to detect from orbit and a single drone pass about fifteen seconds ahead of the Archetype. Dash executed it, taken aback by the dazzling blasts rolling out from the dark-lance's beam as it ripped through the quantum roots of the planet's atmospheric gases. Sentinel had warned him this would happen, but he just wasn't used to the weapon producing anything but a shadowy hint of a beam, the phenomenon that gave it its name.

It was over in a few seconds, the Archetype racing back up into the scudding clouds, the settlement's comms array and three Verity shuttles hidden—not quite well enough—under snow and ice all reduced to glowing wreckage. Dash had also snapped out a shot at a bulky device apparently deployed by the Verity on the edge of the settlement, blowing it to fragments and atomic dust.

"Any idea what that was?" he asked, as the Sentinel swooped back into a storm. "That last thing we shot at?"

"Similar to a portable version of a deep-space comm array. It may also have been a defensive system of some sort. Our destruction of it was rather efficient, so this is merely a guess."

Dash considered that. "Apologies. Would an additional second or so give you time to identify more of the enemy tech?"

"A second would be more than adequate, and thank you for, as you might say, withholding the boom," Sentinel said.

"It's my pleasure. Remember, I'm a gentleman at heart."

"I'll make a note of that status," Sentinel said.

"Dash, I'm down," Leira broke in. "I've set down about five hundred meters from the northern edge of the settlement."

Dash felt himself grimace. Half a klick was an irrelevant distance—until you were on foot, rushing through a blizzard, quite likely under fire. "Why so far away? Are you secure?"

"Because there's a big excavation here, into the ice, about a hundred meters to my left. It looks like someone's been digging for something."

"Ah, okay. Good call, then. No resistance?"

"Nope. And all three shuttles are down. Benzel's getting the troops sorted out—"

"Yeah, Benzel here. Sorry to cut you off, Leira. Dash, the plan was to take the settlement, but this excavation looks pretty—

significant, I guess. Someone's been going through a lot of effort to dig after something. I think we should secure it first."

"Well, at this point, Benzel, it's your show," Dash replied. "There don't seem to be any immediate threats we need the mechs to deal with, so I'm going to join you down there. Just make sure you keep up comms with the *Herald*. Sentinel, that goes for you too. You and Tybalt are going to have to keep a watch out for anything that might come up nasty, either down here, or back up in space."

"Understood."

Dash jackknifed the Archetype and plunged back downward, plummeting toward the surface headfirst. A klick up, he flipped again, then settled the mech a couple hundred meters closer to the settlement than the Swift. As its massive feet sank into the drifting snow, he scanned the nearby buildings. There were about a dozen, mostly prefabs, although a few were clearly repurposed spaceship components. Another dozen or so cargo pods were scattered among them. Thermal signatures glowed from a few—heating appliances, most likely. He saw no other signs of—anything, really. The settlement seemed abandoned.

"Okay, Sentinel, you're on. Keep a particular eye on the settlement in case anyone—or anything—tries to come at us while we're otherwise engaged." He added the anything because powered-down bots would show no heat signatures, and the Golden were fond of their bots.

Dash dismounted into a gusty blizzard. Icy crystals of wind-whipped snow rattled against his tactical goggles and brushed against his enviro-suit. Gripping a pulse-gun, he trudged through the knee-deep snow, immediately missing the warm, quiet interior of the Archetype. It was definitely a lot more pleasant weathering these temperatures inside thousands of tons of high-tech machinery than out here on his own feet, floundering through drifting snow.

"Dash, I'm over to your right," Leira said over the comm.

Dash looked that way and saw her crouching behind a hulking digger. Just beyond her, a gaping hole inclined down into the base of an ice face, itself the leading edge of a glacier bulging out of a mountain valley that vanished into the clouds.

"On my way."

He joined Leira, crouching beside her in the snow. He had to take a moment to catch his breath, though. Beating a path through snow that was, in some places, almost waist deep, definitely put the word *labor* into *laborious*.

"Quite the workout, isn't it?" Leira asked. He couldn't see her mouth under her environmental hood, but he could see the grin in her eyes from behind her goggles.

"I thought leaping and jumping around in that cradle would've had me in better shape than this." He sucked in a deep breath. "Okay, what's the situation?"

Leira nodded toward the excavation. "Benzel's just sent the first squad in. He's holding the other two squads back until they've got a foothold in—whatever the hell is in there."

Dash looked up at the digger. It was an older, clunkier model, once more something that could be found laboring away on hundreds of worlds. This one had seen better days, but its bucket had been replaced with some sort of sleek, gleaming drill.

"That looks like Verity tech," he said. "They're definitely after something down there—"

Leira held up her hand. "I hear shooting."

Dash heard nothing but the boom of the wind—and then a sporadic rattle of pulse-gun fire.

He tapped Leira. "Come on."

Together, they floundered through the snow. Their body armor didn't make it any easier, because although it weighed very little, it still restricted their movements. They arrived at the mouth of the excavation just as Benzel led a second squad inside to reinforce the first. They pounded down a metal ramp and immediately took cover among drilling machinery, cargo cases, pumps, and other sundry gear used for digging out tunnels. Pulse gun shots slammed into the ice ramp behind them with puffs of superheated vapor and eruptions of shimmering fragments.

"Lead squad says they've found a bunch of Verity holed up about a hundred meters in," Benzel said. "Trouble is, there's not much room to maneuver in there. If we want to take them, we either have to assault them head-on, or wait them out."

Dash bit his lip. Waiting would be safest, but Verity reinforcements could be racing toward Burrow right now if they managed to get out a distress call before he'd taken out their comms. Actually, having the Archetype blast dark-lance shots into the excavation and simply obliterate everyone and everything inside was *truly* safest—but it was also out of the question, for the same reasons they hadn't just bombarded the place from orbit. And a frontal assault could be costly, terribly so.

He looked around for something, anything, that might help,

and let his gaze settle on another brutish machine, this one an excavator with a massive dozer blade.

"Do they have any heavy weapons?" he asked. "Anything like that plasma-cannon thing they were using on the Forge?"

Benzel shook his head. "Not that we've seen. But those pulse-guns and laser flash-guns they're using are more than enough to keep us pinned down. Why?"

Dash looked at Leira. "You ever run a big machine like that one?" He nodded at the excavator. Leira's eyes rolled, but then she realized he was serious.

"Do I look like someone who'd have ever driven something like that? I do spaceships and giant mechs, thanks. Not really a dirt girl."

Dash gave her a wintry smile. "True. You're more of a space hooligan."

"Hey—" Leira tried to protest, but Dash grinned to take the sting away, then looked at Benzel, who shook his head.

"I see where you're going with this. Just a sec—Tabor, where are you?" Benzel said.

A woman's voice came over the comm. "Still up top where you left us. Why?"

"Get your butt down here, got a job for you. The three of us are at the base of the ramp, to the right, behind some cargo cases."

A moment passed, then a figure came running down the ice ramp in a crouch. She dove behind the cargo cases covering Dash, Leira, and Benzel, just as another salvo of pulse-gun fire smashed into the ramp less than a meter behind her feet.

She slid to a stop. "What's up?"

Benzel jabbed a thumb at the excavator. "You used to run those, right?"

"Been a while, but yeah."

Benzel nodded to Dash, who knelt and began sketching a plan in the snow. With broad strokes, he watched as the dawn of understanding came over Benzel and Tabor's faces.

"Ah," Tabor said.

"That's a good thing, right?" Dash asked.

"Very. Good plan, boss. I'm ready," Tabor said.

"Same," Benzel added, a hungry look on his face. He then gave orders to the two squads now engaged with the Verity. With a final thumbs up, he trotted away with purpose.

"Okay, let's dish it out," Dash said.

As one, the Gentle Friends rose and opened fire, pouring shots into the excavation. At the same time, Dash leapt over the cargo cases, Tabor and Leira right behind him. A few shots snapped at their heels as they ran for the excavator, but the sheer weight of shooting from the Gentle Friends gave them the few seconds they needed to reach the big machine.

"It's time," Dash said to Tabor. "Up you go, and let's hope it's actually running."

"Only one way to find out," the woman said, clambering into the cab. A moment passed. Okay, maybe this thing didn't run, which means they'd need a plan B—

The big machine hummed, then sparked to life with a shrill, rising whine. Tabor gave a thumbs up of her own and raised the dozer blade, obscuring the cab from the Verity. It was just in time;

pulse-gun fire that would have ripped through the cab flared and sparked against the blade, a massive slab of thick, high-strength composite alloys.

"Okay, here we go," Dash said into the comm as Tabor began maneuvering the excavator, its chunky tracks squealing. As she turned and started down the excavation, Dash and Leira followed behind; the Gentle Friends closed in until an entire squad was crowded in behind the rumbling machine.

They advanced, a hail of pulse-gun fire hammering desperately at the excavator. Glowing chunks of alloy began spalling off the blade and the tracks, but both were meant to grind against rock; it would take far longer than the trip along the tunnel for the Verity to disable the big machine.

Leira and Benzel crowded against him, and Dash tried to count his paces, taking each as about a meter. Fifty. Now sixty. Seventy—

"Get ready!" Benzel shouted.

Seventy-five. Eighty-five—

"Now!" Dash shouted.

Two of the Gentle Friends dodged around the sides of the excavator and threw concussion grenades. A pulse-gun blast hit one of them squarely, knocking him flat on his back. Dash glanced at him and saw him wave, and a scorched pit in his body armor showed he'd survived.

The grenades detonated with a double *WHAM WHAM* that thundered up the tunnel. An instant later, Benzel shouted "Go!" and the Gentle Friends leapt from behind the excavator, pulse-guns, snap-guns, and sluggers firing. Dash had reminded them there might very well be hostages among the Verity, and to watch their shooting; frankly, they all knew there was no way to really guarantee the safety of any captives.

Behind them, the second squad of Gentle Friends came running up the tunnel to join the fray. Dash ran around the excavator going right; Leira went left. Tabor jumped down beside Dash and opened up with her pulse-gun. The next few moments were a blur of running, taking cover, shooting, running again, and dodging. Dash shot a Verity who popped up in front of him at point-blank range.

It fell back and another appeared, slamming a shock-baton into him. It hit his armor and discharged, mostly harmlessly, but there was a sudden, tingling jolt, a fraction of what would have ripped through his body if it had connected somewhere not armored. He struck back with the butt of his pulse-gun, catching the Verity in the throat. It staggered back but lashed out with the baton again. Dash dodged it by millimeters, then kicked the Verity's knee, buckling it. A follow-up pistol whip across its face dropped it, and a double tap of shots into it kept it down.

Someone slammed into Dash, knocking him sideways. He tried to stop his fall, but whoever had attacked him had him pinned against the alloy frame of a drill. Dash shoved desperately back, trying to get some leverage, but saw a keen, curved blade rising—

Before it vanished, the pale hand holding it blew to ragged shreds. Leira yanked the Verity off Dash and finished it with another shot into its throat. Dash gave her a nod and readied himself for his next attacker.

But there was none. Only the Gentle Friends remained on their feet and in possession of the tunnel. All of the Verity were down.

"Dash, we've got some hostages over here," Benzel called.

Limping due to a leg wound he hadn't even felt, Dash moved to where he could see Benzel waving at him. Along the way, he saw a few of the Gentle Friends were down, but all seemed to be alive. More to the point, he saw many instances of seared and pitted body armor. It might be a pain to wear, he thought, but it sure seemed to do the job.

He stopped beside Benzel. There were indeed hostages locked in a contraption made of metal mesh platforms repurposed into a cage. Dash scowled at that. "Let's get them the hell out of there."

Benzel nodded and shot off the lock. The hostages, now survivors, immediately pushed their way out. Dash counted fourteen, including three who had to be no more than twelve or thirteen years old. All were grubby and malnourished. One of them, an older man with a riot of greying hair and whiskers, pointed at the back of the excavation.

"They were after what's back there, some sort of alien tech," he said, then stopped and looked stricken. "Did you rescue anyone from the settlement? They've had us down here for days, using us to dig—" He broke off with a sobbing breath.

Dash shook his head. "We haven't been to the settlement yet. It looks completely abandoned, but we'll check it out."

"Dash," Leira said over the comm. "You've got to come and look at this."

Dash left Benzel and the Gentle Friends to get things under control, then found Leira crouching over something protruding from the ice wall at the very back of the excavation.

"That looks like Golden tech," Dash said, kneeling beside her.

She nodded. "Yeah, it does have that look to it, doesn't it? I've sent an image to Tybalt, and he and Sentinel are—"

"Now able to offer some insight," Tybalt said over the comm. "This indeed appears to be a cache of Golden technology. However, the ring-like object you see protruding from the top of it is consistent with the technology of the Creators."

"The Unseen?" Dash focused his attention on the specific piece Tybalt had described. One ring stuck out of the ice. Another was completely entombed, with about a meter separating the two. Both seemed to be attached to a cylindrical object Dash could just make out deeper inside the ice. "Is this—is this the power core?"

"So it would appear," Sentinel said. "The presence of the two rings suggests that another power core can be stacked in tandem with it."

"A dual power core? What would that be used for?"

"Unfortunately, we do not have that information."

"Yeah, of course we don't." Dash went to scratch his nose but realized it was enclosed in the enviro-mask, so he'd just have to live with the itch. He looked at the ice wall. "Looks like they were close to getting this stuff out of here." He glanced at a fallen Verity. "Good for them to do the heavy lifting. Might've tipped them, if they'd survived."

Leira opened her mouth to answer, but a tremendous explosion shook the tunnel. Chunks of ice came loose from the ceiling and sent them crashing down among those inside.

Dash, Leira, and Benzel once more stopped just inside the excavation, only this time they were facing out into the blizzard. Driving snow limited visibility to a couple of hundred meters at best—far enough to show one of the shuttles that had carried the Gentle Friends down from orbit was now a smouldering wreck. Something rushed overhead with a roar.

"Sentinel, what the hell's going on? Verity reinforcements?" Dash shouted.

"If they are, then how'd they get here without the *Herald* detecting them," Leira said. "And down from orbit, too."

Another brilliant flash cut through the storm, followed by a colossal WHUMP that Dash felt in his chest. Something big had just exploded in the direction of the Archetype.

"Sentinel!"

"We are under attack," came her unruffled reply.

"No shit," Dash snapped. "Who is it? Where are they?"

"Unknown, and generally approaching from the direction of the settlement," Sentinel said. "I would suggest you and Leira remount the Archetype and Swift in order to deal with this new threat."

"Again, no shit! But there are a couple hundred meters of deep snow and blizzard between you and us!"

Something else rushed overhead, a thunderous roar rolling along behind it. Dash caught a glimpse of something delta winged. It was an atmospheric fighter, but not one Dash had ever seen before.

Who the hell was *this*, now? Who was attacking them?

Something huge came plunging out of the sky. Dash gasped as they all made to throw themselves back into the excavation—but it was the Archetype, landing about ten meters from the tunnel opening.

"This should make it easier for you to remount," Sentinel said.

Dash glanced at Leira. "Can't argue with that—"

Another roar thundered overhead. An instant later, a searing flash punctuated the blizzard. Something exploded high above them, showering the field of wind-blowing snow with smoking debris.

"The pilots of these craft appear to be flying what amount to suicide missions," Tybalt said. "The Swift has been struck twice now, with moderate damage."

Dash braced himself to run to the Archetype, but hesitated. He couldn't see the fighters but could hear them maneuvering overhead. It was only ten meters to the Archetype, but then he had to mount and get inside.

"Sentinel," he said. "How about a hand getting aboard?"

The Archetype crouched and lowered a massive hand. Dash threw a quick salute to Benzel, who nodded back. To Leira, he said, "Mount up." Then he ran and leapt into the Archetype's huge palm.

He and Sentinel had practiced this, an emergency mount using the Archetype itself to lift Dash. It was much faster than the usual way of having the Archetype crouch until it was almost prone, but not as safe; he'd be fully exposed as he was lifted, and any explosion might knock him off his perch. Dash gritted his teeth as the mighty hand raised him smoothly toward the open cockpit. Wind gusted around him, buffeting him as he rose further and further from the ground.

Another atmo-fighter streaked overhead. This one loosed a trail of a small objects in its wake. It took Dash a second to realize they were bombs.

And one was plummeting straight toward him.

"Dash, get down," Sentinel boomed.

Cried. She'd *cried* his name. She'd sounded—*emotional*. Human.

Dash was still thinking this when instinct made him drop prone against the cold alloy of the Archetype's hand. Its other hand enclosed him in a metal cocoon. Something clanged against the hand above him; an instant later, something else slammed through his brain like a missile impact.

D*ASH*.

He heard it. Heard a series of sounds, anyway. *Da-a-ssshhh*. It was familiar. Meant something—

Dash.

That has something to do with me, he thought.

"You must wake up—"

Wait. That's Sentinel, Dash thought. She's talking to me.

"Dash!"

He opened his mouth—

"Ow!"

"Dash, I am using the Meld to amplify our communications. It is essential that you mount the cradle and assume control of the Archetype."

Dash sat up. He'd been sprawled on the cockpit floor; Sentinel must have managed to get him inside, but there was no way she could install him in the control cradle. A shrill whine filled his head; pain blasted behind his eyes like lightning bolts every time he moved.

Groaning, he dragged himself to the cradle and clambered into it. "Crap, my head hurts. What happened?"

"A bomb detonated against the Archetype's hand. It did only superficial damage—"

"Felt more than superficial to me," Dash said, wincing as he settled into the cradle. At once, his physical hurts receded into a distant background—pain he was aware of but didn't really feel. Instead, he felt the solid form of the Archetype embrace him. The heads-up flared to life, showing him the situation.

"Leira, you online?"

"Just waiting for you to get out of the way so Tybalt can bring in the Swift. Are you okay? It looked like you had a bomb go off pretty close to you."

"Pretty close doesn't begin to describe it," Dash said, applying power to the graviters and lifting the Archetype skyward. "Join me as soon as you get mounted up. Benzel, keep your people under cover in that tunnel until we can get this sorted out."

They both acknowledged, and Dash turned his focus to the threat indicator. A trio of atmospheric fighters were racing toward him, flying nap-of-the-earth, hugging the rugged, snowy terrain as they closed. "They're coming in awfully fast," he said to Sentinel. Awfully fast, and accelerating. They went transonic and accelerated some more.

Realization hit him. "Suicide attacks."

"So it would appear," Sentinel replied.

Dash did some accelerating of his own, powering the Archetype straight up. The three fighters pulled into a steep climb—at least two of them did. One of them just shattered, apparently ripped apart by the aerodynamic shock of trying to maneuver hard at such high speed. Firing solutions came up; Dash fired the dark-lance, vaporizing one fighter, but the second closed even faster than the few seconds it took the dark-lance to recuperate. Point defense opened up, ripping chunks off the fighter, but the bulk of it slammed into the Archetype and exploded.

Dash yelped as the shockwave tore through the Archetype. The fighters must be loaded with some sort of explosive payload; the blast flung the Archetype backward, momentarily out of control. At the same time, a missile fired by yet *another* fighter struck the Archetype's back. Dash swore and snapped out a dark-lance shot, blowing that fighter apart in a shower of glittering sparks.

"Moderate damage," Sentinel reported, though Dash already knew it through the Meld. "The left hip actuator is offline."

"Yeah, well, I don't plan to walk," Dash growled, and flung himself toward another group of fighters starting an attack run.

"Dash," Leira said. "We've got ground forces coming through the settlement. Infantry—and crap, some tanks or something. I don't think Benzel has the firepower to deal with it."

"I'll take care of the air battle," Dash said. "You help Benzel."

"Will do."

Dash scanned the heads-up and the threat indicator. Flights of fighters raced and wheeled through the air, surprisingly hard targets for the Archetype to engage. The mech was optimized for space combat, and spacecraft couldn't turn, climb, dive, and sideslip the way atmo-fighters did. Worse, he had to be careful with his shots because their enemies were wisely trying to keep the battle as close to the settlement and excavation as possible; otherwise, he'd just fire the distortion cannon a few times and swat the fighters from the sky.

"Looks like we have to do this the hard way, then," he muttered, and flung the Archetype through a wrenching series of evasive maneuvers. Fighters raced past the Archetype, banking hard, desperate to not stray too far. Dash fired the dark-lance, keeping the shots away from the settlement below. The blasts of energy from wounded atoms ripped the clouds apart, and wrecked fighters plummeted earthward. He launched missiles, which relentlessly tracked and blasted apart more of the nimble little ships.

But it didn't go entirely his way. Three more times, fighters managed to slam into the Archetype with heavy, explosive impacts. The mech shuddered under the blows but shrugged off most of the blast effects. Still, the damage piled up.

"Right arm and wrist actuator are offline. Waist actuator is operating at—"

"Yeah, I can feel all of it, Sentinel. That's fine," Dash said, taking a momentary breather. Three more fighters wheeled through a hard turn and burned in fast. But they weren't heading for the Archetype. They were aimed at the settlement, where Benzel's people and the Swift fought against the ground troops attacking out of the cover of the buildings. The Swift would likely be okay, but Benzel and the Gentle Friends had taken up firing positions outside the excavation and were fully exposed.

"Oh, for—cowardly bastards."

Dash targeted the fighters, fired the dark-lance, and missed. Then he missed again. The fighters jinked desperately. Seconds to impact.

"Benzel, Leira, hang on!" he shouted.

"Dash, what are you—" Leira began, but he didn't have time to answer. He targeted the distortion cannon on a mountain peak that seemed far away but was as close as he dared shoot.

He fired.

The mountain collapsed. The surge of gravity simply ripped it apart. Nearby ridges and peaks turned to rubble that plunged into the artificial gravity well. Seismic shock waves ripped through the planet's crust, triggering powerful earthquakes that rattled through the planet, cracking the landscape and triggering avalanches.

More importantly, though, the three fighters were wrenched

into momentary, vertical climbs, as gravity abruptly shifted ninety degrees. The pilots fought to compensate, but the effect ended, the planet's own gravity reasserted itself, and two of them dove into the terrain, vanishing in rolling explosions and clouds of debris. The third rocketed straight upward instead; it gave Dash the chance he needed, firing the dark-lance and blasting it from the sky.

"Dash," Leira shouted. "What the hell?"

"You guys okay?" he cut in. "Benzel?" His stomach clenched hard, waiting for Leira to say that he'd hurt or killed some, or even all, of the Gentle Friends.

"Still here," Benzel said. "That was—shit, let's not do that again, okay? I mean, we're used to sudden shifts in gravity, but aboard spaceships, not on the ground."

Dash breathed. "Are your people okay?"

"A few got hurt, but yeah, I think everyone's still with us. Enemy didn't do so well, though. I think all of their tanks just flipped over."

"Okay. Good." Dash checked the threat indicator. "It's clear up here, so I'm on my way back down."

He dove the Archetype back through the ragged clouds. Dust billowed from landslides triggered by the distortion cannon-shot he'd fired; fresh, dark scars in the snow marked places where hillsides had given way and slumped into valleys as falls of debris. He leveled out and looked for new targets but saw Benzel's people among the buildings, several of which had collapsed. Chunky tanks were scattered among them but, as Benzel had said, most had toppled on their sides when *south* momentarily became *down*.

One had apparently exploded, leaving a ragged, black crater and smoking wreckage.

"We've got prisoners, Dash," Benzel reported. "Fifteen, including their commander. A total of twenty-six survivors, now, from the original settlement, too."

"A moment," Dash said, once more putting the Archetype down, a couple of hundred meters from the now-ruined settlement. He collected his thoughts, feeling his pulse slow by a force of will alone.

This was no place for rage—not now. That could come later. For the moment, he needed to be cold.

Dash let the chill of command take over, just as the Archetype touched down.

"AM I SEEING what I think I'm seeing," Dash said, looking at the line of prisoners. "Are these guys from Clan *Shirna*?"

Leira turned her back to the booming wind. As she did, the ground rumbled again under her feet. "That's what it looks like," she replied. "We're not sure if this is just a remnant of them, or if they've got other forces elsewhere. Either way, it looks like this was the Verity's backup, here on Burrow."

Dash shook his head, wincing as he did; that shrill whine and the concussive pain in his head still hadn't completely faded. Clan Shirna. Dammit, did any of their enemies ever really go away?

The ground rattled again. "Dash," Sentinel said over the comm. "The seismic instability in this region is increasing as the rock mass seeks to find a new, structural equilibrium. It is likely that larger earthquakes are imminent."

"Moreover, I have scanned a large volume of water trapped beneath the nearby glacier, in which the cache of Golden technology, and the Creators' power core, are embedded," Tybalt said. "Even a modest shift in the ice flow will likely release it, flooding the excavation and much of this valley."

Dash put his hands on his hips. "Great. Benzel, what's up with the *Herald*? Did I hear something about a battle up in space, too?"

"You did," Benzel said. Dash turned, because the man's voice over the comm was merging with his actual voice, and saw him approaching, trudging through the snow. A pair of Gentle Friends followed him, escorting a prisoner. "A Clan Shirna cruiser made a run at the planet. Not sure if they were trying to support their friends here, or try to evacuate them, or if it was just a suicide attack like their fighters. Anyway, she was disabled and boarded." As he said it, he stopped a few paces away from Dash, gesturing for the prisoner to be brought forward.

"It looks like they might also have retrieved a power core," Benzel said. "From somewhere, anyway, and had it aboard their ship." He nodded at the prisoner, who Dash saw sported a bandolier made of what looked like jagged scraps of metal. "She probably knows, but she's not talking."

"Not to heretical vermin such as you," a woman's voice said, but Dash couldn't make out any details under her environmental suit—save for her eyes, which glared at him with naked hatred.

Dash just chuckled. "Still on about that holier-than-we-are

religious crap, huh? You don't need to bother, we know that Nathis and his crew were just in it for the goodies the Golden promised them."

"You're not fit to speak his name," the woman hissed.

"Who? Nathis? Hey, I'm the one who killed him, so I think that kind of gives me the right. Especially with your archaic social structure. You're lucky I didn't skin him and wear him as a belt."

The woman lunged at him. Her two guards yanked her back.

"Nathis means something to you," Leira said. "A lover?"

"No. My father."

Dash raised his eyebrows at that. Speaking of eyebrows, though—

He grabbed her face mask and yanked it down. The woman winced as the icy air struck her exposed skin.

She was human.

"All due respect, lady, but Nathis wasn't human, so how—"

"He adopted me," she said imperiously. "And I am his heir. My name is Sur-Natha." Her eyes narrowed. "Remember that name well, because it will be on your lips when you die," she hissed.

Dash sniffed. "I doubt that." He pointed at the bandolier of metal scrap. "And what's this supposed to be?"

"Each piece of metal is cut from the hull of an enemy I've vanquished. I look forward—"

"To adding ours to the collection, blah, blah," Dash cut in. "Yeah, I get it." He looked at Benzel. "Let's get her, the rest of the prisoners, and the survivors of the settlement into—"

He broke off as a heavy tremor shuddered the ground.

Another hillside a klick away slumped into ruin with a rolling crash.

"You don't do anything halfway, do you, Dash?" Leira said. "Fight a battle, trigger massive earthquakes."

"Hey, whatever works. Sentinel, Tybalt, how much time do we have to retrieve that stuff from the excavation before that underground lake or whatever it is gives way?"

"I estimate approximately two hours," Tybalt replied. "With an uncertainty of plus or minus"—he paused, though whether because he was calculating or just for dramatic effect, Dash wasn't sure— "two hours."

Dash looked at Leira. "Well, shit. Guess we'd better get busy then and dig that stuff out while these guys get off the planet. I mean, I'd hate to go through all this and then drown."

Benzel nodded. "Drowning would, indeed, suck."

DASH WATCHED as water roared out of the former excavation, now a deep notch punched and smashed into the face of the glacier by the two mechs. Despite Tybalt's protests about *inducing further instability*, it had been the fastest way to get at the cache of Golden tech. They'd managed to retrieve almost all of it, including the strange power core, before the base of the glacier finally fractured enough to let a small torrent of water come gushing out. In seconds, a small flow emerged, becoming larger as it ate at the ice—and then became a thunderous deluge. They'd hastily lifted the Archetype and Swift from the flood, which was so powerful it was starting to slam boulders into the legs of the two mechs.

The water continued to surge into the valley, filling it faster than it could empty. Soon, it would wash over the battered settlement; eventually, it would all freeze, entombing it in ice fifty meters or more thick.

Dash watched the torrent a moment longer, then powered the Archetype up to head for orbit and the journey home to the Forge.

Behind him, the clustered buildings of the settlement on Burrow vanished beneath foaming water, wiping away any trace anyone had ever been here.

9

DASH STILL LIKED the War Room. The Command Center was amazing—everything a commander could ask for, especially when directing simultaneous, far-flung operations and multiple forces. But the War Room had certain intimacy to it, so he decided to meet Al'Bijea there.

The arrival of the Aquarian leader had been a surprise. His ship, a luxurious cutter named the *Twin Tails*, dropped out of unSpace without fanfare and requested permission to dock. Dash had been standing in a hot shower, letting the warm water sluice over him as he attempted to take the edge off the bleak, frozen memories of Burrow, and had only reluctantly turned off the spray and got dressed. To anyone who lived and worked in space, a shower that never ran out of hot water was an unheard-of perk. He was lucky to get two minutes of it out of the tiny shower cubicle aboard the *Slipwing*.

His hair still damp, he ambled into the War Room to find Al'Bijea, a personal assistant to the ring's governor, and several of his engineers already there. Leira, Harolyn, Benzel, and Wei-Ping sat with them, all of them cutting off whatever conversation they were having as Dash entered.

"Dash," Al'Bijea said, standing with a near-flawless grin and offering his hand. "It's very good to see you again."

"Likewise," Dash replied, taking the proffered hand and shaking it. "Although, I don't think we were expecting you. Is everything alright?"

Dash braced himself. Leira had already informed him Al'Bijea hadn't wanted to talk about whatever business brought him to the Forge over a comm; he only wanted to talk in person. He'd added that it was nothing problematic, but that left Dash wondering what could be so important that it brought Al'Bijea himself here.

Al'Bijea laughed. "You're a terrible negotiator, Dash. I can see on your face that you're apprehensive about my visit. I could easily turn that to my advantage."

Dash smiled back. "Yeah, well, the trouble is that I'm used to negotiating with criminals, smugglers, those sorts—not honest people. It throws me off. All that earnestness and—" He waved his hands, helpless in the face of such nobility.

They sat down and Al'Bijea leaned forward. "I'll get right to the point. We've given this careful consideration and have decided that we're willing to enter into an alliance with you."

Dash blinked. "Oh. That's—well, that's great. Do I sense a *but*?"

"In a sense. We *do* have a few stipulations. This would be primarily a military alliance, at least initially. To that end, we are prepared to place ourselves under your nominal command for the purpose of pursuing military objectives. However, we would retain the right to object to certain uses of our forces, at our discretion. Also, in all other non-military respects, we would be partners with you."

Dash scanned the faces of his colleagues—particularly Harolyn, who he'd named as overseeing their civilian affairs and relationships. None of them seemed to object; Harolyn, in fact, gave a slight shrug, then a nod.

Dash turned back to Al'Bijea. "I think that's all fine, yeah."

"We're really just formalizing the relations we have with you now," Al'Bijea replied, then gestured at his assistant. "Aliya has already seen to the drafting of the necessary paperwork and will execute it with you as soon as it's convenient."

Aliya flashed Dash a charming smile. And, just like the first time he'd seen it, he knew at once that it was absolutely insincere.

"Sounds good," Dash said, smiling back at her. He had to admit, fake smile notwithstanding, Aliya had a certain appeal.

"So, Al'Bijea," Leira said, yanking Dash's attention away from Aliya. "You could have done this over a comm, couldn't you? Did you really need to come all this way?"

He smiled. "I must admit, I was rather interested in seeing this Forge of yours I've heard so much about." He looked up and around. "It *is* very impressive." Now he looked at the three engineers he'd brought with him. "I'm sure my people agree."

"It's—yes, impressive," a woman said. But one of her colleagues just barked a short laugh and shook his head.

"Impressive? It's *stunning*. The technology that must have gone into making this—"

"I think that what my people are trying to say is they would like a tour, if that's possible."

Dash gave an enthusiastic nod. "Sure, we can do that."

"First, though, perhaps we should discuss strategy," Al'Bijea said. "Do you have a star chart handy?"

"Custodian?" Dash said.

The holo image of the star chart appeared, depicting the entirety of the known galactic arm.

Al'Bijea gave an impressed nod, then paused and peered more closely. "This is remarkable. There is information on this chart that we don't have." He stood and pointed at a part of the star field. "Like here. We've considered doing a cometary survey in this system—except your map shows it as three systems, not one."

"It is a dispersed trinary star system," Custodian said. "The three stars in question are affected by each other's gravitation, but the result is an unstable, temporary grouping that won't last another five hundred thousand years."

"Custodian," Dash said. "Upload all of these data to Al'Bijea's ship, or wherever he prefers." He shrugged at the Aquarian leader. "No sense in allies trying to work from different star maps, right?"

He smiled back. "Right indeed. We are most grateful." He

studied the map again. "Can you portray on here where our enemies are active?"

Lines and icons appeared, showing the latest intelligence picture they'd assembled on the Golden and their minions like the Verity. Al'Bijea blinked. "Again, this is remarkable." His face creased in a frown. "And somewhat frightening. According to this, their activities transect a third of the arm."

Benzel nodded. "And we're kicking their asses, but that doesn't stop their influence from growing."

"Probably because more and more Golden are waking up, or powering up, or whatever," Wei-Ping added.

"Plus, we're not really sure how widespread their allies are," Leira said. "We've already encountered the Bright, the Verity, and Clan Shirna."

"Plus a human," Harolyn added. "Don't forget Temo, the guy who tried to sabotage the Forge by pretending to be a refugee."

Al'Bijea sat back down. "This paints an even more dire picture than I'd feared."

Dash leaned forward. "True, we shouldn't underestimate these guys. But we shouldn't overestimate them, either. Like Benzel said, we *have* been kicking their butts. And we're making progress, powering up the station, the two mechs, we're building a bunch of new tech—"

Al'Bijea held up a hand. "Don't worry, Dash, we're not about to back away from this. I'm well aware of the implications of giving your competitors both not enough credit *and* too much. It is just very—sobering, to see the situation depicted like this." He stood again then leaned on the table and studied the map. After a moment, he pointed to a broad line traversing roughly parallel to the long axis of the galactic arm, one that intersected some star systems, but missed many others. "What does this line show?"

"That is the central axis of our enemy's activities," Custodian said. "Whether it has some significance to the Golden or is simply how their various interests have happened to align, we are not certain."

"It makes a useful planning thing, though," Dash said. "Right now, our plan is to move the Forge roughly along this line, pacifying systems along the way, and staking out any for ourselves that might seem beneficial to us."

Al'Bijea's eyebrows raised. "You intend to claim territory?"

Dash leaned back and smiled. "I know what you're thinking. The Cygnus Realm isn't recognized by anybody else, isn't signed up to any of the bazillion treaties that pretend to regulate relations among everyone, so what standing would we have."

"The question does occur."

"Of course it does. And the answer is, we're not sure, over the long run. One option we're pondering is to keep the Cygnus Realm as a purely space-based enterprise, using the Forge, and things like the *Greenbelt* out there, to give us living space that we can also move around with us."

"That, incidentally, is why we're so keen to have you folks aboard with us," Harolyn put in. "We might be looking at doing some big engineering projects—bigger than getting the *Greenbelt* back here, which your people did with incredible professionalism."

"Having access to the comet-harvesting systems on that ship

was ample incentive to be as professional as possible," Al'Bijea replied.

One of his engineers leaned forward. "We're going to be learning lessons from what those Verity did for years. They might be murderous, inhuman assholes, but they aren't dumb."

"No, they aren't," Dash agreed, the eagerness on the man's face making him smile. Harolyn's easy adoption of a smooth diplomatic tone made him smile even more. She'd been a good choice for the Cygnus ambassador.

"That raises a point of concern, however," Al'Bijea said. "We realize that the Verity, and their Golden masters, are advanced far beyond us in terms of technology, and that includes military tech. We have relatively few ships, and they are not heavily armed. You've upgraded the *Comet*, but her master tells me that even with the new systems, she still is not suited for sustained combat with our enemies."

"That's true, unfortunately," Benzel said. "Your ships are in the same situation as ours were, like the *Snow Leopard*. She's a damned good ship, and we've upgraded her as much as her systems allow, but she's still second line at best. To make her first line, we'd, well, pretty much have to just build a brand new ship here at the Forge and name her the *Snow Leopard*."

"Still," Al'Bijea said. "This line—the axis along which you intend to advance the Forge, there are systems a smaller power like us can investigate, and even secure. That would free up your first-line assets for direct battle with the Golden."

Dash nodded, again impressed. Al'Bijea not only had business acumen, he clearly had a keen strategic mind. They'd have to have him involved in their planning—"

Conover burst into the room.

He stood in the doorway, almost hyperventilating. "Dash, everyone, you need to come see what we've found."

"What is it?" Leira asked.

But Conover shook his head. "Better if I show you. You'll need to come down to the fabrication plant."

As they exchanged looks, they all began to stand and Dash gave Conover a bemused look. "Do we really need a dramatic reveal here? Can you at least give us a hint?"

"It's something that might change everything," he said. "It might even be the key to winning this war."

As he turned and began leading them back down to the fabrication level, Leira looked at Dash and shrugged. "Dramatic reveal it is, I guess."

"This was included in the Golden tech you retrieved from that cache on Burrow," Conover said, gesturing at a holo-image of a partial schematic of—something. To Dash, it just looked like a random piece of machinery apparently called a Shroud. There was nothing to indicate what it was for.

He gave Conover a questioning look. "Okay. And what, exactly, does a Shroud do?"

Viktor answered. "Based on the limited data we've managed to retrieve from this Golden tech, they hacked or stole a partial plan for building this Shroud."

"But they couldn't break the encryption, it seemed, and extract any other info," Amy said, crouching beside one of the pieces of Golden tech scattered across the holding bay's deck. Somehow, despite none of the alien items involving lubrication, she'd managed to get something smeared on her cheek that looked like hatch grease. It made Dash smile.

"They got this much out of it, it seems," Conover went on, waving a hand at the schematic. "Then they stashed it, and all this other stuff, on Burrow for—well, reasons. I mean, who knows why they do the things they do?"

Dash nodded. "True." He rubbed his chin. "And there's nothing to indicate what it does? I thought you said this could be a game changer."

Conover's grin turned smug. "I was saving that part."

"More dramatic reveal," Leira said, sniffing. "You guys want a drumroll?"

Conover shrugged. "Sorry, but this is big. See, a Shroud, whatever it is, makes power cores."

A moment passed in stunned silence for Dash and his people, bemused silence for Al'Bijea and his. Finally, the Aquarian leader said, "I gather this is significant?"

Dash turned to him. "Oh. Yeah. More than significant. Conover's right, this would be a game changer."

"Because…?"

"Oh, sorry," Dash said. "Caught up in the moment. All of this Unseen tech—the Archetype and the Swift, the ships of the Silent Fleet like the *Herald*, even the Forge itself—they all run on these power cores."

"And they're really about much more than just producing power, although they definitely do that," Viktor said. "They also make it possible for that power to be distributed to where it's needed, when it's needed."

"They also usually contain information," Conover said. "New data that tells us new things about the Golden, or new tech that we can build, that sort of thing. They're kind of a big deal."

"Which means that being able to make our own would be a *huge* deal," Dash said. "For one, it would save us running all over the galactic arm, and beyond, hunting the damned things down."

Al'Bijea frowned. "The Unseen have scattered these cores all over the place? Why would they do that if they wanted you to find and use their tech against the Golden?"

"That's an excellent question," Leira said. "Even their own AIs don't seem to know their reason for it. We assume it's so that anyone who happened to stumble on their tech—especially the Golden or their agents—wouldn't find something already fully powered up, and would have to be able to retrieve the pieces they needed to get it that way."

"But it might be because they just love sending people on scavenger hunts," Dash said, crossing his arms. "Or it's something spiritual, or that they're just dicks. For that matter, the reason might be an entirely alien one that wouldn't make any sense to us even if we did know what it was. But that doesn't change the fact that decentralized power sources make the Golden that much more difficult to defeat."

"What it is, is frustrating," Amy said. "I mean, these guys

have gone looking for way more of these cores than I have, and it still drives me crazy. Just give us the tech already so we can run off these Golden assholes!"

Dash looked around. "So where's that power core now?"

"Kai has it in the engine room," Conover answered. "We didn't want to install it without your say-so, Dash."

"Oh. Okay. Custodian, can you see any reason we *shouldn't* just go ahead and plug that new core in?"

"None is evident," the AI replied. "However, my protocols are clear. Only the Messenger may allow a power core to be installed in the Forge."

Dash paused, then gave a decisive nod. "Kai, you can go ahead and plug that core in."

"I'm doing so now," came the monk's reply over the comm.

A moment passed. They all waited, some of them looking around as though something momentous might happen.

But nothing changed.

"Well, that was anticlimactic," Al'Bijea said.

Dash gave a wry smile, though. "Hey, when we do something like that and nothing blows up, it's a win."

"Custodian," Conover said, his voice taut with anticipation. "What happened?"

No response.

Now the looks exchanged became nervous ones. Dash put his hands on his hips. "Custodian?"

"My apologies," the AI said. "I was experiencing an upgrade and was briefly offline. The Forge's power levels have been increased by fifteen percent. Power distribution efficiency has increased twenty-two percent. Another section of the Forge has been powered up and is now available for use."

"Oh." Dash nodded. "That's all—well, both good *and* a pleasant surprise. Any more ideas about this Shroud thing, though, or what it actually is? These schematics don't look complete."

"They are not complete. As surmised, the schematic you are viewing was all that the Golden were able to extract from this core. These are the complete schematics."

The image changed. It was the same machine, but with far more detail included.

Viktor and Conover both studied it closely. "It says something here about power cores and Dark Metal," Conover said.

"Yes," Custodian replied. "In essence, the Shroud uses Dark Metal to fabricate power cores."

"I sense that things may be coming together," Al'Bijea said. "We have the remains of a facility on the Ring that was apparently used by the Golden to produce Dark Metal. And now you have a means of turning Dark Metal into these power cores, which are fundamental to the war effort."

Dash turned to Conover and slapped him on the shoulder. "I know this was a team effort, but damn, kid, you were right. This could be the key to winning this war."

"Dash," Sentinel cut in. "I have an urgent matter to bring to your attention."

Dash winced and automatically looked around. The last time something urgent happened, it was a Verity force infiltrating the

Forge, followed by a ferocious brawl. The damage was *still* being repaired.

He recovered quickly, shaking off the echo of that firefight. "What are you talking about, Sentinel?"

"This is a matter with security implications."

Dash looked around at his companions, including Al'Bijea and his people. "Go ahead. Everyone here is part of the team."

"During a routine test of the Archetype's comm systems, I noted an anomaly in a sideband range to one of the radio spectrum frequencies we normally use. After analysis, I was able to determine that it is a transmission that has been hidden in that sideband range as radio noise. It is, however, modulated and contains information."

"What sort of information?"

"Unknown. It is encrypted in a way that neither Tybalt nor I can readily break."

"That doesn't sound like standard tech," Amy said. "That sounds like something the Unseen would use—or the Golden."

Dash nodded. "Yeah. So where is this signal coming from?"

"From inside the Forge. And someone appears to be responding, also from inside the Forge."

"We've got spies aboard," Leira said.

Dash nodded again, grimly. "Yeah. Where's that guy we caught trying to sneak tech off the Forge—Sturdivan, I think his name was? We shipped him away, didn't we?"

"We did," Benzel said. "But he might have had accomplices."

"I have isolated the general location of both signals," Custodian put in. "I am showing them now."

A schematic of the Forge replaced the Shroud, with two locations marked as flashing icons.

"Okay," Dash said. His voice was rich with disgust. "Let's run these bastards down."

"Most of the Gentle Friends are off the Forge," Wei-Ping said. "They're aboard the *Herald* and the *Snow Leopard*, doing maintenance and repairs, plus we still have some teams sweeping the *Greenbelt* for any more hidden Verity. We don't have many people *on* the Forge right now, and it's going to take a while to bring them back."

"Go ahead and call at least a few squads back," Dash said. "But we're not going to wait. Viktor, you and Amy stay here with Al'Bijea and his people, protect them and this tech. Leira, take Benzel and whatever Gentle Friends you can find to go find this one." He pointed at one of the flashing icons. "I'll take Wei-Ping and go after the other."

Harolyn stepped forward. "I realize I'm no soldier, Dash, but you don't do geological surveys on remote fringe planets without learning something about fighting."

Dash looked at her, then nodded. "Fair enough. You know how to shoot?"

"Point the gun, pull the trigger, make the bad guy go away." Harolyn shrugged, earning a smile from Dash.

"Clean and simple," Dash said.

"Not if I shoot them," Harolyn replied, her lips a grim line.

DASH STOPPED, the pulse gun he'd retrieved from the armory ready, and peered around a corner along a corridor just one level above the main fabricating plant. This was *déjà vu* for sure; hadn't he just done this a short while ago, hunting and fighting the Verity? And that was on top of the whole Sturdivan thing? Why were they suddenly having so many security problems aboard the Forge?

He filed that thought away as something to discuss with Ragsdale, who had been aboard the *Greenbelt* when Sentinel's security came up. The Security Chief was rushing back now, preceded by a stream of curses over the comm that would have made a dock worker on Passage blush.

Dash glanced back. Harolyn was right behind him, and Wei-Ping behind her. He gave them a *wait* sign, then said, his voice hushed, "Custodian, any update on the location of that signal?"

"The last transmission originated ten meters from your current position," Custodian replied, the volume of his speech likewise reduced. "Along the corridor to your right, and then immediately to the left around the next bend."

Dash looked back again, gave a nod, and rounded the corner. He crept along the corridor, trying to keep his footfalls silent enough to be lost in the background rumble of the Forge's multitude of operating systems.

He stopped again, just short of the corner, then he crouched and looked around it.

A man knelt in the corridor about five meters away. Dash vaguely recognized him as a refugee from Burrow. He'd removed an access panel from the bulkhead, and now fiddled with a piece of tech in his hand, something he apparently wanted to insert into whatever circuits or conduits he'd exposed.

Dash looked back at his companions, nodded, then stepped around the corner, his pulse-gun leveled.

"Stop, back away from that bulkhead with your hands where I can—"

The man spun and fired a small slug-pistol he'd apparently been holding out of sight, three shots in rapid succession. Two shots snapped past Dash like whip cracks, and one struck the bulkhead beside him and fragmented. Something touched Dash's neck with a bright flare of pain.

He spat a curse and dodged aside, firing the pulse-gun. The shot flashed down the corridor, striking another bulkhead near the next intersection. The spy fired his slug-pistol again; this time, the round smacked into the pulse-gun, which gave a shrill error beep.

The entire exchange lasted three seconds. Dash flung the disabled pulse-gun at the man and meant to dodge back into the side corridor with Harolyn and Wei-Ping. But some instinct drove him forward instead, and he charged the spy.

The man flinched as he ducked the thrown pulse-gun, then his eyes widened as he saw Dash charging him. He fired again, two shots, but they cracked past Dash. Someone behind Dash uttered a sharp cry, but Dash didn't have time to turn back or do anything but stop this man. He slammed into him with a body tackle, knocking him back with an explosive breath and the dull snap of a rib.

Dash lost track of the slug-pistol, but there was no time to do anything but get his arms free to swing. He landed a solid blow on the side of the man's head. The man grunted then headbutted Dash back, making the world flash green and another of those shrill, endless whines flood his skull. Dash lashed out blindly, satisfied to hear the spy's nose crunch and crumple.

The man heaved, threw Dash aside, and lunged for something—the device he'd been intending to plant behind the bulkhead. Dash grabbed him and pulled him back, making his clutching fingers fall just a few centimeters short. Beyond the man, he saw Harolyn standing with a pulse-gun, desperately trying to line up a clear shot; Wei-Ping was down a couple of meters behind her. He had no time to even think about that.

"Harolyn, grab that device!"

She lunged forward, kicked the man's hand away, then scooped up the device and yanked it away. The spy reversed and lunged back, slamming a fist at Dash that almost caught him square in the face. Dash hit back, and the next few seconds passed with the two of them rolling across the corridor, each desperately trying to land a solid on the other.

This man was, Dash realized, both stronger and more skilled than he was. A knee drove into his gut, and a fist finally connected, snapping his head to one side and amping up that damned whine. Worse, he saw the slug-pistol was still in the man's hand, and he was trying to get it back into play. Dash saw the muzzle coming around—saw that they were now piled against a door.

"Custodian," Dash shouted. "Open the door!"

The portal slid open and they both toppled partly into the

compartment beyond. The man swore and brought the pistol up again.

Dash threw himself back, keeping his weight on the man's waist and legs. "Custodian, close the door!"

It closed with the spy still sprawled halfway across the threshold. He screamed, an awful, rising shriek that suddenly cut off when the door shut fully, seated inside the frame.

Dash fell back, gasping.

Harolyn appeared beside him, kneeling. "Dash, can you hear me? You okay?"

"Yeah. Shit—yeah." He sucked in a breath. "Wei-Ping. How's Wei—?"

"I'm fine," she snapped, clutching at her leg. "Asshole caught me with a lucky shot—damn, but that feels like fire in my veins."

Harolyn helped Dash sit back against the bulkhead opposite the now very-messily dead spy. "Leira—status?"

"Dash? You okay? You sound—"

"Bit of a tussle. I'm fine."

"We caught the spy," Leira said. "She came at us with a carbon-knife. Conover shot her."

Dash remembered the only other time he recalled Conover shooting and killing a man, on Shylock, when they'd been racing to get off the planet with Kai and his monks. The experience had shaken the kid, badly.

"Conover, how about you? Are *you* okay?"

"Uh—yeah, I'm fine. Not a scratch."

"Yeah, but you—you know, shot someone."

"Yup. It's funny, it was a lot easier this time," Conover said, his voice seemingly unconcerned.

Dash let his head sink back against the bulkhead, suddenly weary beyond words—and not just because of the fight.

Because of this war, Conover had gone from a wide-eyed kid who romanticized space and everything about it, to a young man who could shoot and kill someone without much care.

Conover had said, *It's funny*. But there was nothing funny about that at all.

THEY'D TAKEN Wei-Ping to the infirmary to have her gunshot treated. It was a nasty wound, but only through the meaty part of her thigh and relatively easy for the Forge's medical systems to patch up. Dash also had his neck wound treated; an even more minor wound, thankfully.

"The slug fragment that struck you penetrated your neck and passed four centimeters from your jugular vein," Custodian said, while a pair of articulated arms deftly attended to his wound. "Had it opened the vein—"

"You don't need to go into details," Dash said. "I get the picture." He looked at Harolyn, who'd raised her eyebrows and now gave Dash a *wow* look.

"That wouldn't have been good," she said.

"Especially from this side," Dash agreed.

They'd taken what they could from the bodies of the two

spies and returned to the War Room. Harolyn placed the device she'd retrieved on the table. "Custodian, can you identify this?"

"It is a remote broadcasting unit. Had it been installed as the spy intended, it would have been able to transmit data collected from the data conduit to which it was attached."

Dash frowned. "What sort of data moves through the conduit?"

"Primarily operating instructions for the fabrication systems in Bays three through six."

"So they would have been able to see details about some of the things we're building here," Ragsdale said, arms firmly crossed. He'd only just made it back to the Forge, and Dash could tell he was both frustrated and furious at having been caught away.

"It couldn't have very much range, though," Leira said. "It's not that big a device."

"It is Golden technology," Custodian replied. "It will take careful study to determine the details and its specific characteristics, but it does contain Dark Metal. I am presuming, therefore, that it could transmit its data through the Dark Between."

"Which means the receiver could be virtually anywhere in the universe," Dash said.

"That is not correct; even transmitted through the fringe zone of unSpace, there is a finite—"

"That's okay, Custodian, it just makes the point." Dash looked at the rest of them. "We have a more serious problem."

Ragsdale nodded once. "We have spies on board."

"Lots of them, it seems," Leira said. "First Temo, then Sturdivan, and now this."

"Okay," Dash said, rubbing his eyes. "We can't afford this sort of uncertainty. It's going to eat away at our confidence in our people, and their confidence in each other. It's also going to divert effort and attention from this war. So from now on, I want all incoming refugees assigned to a locked-down part of the Forge, some hab levels that are currently empty. I want them thoroughly searched and screened. Anyone we suspect at all will be shipped off the station." He looked at Ragsdale. "Let's start with every refugee we have on board right now."

"On it."

"And what if we find spies?" Benzel asked. "What do we do with them?"

"My instincts say to kill them, and to do it publicly," Dash said. "But I'm not sure that's an option for us—not as a realm, and not as a species. No matter how pissed I am right now, I can't allow myself the luxury of cold-blooded revenge. That doesn't mean they won't pay, but it *will* be public, at least in part." He sighed, feeling older than his years. "We'll exile them, but first, I'm going to... well, I won't ask any of you to take part, but I'm going to use force to make an example. Non-lethal, but still force, and it's going to be ugly."

Leira looked uncomfortable but nodded. Benzel and Wei-Ping obviously had no qualms. Viktor opened his mouth but closed it again.

"The cost of doing business," Al'Bijea said in the heavy silence, nodding. "One way or another, it must always be paid."

10

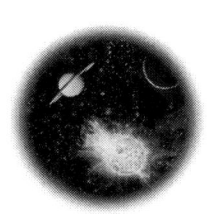

"THE GOLDEN HAVE A WORKING SHROUD," Custodian announced.

The news ripped through Dash's Inner Circle like a tsunami. If it was a potentially war-winning technology for them, then it stood to be the same for the Golden. Dash's reaction to that was simple and swift.

"We need to destroy it."

"First we need to find it," Benzel said. "Custodian, how can you be so sure the Golden have one of these things and its operating? I thought you said they never completely deciphered its schematics."

"They did not. However, data now retrieved from other examples of Golden technology retrieved from the Burrow cache makes it clear that they are, indeed, able to manufacture power cores using a version of the Shroud."

"They must have reverse engineered it from the partial plans they did have," Viktor suggested, and Custodian agreed.

"That is a reasonable conclusion. They are as technologically advanced as the Creators."

Huddled in the Command Center, they talked a long time and finally came to agree with the recommendation put forward by Custodian, Sentinel, and Tybalt—the Forge had to be their priority, taking precedence even over fighting the Verity. Custodian noted they could build their own Shroud from the complete schematics they possessed, but it would be a long process and would require enormous amounts of Dark Metal.

However, Dash realized, if they could find the Golden version of the Shroud and capture it, not only would they deny a critical capability to their enemies, but they'd take it for themselves. Even if, in the worst-case scenario, they were forced to destroy it, they could still harvest its Dark Metal and use it to construct their own Shroud.

"Custodian," Dash said. "Let's come up with a way to find that Golden Shroud. Conover, Viktor—hell, anyone without anything better to do, you'll help. Finding that thing is now our absolute, top priority."

They moved to get their burgeoning fleet organized. They added six new ships, another Silent Fleet retrieved from orbit around a distant pulsar. This gave them nine ships with similar capabilities to the *Herald*, Benzel's flagship. They also now had a second minelayer like the *Horse Nebula*, called the *Rickover*, and another ship based on the same design that would act as a dedicated drone controller, called the *Spider*. Amy suggested the name, saying, "You know, because it sits in the middle of a web of drones, running them all?"

So the Spider it was. This freed up the *Snow Leopard* and the *Slipwing* from their drone-control tasks, allowing them to be further upgraded. Dash could only stare in wonder at the *Slipwing* squatting in the docking bay. Once a scruffy little courier vessel forever on the edge of falling apart or blowing up, she was now a slick, powerful fighting machine, armed and armored with Unseen tech. She still wasn't quite up to going toe-to-toe with, say, a Harbinger, but she made up for it by being small, fast, and elusive. If Dash had had *this* version of the *Slipwing* while plugging along as a courier, he'd have had no trouble doing any job on the Needs-Slate, no matter how demanding or hazardous.

Hell, she probably was, ironically, now one of the powerful and dangerous ships in the whole freaking galactic arm—at least, one not actually built by either the Unseen or the Golden themselves.

Dash worked with Benzel and Wei-Ping to organize their growing fleet into squadrons, which would then begin to run simulations and exercises individually, and as part of the whole fleet. So far, their approach to war fighting had been relatively *ad hoc*—and, indeed, no plan survived contact with the enemy, so *ad hoc* was, ultimately, how most battles were fought anyway.

But there were definite advantages to having people and forces that were going to fight together, train together. They agreed that Benzel would remain in overall command of offensive operations, but Wei-Ping, in addition to her duties as defensive commander, would take over running the training. This would get their forces used to working in an integrated way with the Forge, which had become their single greatest source of firepower by a *wide* margin.

"But we don't do any offensive ops against the Verity until we take care of that Shroud," Dash said, walking through the docking bay with Benzel and Wei-Ping, checking out not just the *Slipwing*, but also the *Rockhound*, which had had some upgrades of her own. She was still very much a non-combatant vessel, but with improved control systems, better armor, and a trio of point-defense batteries, she could at least protect herself. A pair of pulse-cannons replaced her decrepit particle guns, giving her some teeth.

"Are you sure about that, Dash?" Benzel asked. "We're basically surrendering the initiative to the Verity." The man stopped, his hands on his hips. "I think we should keep the pressure on the Verity, now that we've pretty much got them on the run."

"I agree," Wei-Ping said, wincing slightly at the dregs of the leg wound she'd take from the spy's slug-pistol. "It might take us a long time to find that Shroud thing belonging to the Golden. And the whole time, we're just going to let the Verity regroup, recover—"

"I know," Dash said, holding up a hand. "Believe me, I've thought all the same things. But if we just keep fighting battles with the Verity, we're trying to patch up a breached hull with our fingers and toes. Eventually, we'll run out of fingers and toes. But they'll just keep making good their losses, mainly because of that damned Shroud."

Benzel scrubbed a hand through his hair. "I suppose. But I don't like it."

"I think it's a mistake," Wei-Ping said, but Dash cut her off.

"I know you do, and I trust you. But for this, I have to trust myself as Messenger."

Wei-Ping shrugged. "Okay, but—"

"Look, I'm asking for something that's hard to give—your trust," Dash said. "I will always listen to what you have to say and give it careful thought. But since I've been tagged as the Messenger, it seems the decisions eventually come to me to make. And know that I make these decisions with two goals, always: protecting your lives and winning this war. No variation. No doubt. I will *never* treat your blood as if it's cheap. You have my solemn word."

Wei-Ping opened her mouth but closed it again and looked a little sheepish. "You're—okay, boss." She glanced at Benzel. "We've made our decision to help with this, and we're sticking with it. Least we can do is the same for you."

Benzel nodded. "Agreed. We still don't have to like it, though."

Dash nodded back. "If it makes you feel any better, I don't like it either. This is what I might call a nuanced decision, and I see your side. I also see mine, and the picture beyond."

After a moment of glum silence, Dash added, "And if that doesn't make you feel better, maybe this will. The instant we've secured that Shroud, we'll put together a strike package and go hunting ourselves some Verity."

Benzel and Wei-Ping both offered smiles bordering on feral, and Benzel gave a thumbs-up.

"Okay, now *that* does make me feel better."

WEI-PING HAD BEEN WRONG, though. It hadn't taken long for Custodian to work out the probable location of the Shroud. All the intelligence work they'd done to date had dramatically narrowed the possible options; Custodian had then worked with Conover to reconfigure the Dark Metal interferometer they'd deployed around the Forge. It now consisted of three detector platforms centered on the Forge and spanning a hundred million kilometers. Custodian had then reasoned the single strongest Dark Metal signature was likely to be the Shroud. Sure enough, thanks to the improved sensitivity and resolution of the interferometer system, they'd soon located an intense Dark Metal return from a system on the edge of a stellar nursery, a vast expanse of dust and gas that was giving birth to new stars.

"The sheer strength of the neutrino emissions from these new, very active and tightly packed stars tends to swamp the detectors," Custodian explained. "That is a limitation, of course, since Dark Metal is impermeable to neutrinos, and we rely on the resulting neutrino shadows to detect it."

Conover nodded. "This new detector setup makes it so we can detect subtle differences in the neutrino flux from points that are really far apart. When we combine them, we get this."

This had been a deep, fuzzy shadow in the stellar nursery—

which was where Dash and Leira were now, in the Archetype and the Swift.

"Okay," Leira said. "This is incredible. I thought I'd seen pretty much everything space has to offer and then, *pow*, you run into something like this."

Dash nodded and indulged himself in a moment of staring at the Archetype's heads-up in wonder.

Enormous clouds of gas billowed across light-years of space shot through with fierce glare of thousands of intense, new stars. The youngest, Sentinel had said, was less than a million years old, making them newborns in the greater, stellar scheme of things. More stars, buried deeper in the sprawling cloudscape, weren't directly visible; instead, they lit the dust and gas from within, making it glow. And superimposed on all of it were soaring towers of dust, colder and therefore darker than the starlit gas beyond it, giving the whole panorama a depth and texture that just drew the eye deeper and deeper, in search of finer and finer detail.

Leira was right. It was incredible—at least insofar as any word could describe such a scene. It humbled Dash to think that whole solar systems were being born right before his eyes—planets, asteroids, comets, and, on some of them, eventually life.

But they weren't here just to sightsee, so Dash pulled his eyes away from the view and put them firmly on the threat indicator.

It was still dark but, if Custodian was right, it would soon be fully lit up.

"It looks like we haven't been detected," he said. "And I make us a billion klicks from our target system. That about right, Sentinel?"

"It is reasonably close."

He opened his mouth to talk to Leira again but closed it as something else occurred to him—something he'd wanted to ask about, ever since the battle on Burrow.

"Sentinel, back on Burrow, when you scooped me up in the Archetype's hands, and that bomb hit—I heard you shout my name with some—emotion, I'd call it. What was up with that?"

"I reasoned that I was more likely to get your immediate attention by using your name in an urgent manner that sounded more—human."

Dash narrowed his eyes. "I think you're lying."

"I am not capable of—"

"Lying? Oh, sure you are. If you're truly self-aware, then you have to be able to lie. It's kind of basic for the *intelligence* part of *artificial intelligence*."

After a pause, Sentinel replied. "I am not sure I accept your premise—"

"Come on, Sentinel, you've helped me do deceptive things when we fight the Golden and their various lackeys. Deception is nothing *but* lying."

Another pause. "Since we are about to engage in battle, I do not believe this is the correct time for this conversation."

Dash smiled. "You're probably right. Oh, but Sentinel?"

"Yes?"

"I like you, too."

Sentinel said, "I am ready to initiate this action on your command. I will address your emotional outburst later, after we are victorious."

Dash, still smiling, nodded. "That's the spirit. Let's go get 'em."

"I HAVE LINKED WITH TYBALT, and we are analyzing the Dark Metal data now," Sentinel said.

Dash waited. He and Leira had moved the two mechs about twenty million klicks apart, and now they'd linked the Dark Metal detectors of both in a way that mimicked Conover's interferometer. The resulting resolution wasn't as good as that one, but they were far, far closer to their target, so they actually observed far more detail anyway.

A fuzzy image appeared on the heads-up. Dash was looking at something oblong and black, outlined by a diffuse halo of greyish light, the neutrino background glow from the stellar nursery. He recognized the shape of the Shroud silhouetted against it from its schematics right away. So that confirmed it, they were in the right place. However—

"What are those little black dots moving around the Shroud?" he asked.

"They appear to be drones—actually, the Dark Metal components of drones. They are moving in what is, to the best of our ability to determine their trajectories, a random pattern."

"Drone pickets, huh? That's new."

"For something this important, I'd have expected a flotilla of Golden ships and Harbingers, not a bunch of drones," Leira said.

"I think they're counting on using stealth to protect this thing," Dash said. "Hiding it here in this stellar nursery."

"We should not underestimate the effectiveness of those drone defenses," Tybalt said. "In sufficient numbers, drones can be very powerful."

"Good point," Dash replied. "And we won't." He narrowed his eyes at the imagery. "That whatever-it-is on top of the Shroud—that wasn't on the schematic, was it? I don't remember it."

Sentinel overlaid the schematic on the shadow cast by the Shroud against the neutrino glare. Indeed, it matched almost exactly, except for what looked like some sort of antenna or sensor array mounted on it. "To the extent we can determine details at this resolution, it would appear that that array is pointed into deep space, at approximately the following coordinates."

Dash looked at where that was on the star chart, but it was nothing more than a random direction leading into the deep black. He filed that thought away for later. "Okay, we need to do this with maximum speed and violence," he said over the comm. "But we also need to use as much stealth as we can. I'm worried that there are surprises that might pop up while we're doing this, and I want to be ready for them."

Their encounter with the linked Verity fighters, that had

almost succeeded in crippling or even destroying both mechs still burned fresh in his mind, had been a completely unexpected turn, too.

"So how do you want to do this?" Leira asked.

"I'm thinking we translate in as close as we can, each fire a salvo of missiles, then race in behind them to attack and punch holes through that drone screen. We design our course to take us back to the next nearest safe translation point, jump back into unSpace, then maneuver to come at them from an entirely different direction, and do it again. I'm willing to bet those drones aren't translation-capable, so we should be able to change our attack vectors by a lot with each run. Anyway, we keep doing it until we've got the defenses down, and we can take the Shroud.

"Sounds good, although we might want to pay special attention to that comm array or whatever it is," Leira replied. "Since it doesn't seem to be part of the Shroud from the plans, then we should be okay taking it out. I'd rather *not* have them calling for reinforcements."

"Yeah, good idea," Dash said. "Sentinel, Tybalt, get the firing solutions ready for our missiles."

The two AI's acknowledged and, after a final check to make sure all their systems were green, both mechs translated into unSpace and started their first attack run.

DASH WATCHED as the drones configured themselves to plug the gaps their missiles had blown in their screen. They were fast, nimble, and adaptable. Each sported a pulse cannon—albeit, not an especially powerful one, since the drones were only about five meters long—and they worked together to concentrate their fire. The Archetype shuddered as pulse-cannon shots slammed into its shields like hail from a storm, but he ignored it and lined up darklance shots, taking out one drone and then another. A moment later, as they flashed past the Shroud, he fired a quartet of missiles at point-blank range. A drone exploded with a tremendous flash, not hit by a missile, though; it seemed to destroy itself to knock his missiles off their trajectory.

"They're pretty happy to suicide these things," Leira snapped. "I've had two blow up in my face."

"Let's just stick with the plan," Dash called back. "Okay, translation point coming up, and—*now*."

Both mechs flung themselves back into unSpace. Dash waited to see if any of the drones chased them into the darkness that was both infinite and dimensionless, but none did.

"Well, at least that hunch paid off," he muttered. "Okay, let's attack next from…" He decided on a trajectory and passed it through Sentinel, to Leira and Tybalt. They confirmed it, and the mechs maneuvered themselves to their new translation point.

On Dash's command, they dropped back into real space. This brought a glaring deficiency in the Golden's choice of this stellar nursery as a hiding place for the Shroud. Ordinarily, the deepest into a system a safe translation point would be was defined by its star's gravity well. But the nearest star to the Shroud was a small one, a youngster still accreting new matter from the surrounding dust and gas. Its gravitational influence was almost negligible, meaning they could translate in almost as close to the Shroud as they wished. In fact, the only real limit was how close to it they wanted to pop back into normal space, while still having enough time to engage in battle.

Ahead of them, Dash saw the drones flinging themselves through myriad, gyrating accelerations, trying to accommodate their new approach vector. Again, the Archetype and the Swift fired salvos of missiles, then bore in hard behind them. Then the drones opened fire.

They raced past the Shroud, firing missiles at nearly point-blank range. One detonated close to the facility but failed to take out the array, which Sentinel confirmed was a comm system. Dash cursed as they swept into their outbound run and prepared to translate. Repeated, massed pulse-cannon fire from the Golden drones was taking its toll on both mechs. Their shields were down, and both had minor damage to various systems.

Both were also still combat-capable, but as usual, time stood as fierce an enemy as the Golden themselves; if the Shroud had managed to send a distress signal, they might soon face much more powerful reinforcements. As they translated and maneuvered to attack from another vector, Dash decided that if other enemy forces did show up in strength, they'd just run. As much as he wanted this shroud—or to put it out of action—he would not risk losing their mechs over it.

As they snapped back into real space and began to accelerate, Dash called up Leira. "If we don't do something decisive to shut down these defenses and set it up for capture on this run, then we're just going to destroy this Shroud thing."

"Got it," came Leira's terse reply as they zoomed back into the maelstrom of drone fire.

The Shroud grew in the heads-up; firing solutions resolved and the missiles armed, ready to launch. On instinct alone, Dash decided to configure the missiles to use a more scattered approach, forcing the drones playing close-in defense on the Shroud, and its own point-defense systems, to take a tiny bit longer to acquire targets and shift fire among them. At the same time, two of the missiles would hang back and approach in a spiraling corkscrew, making them a little harder to acquire in the first place. As he launched the missiles, Dash knew it was a trade-off, giving their enemies more time to engage, but making it harder for them to do so. He could only hope the latter overrode the former, even just a tiny bit.

But it was a gamble that paid off. One of the spiraling missiles flashed past the defending drones, somehow dodged a last-ditch storm of point-defense fire, and slammed into the comms array. The explosion blew the array to pieces, the blast and resulting shrapnel ripping into the Shroud's hull.

As they once more started their outbound leg, Dash saw that the drones seemed to suddenly lose their smooth coordination, the maneuvers becoming erratic, their fire more sporadic. Sentinel confirmed it.

"The drones are now operating at a much lower level of efficiency. It would appear that whatever control system directed them from the Shroud has gone offline."

Dash made a snap decision. "Leira, reverse course! Let's attack right now, before they get a chance to do any repairs!"

The Archetype and Swift both jackknifed through course reversals, then accelerated at full combat power, slowing, stopping, then driving back along a back trajectory. Dash began pumping out dark-lance shots, while Leira opened up with the Swift's nova cannon. Soon, fragments of wrecked drones spun and tumbled around the Shroud; by the time they'd zipped past it, only a few remained operational. While Leira finished them off, Dash put his attention on the Shroud itself. It still poured out point-defense fire; it wasn't much of a threat to the Archetype, but it needed to be silenced if they were going to recover this thing.

"Sentinel, can we dark-lance those point-defense batteries without wrecking the Shroud?"

"Inadvisable. The energy release from the dark-lance impacts will likely do considerable damage to the facility, perhaps even destroying it."

"So it's a club, and I need a scalpel." His mind raced. "How about our own point-defense systems? Can we use those?"

"We would have to close the range considerably. However, they would do much less collateral damage, yes."

Dash flung the Archetype directly at the Shroud, switching the mech's point-defense batteries from autonomous, reactive mode to a reactive, command-input mode. The instant they entered range, he opened up.

For the next few moments, Dash found himself embroiled in one of the strangest battles of this entire war. The Shroud and the Archetype traded barrages of point-defense fire, shots meant to be a last-resort defense against incoming ordnance. The result was spectacular torrents of fire exchanged between the mech and the Shroud, but it didn't actually *do* very much to either one, at least not quickly.

Despite the tension of the situation, Dash had to grin. "I think I could spit on the Shroud and do about as much damage," he said, watching as the dazzling display of shooting played out. It was like two guys locked in an awkward slap-fight, one unable to throw any punches, the other unwilling to.

"Need a hand?" Leira said.

"Yeah, it'd be helpful," Dash replied. "This is going to take forever."

Tybalt coordinated the Swift's fire with the Archetype's, timing the shots from the two mechs so they'd impact simultaneously, on common targeting points. With the added weight of Leira's fire, the Shroud's defenses were finally silenced, one by one.

The threat indicator had gone dark. Dash warily moved the Archetype in closer to the Shroud, ready for it to light up again.

It didn't.

He let himself relax a notch. "Okay, looks like we've got this. Now, to get it out of here before more bad guys show up."

"Dash, I don't see any way of actually boarding this thing," Leira said.

Dash scanned the oblong bulk of the Shroud for anything that resembled an airlock. He saw lots of relatively minor battle damage, albeit still enough to seemingly knock the facility completely offline. But he saw no way in.

"That is because it is an entirely automated facility," Sentinel said, answering the question Dash was just about to ask. "It is meant to operate autonomously. There is a small maintenance facility, but it is isolated from the interior of the Shroud, where the fabrication functions are performed."

"I would speculate that the fabrication processes for power cores are not compatible with the existence of organic life," Tybalt added.

"Makes me a little nervous having one of these things operating aboard the Forge," Leira said. "Of course, I get nervous whenever I hear that something is *incompatible with organic life*—you know, being organic life and all myself."

"We might have to operate it like a standalone thing," Dash said. "But that's a problem for later. Right now—Amy, you there?"

"Roger that. Standing by."

"Okay, come on in and get this thing hooked up so we can get the hell out of here."

"Be there in a flash."

A few seconds after she'd spoken, the *Slipwing* and the *Rockhound* both dropped out of unSpace, each with a tug drone in company. While they moved in, the Gentle Friends aboard the *Rockhound* proceeded to get things in place and hooked up with their usual, brusque efficiency. Dash and Leira took up stations a few tens of thousands of klicks on opposite sides of the Shroud and maintained a careful watch for any new, incoming threats.

It seemed to take the Gentle Friends forever to get the Shroud rigged for towing. Dash knew it didn't really, but he couldn't forget that comms array, pointed into what seemed like empty blackness. It made him wonder, and wondering made him start using his imagination, and none of the things he imagined were good.

Had the threat indicator flickered? "Sentinel, did I see a brief contact there?"

"I have detected nothing, and the Archetype's sensors are showing as fully—"

"That's fine," he said. "Guess I'm just jumpy."

Dash tried to make himself relax and stop seeing more flickers from the threat indicator, or more things suddenly moving against the starfield, then vanishing as soon as he looked at them.

I need a vacation, he thought.

"Okay, Dash," Amy said. "The Gentle Friends are ready."

"Excellent, let's get out of here."

"In a hurry?"

Dash frowned at his own anxious tone. Yup, definitely a vacation, sometime soon.

"I'm always in a hurry, Amy," he finally replied, making his tone as light as he could, this time.

Still, he was profoundly glad when they finally entered unSpace, heading back for the Forge and leaving the spectacular menace of the stellar nursery behind.

11

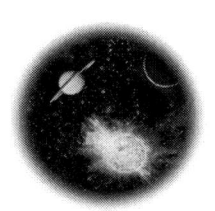

Dash strode along a corridor, reading a datapad as he went. Custodian had given him one of his typically *too*-complete status updates; it recounted all sorts of specific parameters about things that Dash either didn't really understand, or frankly just didn't really care about. He was used to it, though, and was able to quickly sift out the things that were important—at least, to him.

The Forge continued its stately progress toward Verity space and would cross what seemed to be the boundary in about five or six days.

Power levels for the Forge and the two mechs had stabilized; the latter had also now been fully repaired and were ready for battle.

Benzel had finalized the configuration of the fleet, and Wei-Ping had started a series of exercises and war games to hone their skills and tactics, and to get them used to working together in their new squadrons.

The smelting and fabricating systems were running flat-out, producing new ship components, missiles to restock and expand their inventory, even more mines.

Dash slammed to a stop and reread the section he'd just finished.

"Custodian?"

"Messenger."

"What's this about new mechs?"

"Sentinel was correct."

"Uh—what?"

"She suggested that if I simply included that as an unremarkable line item in a routine status report, it would evoke this very reaction from you."

"She—wait. You mean Sentinel put you up to something?"

"*Put you up to something* is an idiom with which I am unfamiliar."

"It means that she encouraged you to do something meant to...well, affect me in some way. Usually, it's some sort of trick or joke."

"This is neither. The Forge really is now capable of constructing new mechs."

"Yeah, I get that, but—" Dash broke off, smiling and shaking his head. He knew these AIs communicated with one another all the time, but he'd always just assumed it was about AI things, swapping data, that sort of thing. But they were also conspiring to screw around with him?

He needed to talk to Leira and the others about this. The AIs were clearly starting to show human quirks and characteristics, and while that was both amusing and fascinating, was it also going to start affecting their ability to do the things they'd come to count on them doing?

For now, though, he just put that aside. "So tell me about these new mechs. Where did the schematics for them come from?"

"From the data stores in the tandem power core retrieved from Burrow and installed in the Forge. I have been evaluating them, and have concluded that, with some modifications, the Forge would be capable of constructing both types of new mech."

"Okay, so what are they like? What abilities do they have? How many?"

"If you come to the fabrication plant, I can better explain."

Dash glanced at the time on the datapad. "I have a meeting with Freya in fifteen minutes. I'll be there, say, in an hour."

"I shall be ready."

Dash resumed his way along the corridor. Freya had been coy, too, about what she wanted to talk to him about. It seemed that this was a day for surprises.

That some of them were coming from the AIs just made him shake his head again.

DASH CARRIED ON, following the directions given to him by Freya.

They were leading him into a part of the Forge that had been open and powered up for some time now, but that they hadn't put into use. It was, as far as Dash knew, all hab and storage—good to have available, but not immediately required for anything. He wondered just what the hell Freya had been up to in here.

He rounded a corner and saw Freya just ahead, standing in front of a big blast door. It opened, as far as Dash could recall, into a series of cargo bays. She smiled and nodded as he approached.

"Hello, Dash. Glad you could make it."

"Well, you made it sound important. Also, you're my supplier for plumato wine, pomegranate whisky, and whatever the hell that turquoise stuff is. You know, the one that glows a bit."

"Oh, right. I haven't named that yet. It's got a base of potato vodka, and then it has extracts from a couple of types of hybrid berries from that crashed Golden ship near Port Hannah."

"You sure that stuff is really safe to drink?"

"Very. In fact, there are compounds in the berries that actually offset the toxic metabolic effects of the alcohol, so you get the drunk part without the hangover part."

"Sold!" Dash said, grinning. "I now have a new favorite drink, named or not." His grin became thoughtful. "Now *that's* something we could look at selling sometime. Holy crap, never mind blowing up stars or things made out of Dark Metal, drunk without a hangover would be worth a *fortune*." He looked at Freya. "You're officially my new hero. But I assume you didn't want to bring me here to talk about booze."

"I did not. I want to show you something I've been working

on. I've had Custodian helping me, mainly by keeping what I've been doing here secret."

Okay, now Dash had to resist a frown. They'd first met Freya in Port Hannah, on Gulch, where she'd been secretly slipping inside the crashed Golden battlecruiser buried nearby. Although Dash knew she hadn't intended it, she could very well have roused the multitude of bots left dormant inside the Golden ship and provoked them into attacking Port Hannah. In other words, the woman had a history of questionably secretive judgment.

Although if Custodian had at least been aware…

"Okay, well, show me what you've got," Dash said.

She nodded, turned, and touched a panel, opening the blast door.

Light spilled out. With it came a waft of warm, humid air, and a smell Dash could only describe as *green*.

He followed Freya through the open blast door then stopped and gaped.

He stood in a park.

Grass underfoot. A riot of color from flowering shrubs. Trees, some twice Dash's height, with a lot of room yet to grow under the compartment's ceiling. A path wound away from the blast door, vanishing among a stand of what Dash thought might be some sort of hybrid maples, but he was no plant expert and just guessed at it, from the flame-toned foliage.

Freya's grin went from ear-to-ear. "What do you think?"

"Uh—"

Dash found himself literally speechless. Freya just waited for him to find his voice again.

"Okay, holy shit," is what he finally said.

"Holy shit is a good reaction," she said. "Pretty much what I was going for, in fact."

"Freya—I mean, holy shit. How did you *do* this?"

"Well, the Forge has stocks of a growth medium that I was able to use for soil. It can also make the stuff from almost any organic feedstock."

Dash narrowed his eyes at that. "Such as?"

Freya smiled back. "Do you really want to know?"

Dash looked at the grass, the soil beneath it. It looked like regular dirt. He decided to keep it looking that way and shook his head. "Not really."

"Anyway, once that was ready, I was able to start seeding the place." She gestured around. "And here we are."

"Most of these plants look like they've been around for, well, more than just a few—" He paused. "How long have you been working on this, anyway?"

"A couple of months."

"A couple of—" Dash shook his head. "You've been doing this for a couple of *months*? How the hell did you keep it a secret?" He shook his head again. He'd been worrying about security issues on the Forge before this, but the fact Freya could get away with something this elaborate—

Freya, still smiling, shrugged. "I had help. Custodian and Ragsdale were both in on it."

"Oh." Dash blinked. Well, that helped explain that.

"Ragsdale too?"

"After what happened with that crashed Golden ship on

Gulch, there was no way I was going to try going behind his back on something like this."

It was a good point, one that Dash gave a nod of admiration. "And Custodian, the AI who's supposed to be all deferential to me, you know, the Messenger?" He raised his voice a little at the end of that and shifted his attention away from Freya.

"In all matters I normally do defer to you," Custodian said. "However, your health and well-being are also of concern to me, and Freya made a strong case regarding why this particular endeavor of hers should be kept from you."

He looked back at Freya. "And that case was?"

"Dash," Freya said. "How did you feel walking in here just now?"

"How did I feel? Well, surprised. And impressed. Actually, kind of awed."

"Excited that we have this greenspace on the Forge now? A place to come and relax, get away from ships and Dark Metal, and mines and missiles and—"

"I get it. And, yeah, I guess I am." He smiled. "You didn't do this just for me, though."

"No. For everyone. See, that's the benefit of not being a soldier, or an officer, always thinking about strategy, the next battle, defending the Forge, all that. I'm an outsider, looking in at you guys. And what I'm seeing is a lot of people who're starting to look...I don't know, stretched too thin, I guess. Tired all the time. Doing too much, for too long, in the middle of something that's scary in ways I can only probably try to imagine." She looked around and shrugged. "I want you guys to have a place to, if not get away from it entirely, then to at least take the edge off it for a while." She finished on a smile. "Plumato wine and glowing green stuff only goes so far."

As she spoke, Dash thought about their recent recovery of the Shroud, and particularly about that time he spent just hanging in space while the Shroud was rigged for towing. How vast and cold and empty space had felt. How worried he was that they'd be counterattacked and have to fight again, maybe against much superior forces.

How risky it all was.

How tired he was.

Instinct kicked in. Dash stepping forward, grabbed Freya, and hugged her.

"Thank you," he said. "Thank you for doing this."

She hugged him back, then he stepped back and looked around again. "You still haven't told me why this place looks so... established. I can't believe these plants are just a couple of months old. Especially those trees."

"Actually, for most of these plants, this really is just two months of growth. For others, like the trees, I used botanical sleight of hand and modified their biochemistry to make them grow much faster. Unfortunately, it also means they're going to die much sooner, probably in no more than, say, three or four years. By then, though, I plan to have trees about the same size here, grown the old-fashioned way."

Dash nodded, then followed Freya as she offered him a tour. The park filled this first compartment, plus about half of the adjoining one. By the time they reached the point where the soil gave way to deck plating, Dash was already pointing into the remaining adjacent compartments stretching off in a gentle arc, following the curve of the Forge.

"I am totally convinced," he said. "Let's plan to fill all these compartments with parkland. I think we can afford the space, and this is—well, it's what we need. It's life."

Freya beamed at the praise and the implicit blessing to carry on with her project but gave a self-deprecating shrug. "That's the downside of not being a soldier. Sometimes, I feel like I'm not really contributing much."

"Well, you are officially a huge contributor to what we're trying to accomplish here, Freya," Dash replied, giving her a firm nod. "I figured we might be able to use the *Greenbelt* for something like this, but it's a pain shuttling back and forth to it. This—" He nodded once more. "Yeah, this is much better. The immediacy of this is what we need. What all of us need, really."

He left Freya to get to his meeting with Viktor in the fabrication plant. As he did, he thought about something she'd said.

Unfortunately, it also means they're going to die much sooner, probably in no more than, say, three or four years. By then, though, I plan to have trees about the same size here, grown the old-fashioned way.

She was thinking ahead three or four *years*. Dash had trouble seeing beyond three or four *days*. But, if he tried, he could envision himself being here three or four years from now, with the war hopefully long won.

Which meant he could think of the Forge as more than just a munitions factory and a weapon. He could think of it as *home*.

"Did you know that Freya has been building a park aboard the Forge?" Dash asked Viktor.

Viktor stooped beneath a mechanical arm moving to lift a freshly cast component of a new mine layer out of a mold. "I'd heard rumors, yes."

Dash frowned. "Really?"

"Really."

"I ran into Benzel and Harolyn on the way here, and they both said the same thing. Have you guys all been working together to keep this a secret from me?"

Viktor smiled. "You can blame Custodian. As soon as it ever came up in conversation, he asked us to stop talking about it, especially around you. I guess it was meant to be a surprise—well, to you, anyway."

"Well, it was. A really nice surprise." He raised his voice a little "Although it makes me wonder what else these AIs are keeping from me."

"Nothing of direct relevance to the war effort," Custodian replied. "Of course."

"I believe you," Dash said. "Really, I do." He cocked his head and narrowed his eyes in suspicion. "But that answer implies there might be things *not* of immediate relevance to our war effort that you *are* keeping from me."

"Many things, actually," Custodian said. "However, I assume you are not interested in second-to-second details of power distribution in the Forge, or continual updates on atmospheric pressure in the docking bay."

"Yeah, no. That's fine." Dash looked at Viktor. "Sometimes less really is more."

Viktor nodded, but Custodian continued talking before he could speak.

"That said, there is a matter of direct relevance to the war effort you do need to consider, Messenger."

"I was just going to get to that," Viktor said. "Custodian and I were discussing updates and refinements to our production schedule, and he mentioned that we actually have a lot of Dark Metal available—enough that we have some options. And, since you asked me and Conover to oversee this stuff, I said we should come to you with those options and see how you want to proceed."

Dash ducked as another automated arm passed overhead. Nearby, a mold rumbled closed and began to fill with molten metal. Dash took Viktor's arm and led him away, saying, "Let's go stand somewhere where we're not likely to get clocked by a robot arm, or accidentally knocked into a vat of something super hot."

"The chances of you being injured by the operations of the Forge are—" Custodian said, sounding a little aggrieved—"

"Fifty-fifty," Dash cut in. "It either happens, or it doesn't."

"That makes no sense."

"Tell Sentinel that. It's her joke."

Viktor grinned. "Really?"

"Yes, really." They stopped in a clear space, away from the

operating fabricators. It struck Dash that this very space had been swept with pulse-gun shots exchanged with the Verity who'd infiltrated the station. Not a trace of that battle remained, which made Dash fiercely glad; it meant those Verity had died for nothing, which suited him just fine.

"Anyway, what are these options you're talking about?"

"Custodian says we can build more mechs."

Dash raised his eyebrows. "Okay, that is good news. Another Archetype or Swift would be *really* helpful."

"Oh, we've got more choices than that. Custodian?"

A holo-image appeared. Dash had come to realize that Custodian could project them virtually anywhere in the Forge, thanks to a built-in property of its basic structure. This image showed two mechs, both very different from the Archetype or the Swift. One, labelled *Talon*, was a lighter mech, similar to the Swift, but apparently massing even less, so it was faster and nimbler, but more lightly armed. The other, called a *Pulsar*, was the opposite—bigger, even more heavily armored than the Archetype, but apparently meant more for support roles in combat—particularly electronic warfare, both offensive and defensive, and the evaluation and retrieval of tech.

As Dash studied the two schematics, Viktor went on. "It seems that both these mechs are meant to complement the ones we've already got. One is optimized for reconnaissance and skirmishing, while the other is meant to hang back and support the other three."

"I assume these are newly discovered plans?" Dash asked.

"Yes, they were included in the data stores in the tandem power core you recovered from Burrow," Custodian replied.

"And we have enough Dark Metal to build both of these *and* get the Shroud online?"

"We do," Viktor said. "The Shroud will have to be rebuilt anyway because of battle damage. But it turns out that the way the Golden reverse-engineered the Shroud from the partial schematic they had for it used a lot more Dark Metal than was necessary. When you have the full, correct plans, though, you can build it properly, and that's going to save us hundreds of kilos of the stuff."

Dash crossed his arms. "How long until that's done and we have a working Shroud? Because these new mechs will need power cores, right?"

"At least several weeks," Custodian replied. "We can fabricate components for the new mechs at the same time so that they are complete at about the same time the Shroud is able to begin producing power cores which, as you note, they will require."

"Of course, this raises a whole other question," Viktor said.

"Yeah. Who will pilot them?"

"I have a couple of suggestions."

Dash looked at Viktor. "I'm all ears."

DASH WAS STILL STUDYING the schematics of the two new mechs, now projected as a holo-image in the War Room, when Viktor entered with Conover and Amy.

"We in the shit for something?" Amy asked, sounding absolutely unconcerned about the prospect.

Conover, though, saw the schematics and immediately stepped close, eagerly studying them. "These are new," he said. "Two new mechs…"

Dash smiled. "Yes, they're new mechs. And no, you're not in shit—this time, anyway."

Amy joined Conover in peering at the schematics. After a moment, she giggled.

Dash gave her a bemused look. "Okay, so what's funny about a plan for a giant mech?"

She pointed at the Pulsar. "Well, from this angle, if you look between its legs, it looks like it has a—"

"Yeah, that's fine," Dash said, shaking his head. "I get where you're going with that, which is…"

His voice trailed off. Actually, from this angle, it *did* look like the mech had a—

"Anyway," he said, pulling his gaze away and putting it back on a grinning Amy. "I wanted to talk to you guys about these things. We're planning on building them to augment our fleet. And we're considering you two to pilot them."

The both looked stunned. Then Amy said, "Ooh, I call dibs on the one with the—"

"That's not how this works," Dash said. "I've talked this over with Viktor—who's actually given this a lot of thought himself, because he's one who suggested you two—and with Leira, Custodian, Sentinel, and Tybalt. We've come to the conclusion that the lighter mech, the Talon, is a better fit with your personality, Amy.

The bigger one, which is more about electronic warfare and tech, would work better with Conover."

"What about the *Mako*?" Conover asked, referring to their prototype atmospheric fighter with the big blast-cannon. "I thought I was tagged to fly that."

"We'll find another pilot for that. You're definitely a much better match with the Pulsar, the bigger mech." Dash glanced at Amy. "Yes, the one that looks like it has a—you know."

She giggled.

Conover turned his attention back to the schematic. He lifted a finger toward the Pulsar, then let it slowly drop. "Piloting this would be—" He nodded. "It would be—" He nodded again and looked at Dash. "I'll come up with the right words eventually."

"It would be *awesome*," Amy said. "That's the word you're looking for—*awesome*." She clapped her hands. "When do we start?"

"Not for a while yet," Viktor said. "These mechs haven't even been built yet."

"And we have to wait to get the Shroud up and running to make power cores for them," Dash added.

"In the meantime, however, I am conferring with Sentinel and Tybalt to determine which AI best suits your particular biophysical and personality profiles," Custodian said. "Additionally, I will need to run each of you through a series of psychological tests. Once that is complete, I will activate your respective AIs and you can begin simulator training with them."

Amy grinned. "This is exciting!" But her grin faded some. "What about the *Slipwing*, though? Who's going to pilot her?"

"That would be me," Viktor said.

Amy gave him a surprised look. "I didn't know you were a pilot."

"It's how I started out. Once, long ago, I helmed a freighter, and then switched to a courier ship, flying it on behalf of its owners. They were cheap bastards, never wanted to spend the credits to fix anything, so I had to learn how to make things work and keep them working. When I met Leira, and she said she needed an engineer because she was too broke to keep things working, it gave me a chance to switch jobs—you know, become more my own man."

"I now know more about you than I think I ever did," Conover said.

Viktor smiled back at him. "We're all books with unturned pages, aren't we? Someday, I'd like to hear the story of how you got those eyes of yours."

"Actually, I'd like to know as well," Dash said. "You've never told us."

"I have an incoming message from Al'Bijea," Custodian cut in. "He says it is an emergency."

"Okay, hold that thought," Dash said with a sigh. "Because it looks like it'll have to wait for another time."

12

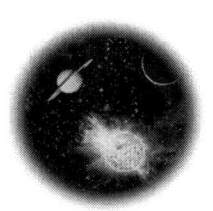

"So you want us to essentially be bait for a trap," Al'Bijea said.

Dash looked at the oversized image of the Aquarian leader, projected into a window on the big display in the Command Center. Al'Bijea's head stood at least two meters high, gazing at him like an oversized saint from the deep past. "That's what it amounts to, yes."

The door opened, admitting Benzel and Wei-Ping. "Sorry about that," Benzel said. "We got caught aboard the *Herald*. What's up?"

"Al'Bijea's people have detected what seems to be a Verity strike force heading his way," Dash said. "He's got scout ships falling back ahead of them, maintaining contact and keeping them under observation."

"What he doesn't have is heavy warships," Leira put in. "The Aquarian ships are well-armed."

"Yeah, I remember that gamma-ray laser they used," Wei-Ping added. "That thing was terrifying."

"And very effective," Al'Bijea said. "But we only have a half dozen of them ready. We've also currently got the *Comet*, which you have upgraded and is back at the Ring for a crew rotation. But that's about it. Based on the reports I've read of your encounters with them, none of our other ships are really capable of taking on the Verity head-on."

"So I've asked him to delay them as much as he can while we get a strike force of our own deployed," Dash said. He pointed at a particular region of space about a light-year from the Ring, one bordered by an expansive nebula. "If he can draw them into that area there, then we can use the nebula to come at them without being detected pretty much until we're right on top of them."

"That would be the *using the Aquarians as bait* part of the plan, which is what we were discussing just as you came in," Leira said.

Benzel took a moment to study the star chart depicted beside Al'Bijea's image, then turned and had a brief, hushed conversation with Wei-Ping. They both nodded and he turned back.

"Okay," he said. "We've already got the fleet broken down into two basic force packages, and they've been exercising together for a while now." He glanced at Wei-Ping. "This would be a good chance, we think, to test them all at once."

"Use the whole fleet?" Dash asked. "Leave nothing here at the Forge?"

"I think the Forge is pretty good at taking care of itself," Wei-Ping said. "Custodian and I have been talking about defending this place, and I think we've concluded it's safe on its own for a while."

"I would concur," Custodian said. "The Creators' intent was that the Forge function in several capacities: manufacturing facility, habitation, base for military forces, and as an independent maneuver element."

"It's meant to basically be a fleet all on its own," Wei-Ping added.

Dash looked back at the star chart. The Forge's path along the axis of the galactic arm had brought it closer to inhabited space, including the Aquarian Ring system. The fleet would be, at most, a few hours translation time away.

But a *lot* could happen in a few hours.

Dash thought about the park Freya had built, and how it had made him think of the Forge as more than just a military installation, or a factory, but as what was becoming home. The idea of losing it was probably the most wrenching thing about this war, next to losing the war to the Golden entirely.

But it was a war, and it had to be won.

"Okay, if you guys are good with this, so am I," he said, and turned to Benzel. "Get the fleet deployed."

"Already given the orders," Benzel said, grinning. "Figured I'd get a jump on things. We should be ready to launch in about an hour."

"Okay, then," Dash said, then he started to turn away but paused. "How could you be so sure I'd say yes that you'd start getting things deployed? And before you even really knew what we were planning?"

"To answer the second question, Custodian gave us updates along the way as we came here. And to answer the first"—Benzel's grin widened, and now Wei-Ping smiled along with him—"we've come to know you pretty well, Dash. We knew you'd want to go all in on attacking these bastards, because it's what we would have done." He put a hand on Dash's shoulder. "You would have made a great addition to the Gentle Friends, you know."

"I think he'd count as an honorary member now," Wei-Ping said.

Dash smiled and shrugged at their words, but honestly, it was one of the greatest compliments he'd ever been given.

Dash watched the skirmish between the Verity force and the Aquarians play out on the Archetype's heads-up. The imagery and data were being relayed to them from the Ring; racing through the tenacious dust and gas of the nebula they'd chosen to cover their approach, they were blind to what was happening more than about a hundred thousand klicks away.

"Those Aquarian ships need to break off," Leira said. "They're getting their asses kicked."

Dash gave a grim nod. The Aquarian scout ships were about as durable as dry paper in the face of the Verity attacks. They had scored one solid hit with a gamma-ray laser that had raked a light cruiser from bow to stern, gutting it, but Leira was right—they were getting their asses kicked.

Dash called up Al'Bijea. "Your people have done all that was needed," Dash said. "Hell, I think they've done all that they *can*. Get them out of there."

"The commander of the *Comet* has already ordered a withdrawal," Al'Bijea replied. "I think you're right, we've done what we can. It's over to you now, Dash."

"We'll be deploying for battle in about twenty minutes," Dash said, glancing at the chrono. "Don't worry, we'll take these assholes out before they get anywhere near you."

"I hope so. Al'Bijea out."

Dash heard everything he needed to in that *I hope so*. What the Aquarian leader was saying was, *I've decided to throw in my lot with you. Now, you have to convince me it's worth the blood of my people.*

"Dash," Sentinel said. "There are anomalous scanner returns from ahead and to port on the bearing shown."

Dash looked at the heads-up, showing the tactical display. It did show what seemed to be a localized source of neutrinos, hidden somewhere in the billowing dust. It might just be the emissions from a star the charts showed as laying in that direction but otherwise hidden from them by the nebula. Sentinel was right, though; the exact characteristics of the neutrino emissions were off; they were detecting more of the elusive particles than should be emanating from a star of the class shown. There seemed to be astronomical exceptions to everything, though, so it could be some natural effect.

Or it *could* be a spaceship trying to conceal its reactor emissions by putting itself in front of a more distant star.

"Leira, I'm going to take A squadron off in the direction of that anomaly, just in case. You and B Squadron keep on your current course and get ready to intercept that Verity fleet approaching the Ring. We should only be a short distance behind you."

"Roger that."

Dash veered the Archetype onto a new trajectory, heading straight for the anomaly. The rest of A Squadron, led by the *Herald*, followed in his wake. Dash hated calling them A Squadron and B Squadron. They needed to come up with something more personalized that would instill pride.

The threat indicator lit up. At the same time, a pair of big ships emerged from a cloud of electrostatically charged dust.

"Two Verity heavy cruisers ahead," Benzel said, and began snapping out a series of coded orders that made the squadron smoothly rearrange itself into a battle line. At the same time, the *Herald* erupted with a torrent of fire, pulse-cannons, dark-lances, and missiles ripping into the closer of the two cruisers. This Verity force was likely trying to use the nebula the same way they were, as a covered approach to the Ring, so they could take the Aquarians in the flank. They hadn't counted on Dash and the Cygnus fleet using the nebula in much the same way, and seemed to be in the middle of trying to spring an ambush. They would have gotten away with it, too, if not for Sentinel very much living up to her name.

The cruiser staggered under the weight of the *Herald's* fire. It managed a few desultory return shots, and a few more from its surviving point-defense systems as the *Herald*'s missiles raced and slammed home. Leira hit it with a nova-cannon shot even as she raced by, leading B Squadron to the rescue of the Aquarians still doing battle beyond the opaque veil of the nebula. Her blast hit the drive section, leaving the cruiser stricken, coasting helplessly along on her last trajectory, slew a little to one side as she vented atmosphere from the rents in her hull.

Dash turned his attention to her companion. The other cruiser was burning hard, changing her course to vanish back into a thicker part of the nebula. She knew she was outgunned, and badly at that, facing the entirety of A Squadron. A flotilla of lighter ships, a frigate, and a half dozen corvettes darted forward and launched missiles, desperately trying to screen the bigger ship as it fled.

"Benzel, that damaged Verity cruiser looks pretty much intact," Dash said. "Think we could take her as a prize? She's got to mass about as much as the *Herald*."

"Why not? Wei-Ping, can your squadron and Leira deal with whatever's attacking the Aquarians?" Benzel asked.

Wei-Ping answered immediately. "Based on the data they're sending us from the Ring, yeah, I think so. We just need to keep an eye out for that heavy cruiser that you guys chased off."

"The last maneuver detected for that vessel had it accelerating at a high rate directly away from, and above, the ecliptic plane of the galaxy," Sentinel put in. "Unless it uses some method or technology we have yet to encounter, it will take at least an hour to return to the current battlespace."

"Pfft, that gives us lots of time," Wei-Ping said. "Leira, you okay with this?"

"Of course. Dash, you and Benzel go get yourselves a new ship for the fleet," Leira replied.

"Okay, then," Dash said. "Benzel, I'll meet you outside the rear-most airlock."

The reply that came back rang with fierce anticipation. "We'll be there!"

Dash pulled himself along a corridor lit by fitful, flickering lights. A squad of Gentle Friends ranged ahead, clearing the way. Benzel led another squad forward, heading for the bridge.

"We've got another sealed bulkhead up here!" the squad leader called back. "Dash, can your mech do anything about that? Open it for us?"

"I'll check. Sentinel, have you hacked in yet? Can you open that?"

"I can," Sentinel cut in. "But there is a more urgent matter."

Dash noticed that Sentinel had replied on a private channel, so whatever she was about to say she'd obviously intended for Dash's ears only.

His stomach clenched.

"What's going on? What's wrong?"

"There is a scuttling program running. It will detonate the remaining ordnance aboard the cruiser in just over two minutes."

"Oh. *Shit*. Can you stop it?"

"I am attempting to do so now."

"It's going to take us longer than that to get out of here, you know."

"I am aware of that."

"Dash," the squad leader called back. "Any word?"

Dash switched the comm to the tactical channel. "She's working on it. Just stand by." He switched back to the private channel. "How's it going?"

"I am still working on it."

It struck Dash that he'd actually not lied to the Gentle Friends squad leader—Sentinel was working on *it*, even if *it* was something entirely different. All it did was buy him a moment of clearer conscience though; he was going to have to decide, sometime in the next few seconds, if he was going to even tell the Gentle Friends about their danger. Not that there was anything he, or the rest of them, could do about it.

"I anticipate that I am going to be unable to terminate the scuttling program in time," Sentinel said.

Dash stared up the corridor and at the Gentle Friends, who were glancing back from the sealed bulkhead, at him, waiting.

Shit. Do I tell them, or just let this happen? Dash thought.

As he confronted the quandary, Dash had a sudden vision of Freya's park back on the Forge. He remembered that moist, green smell, the riot of colors from the flowering plants, the grass under his feet.

He wished that's where he was right now. More than anything, that he was—

Wait.

"Sentinel, you said the scuttling program will detonate all of the ordnance?"

"That is correct. In about forty-five seconds."

"How much ordnance is aboard?"

"Almost the entire load out. The *Herald*'s attack prevented the launch of—"

"Can you access fire control?"

"Yes. The Verity failed to lock down that system against intrusion." She paused, then said, "You want me to launch the ordnance, don't you?"

"Can you?"

In answer, tremors ran through the ship, again and again. The Gentle Friends tensed, and the squad leader called back, "Status update! What's happening?"

"Just keep standing by," Dash replied, then switched channels again. "Sentinel?"

"I have launched all ordnance, except for a single missile jammed—"

A heavy shudder rippled through the ship, flinging them all sideways.

"That *was* jammed in a launch tube," Sentinel finished.

Dash took a long breath then let it out. "Okay. Now that my heart is starting to beat again, can you open up this door ahead of us?"

"At your command."

Dash switched back to the tactical channel. "You ready? Sentinel's going to open the blast door."

The squad leader gave a thumbs up and rattled orders to his people.

"Okay, Sentinel, *now*." Dash called.

The door slid open. As soon as it did, a blinding flash flooded the corridor. Dash's last thought was, *guess Sentinel was wrong about that ordnance.*

THE LACK of atmosphere saved them from what could have been a catastrophe. With no medium to carry a shockwave from the Verity booby trap, there was no blast effect along the corridor. There was still shrapnel, of course, from the charge casing; three of the Gentle Friends had their vac suits breached, and one of those probably would have been killed if not for their new body armor.

Still, it made them far more cautious as they advanced toward engineering. They encountered three more charges, two of which the Gentle Friends were able to disarm. The third, unfortunately, went off and badly injured one of their number with a fragment that punched right through her helmet and lodged in her neck. As she was evacuated back to safety, the rest of the squad pressed on, working their way through the inconstant lights strobing along the passages and in the compartments they passed.

"Dash, Benzel here. We've got the bridge—" He paused then went on. "The fire control board is showing a massive ordnance launch not long after we boarded. Was that what we felt, that shaking?"

"Yeah, it was."

"What was that all about?"

"I'll tell you later. We're right outside main engineering, about to enter—"

Another tremor ran through the ship. Dash frowned at that. Now what?

"Benzel, did you just do something? Launch something?"

Sentinel answered. "That was the launch of several escape pods. They have already translated away, their trajectory toward the galactic core."

As soon as she finished speaking, the final blast doors leading into engineering rolled open partway, then stopped. The Gentle Friends threw in a broadband charge; a few seconds later, it detonated with a dazzling visible-light flash and a pulse of energy that would momentarily swamp much of the EM spectrum, short of the far gamma and radio-frequency bands.

They immediately raced in. Dash heard shouts and saw pulse-gun discharges; he piled in after them and found himself embroiled in a vicious firefight. The next few moments were search, find target, shoot, and take cover, over and over. But they knew now that the Verity despised getting into close quarters, so they deliberately pressed in against them, closing and, in a few instances, engaging Verity in melee with boarding cutlasses, axes, and the butts of snap- and pulse-guns.

Dash got in a few hits of his own, knocking two Verity aside to set up attacks from nearby Gentle Friends, then taking down a third with a kick, a fist to knock aside a wild return swing with a shock baton, then a bash from his pulse-gun across his opponent's helmet. The Verity stumbled back, and Dash yanked out his slug-pistol and fired it, all in one smooth motion that was faster than trying to reorient the pulse-gun. The round slammed through the Verity's chest, spraying viscous, whitish fluid in globules that wobbled and spattered against the bulkhead behind it.

"Engineering's secure," the Gentle Friends squad leader said, gasping into his comm. "No more resistance."

For the next few minutes, they confirmed that all of the Verity were down and dead, then they gathered their own wounded back to the *Herald* for treatment. In the midst of it all, Benzel showed up with more Gentle Friends.

"We've got a hold up," Benzel said when he found Dash. "There's quite a battle being fought out there. And I don't mean just Leira and Wei-Ping with B Squadron, although it sounds like they arrived in time to save the Aquarians and kick the Verity's ass out past this nebula. I mean literally right outside this ship."

Dash stared at him through his faceplate. "A battle? Who's fighting? Sentinel, what's going on?"

"The Verity light ships, a frigate, and several corvettes did not accompany the heavy cruiser when it withdrew. They have returned and are attacking, apparently—"

A heavy thud shook the ship around Dash.

"—intent on destroying the ship you have just secured, rather than letting you take it as a prize."

Dash started for the corridor leading forward. "I'm on my way!"

"Actually, Dash, you should remain where you are. You could not safely re-enter the Archetype, given the current tactical situation. Moreover, the *Herald* and the rest of her squadron are, with my assistance, dealing with the matter."

"You're running the Archetype in battle?" Dash made a *hmph* sound. "Hey, does that mean I'm out of a job? I can go back to the Forge and just spend my days drinking plumato wine?"

"The Archetype was meant to be piloted by the Messenger. I am only meant to operate it in exceptional circumstances, such as this one."

Dash gave a wry smile. "And here I thought I could retire."

"Operating the Archetype with you is not the same."

That made Dash's eyes widen. "Are you saying you miss me?"

"I am merely stating a fact. The Archetype does not function as efficiently or effectively without you piloting it. Therefore, it is not the same."

"I think you miss me."

"Please standby, Dash. I have a battle to fight. Sentinel out."

Dash turned to find Benzel grinning at him. He scowled back. "What?"

"That was on an open channel," Benzel replied. Then he sang out, "Dash has a girlfriend."

The Gentle Friends—all of them—laughed, and one of them said, "You need a better body for her than the Archetype, Dash. I don't think you'd last long slow dancing with that mech."

More laughter came, and Dash just shrugged. "Can I help it if I'm popular with the ladies? Even the virtual ones?"

Benzel laughed yet again, along with the rest, but he switched over to a private channel. "So that big ordnance launch—that was to stop this thing from self-destructing, wasn't it?"

Dash looked at Benzel's face through their helmet faceplates, making eye contact with him, and nodded.

"Yeah, it was."

"How long did we have?"

"Less than a minute. Guess they wanted to give themselves time to get away."

"Well, they screwed that up. Those escape pods launched later." Benzel's eyes narrowed. "Were you going to tell us about it, or just let us find out when we went *poof*?"

"Which would you have preferred?"

He saw Benzel ponder it for a moment, then shrug. "Don't really know."

"Yeah. Neither do I." He shrugged back. "Which means I'm just going to hope I never have to actually make that decision."

Benzel punched a gloved hand into Dash's shoulder. "You and me both, brother. You and me both."

13

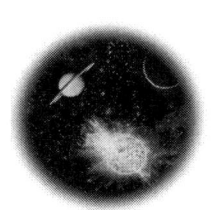

"We lost four scout ships and their crews," Al'Bijea said. "Twelve in total. Overall, a relatively small loss—but we don't have a lot of people, so we feel every death keenly."

Dash leaned on the table and nodded. They were back in the sumptuous meeting room aboard the Oasis, the remote station the Aquarians had established a few tens of thousands of klicks from their artificial home world, the Ring. This was where Dash had first met Al'Bijea, and it made a convenient place to meet now, while the fleet reorganized itself and patched up its battle damage. The thick carpet, wood paneling, and subdued lighting made it seem so incongruous, though, as a place to talk about the war.

"I understand exactly what you mean," Dash said. "We don't have a lot of people, either. I hate losing any of them."

"Which means we had best end this war sooner rather than later, to keep all our losses as low as possible," Al'Bijea replied.

"Couldn't agree more."

Al'Bijea touched a control on his side of the polished table, calling up a holo-image of a star chart. "At least those who died did not do so in vain. They were able to establish the detailed trajectories of the Verity force that was attempting to attack us, allowing us to reverse-track it." He touched another control, and a line appeared, solid at the point where the battle had occurred in and near the nebula, then extending back toward the galactic core, broadening into a widening cone as it did so. "This is their projected course; it widens, of course, based on what we understand to be the maximum acceleration of their vessels. Even then, it is a supposition."

"Doesn't matter," Dash replied. "Those are still damned good data." He followed the widening line back until it vanished into complete uncertainty. He then turned to Leira, Benzel, and Wei-Ping, who were sitting on either side of him.

"We need to take advantage of this," he said. "We're moving the Forge and all our efforts in the right direction, right up along the axis of the arm, toward the galactic core." He pondered the chart for a moment, then turned to Benzel.

"How badly damaged are our ships? Are there any that need to go back to the Forge for repairs? That can't be repaired right here?"

Benzel gave a thoughtful frown, then shook his head. "We really didn't take much damage. I'd say anything we can't repair here is minor. Except for that Verity cruiser we captured, of course. That had the shit kicked out of it. We can repair her and get her into our line, but not any time soon, and not here."

Dash nodded. "Okay, then. We'll press on, right from here. We'll push the fleet right along the axis Al'Bijea's people have identified and take out whatever Verity we encounter."

Benzel and Wei-Ping exchanged a glance, then Benzel crossed his arms. "That's pretty ballsy, Dash. Have to admit, I thought I was aggressive, but—"

"It does seem risky, to launch right into another offensive," Leira said, and even Al'Bijea nodded in agreement.

It was Dash's turn to frown in thought. He got the others' wariness, but his *felt* right. The Verity probably figured they'd finally get a quick victory over the Aquarians, only to have the Cygnus fleet intervene and spoil their plans. They were probably frustrated, which meant they wouldn't be making the best decisions and were likely now scrambling to regroup themselves.

Dash stood. "I hear you guys. But think about this way. If none of our damage is significant, then the fleet's ready for action, right? And if we were at the Forge, and I said we're going to launch an attack, would any of you object then?"

"You got us," Benzel said. "No, probably not."

"Since when did you start making so much sense, anyway?" Leira asked.

Dash shrugged. "Probably about the time I realized I was running a freakin' war."

He smiled as he said it, meaning it to be funny.

But it really wasn't.

Dash couldn't deny he was proud of the fleet, and proud of the work Benzel and Wei-Ping had done in getting it trained and exercised. Each squadron ran like a smooth, well-lubricated machine, while also blending, as necessary, into a seamless whole. Benzel was running them through simulations and drills even as they progressed along the axis of what was apparently the main Verity activity, keeping them honed to a keen edge and ready for battle.

Now, they just needed something to fight.

Dash immediately eyed the threat indicator as they dropped back into real space in yet another system along the path Al'Bijea's people had calculated. This one was a neutron star of a type known as a magnetar, a one-time giant star that had collapsed into something not much bigger than the Forge. It had been a colossal explosion, a supernova with debris in the form of dust and gas surrounding the stellar corpse in a tenuous nebula. The star's gravity had then crushed its remaining matter to the point that protons and electrons were squashed into neutrons. Add to that an insanely powerful magnetic field—one that could rip the iron atoms right out their blood, if they strayed too close—and this was *not* a system very friendly to life. Not surprisingly, the threat indicator remained blank.

"Holy crap," Benzel said. "That magnetar is spinning...I'd say fast, but that doesn't cut it. It's rotating, like, ten times a *second?*"

"Just let's not get too close to it," Wei-Ping replied. "These readings for radiation, magnetic flux and the like are *crazy*."

"We won't be here long," Dash said. "The Verity aren't likely to use this system for anything. I mean, there aren't even any planets."

"If there ever were, they were blown to vapor when this star blew up," Leira said. "And to think I actually made a star go partway in that direction."

She was referring, of course, to their desperate gambit to avoid her plunging into the star around which the Forge had originally orbited, aboard an out-of-control *Slipwing*. Sentinel, though, cut in.

"As I have noted before, Leira, that star was too small to have collapsed into a neutron star. A white dwarf would have been more likely."

"But still with a supernova explosion."

"Yes."

"Same outcome, as far we'd have been concerned," Dash said. "Anyway, Sentinel, I gather we have no reason to stay here?"

"As is to be expected, given the extreme conditions around the magnetar, there is no evidence of any activity in this system by the Verity or anyone else."

Dash nodded. They just waited for Tybalt, now; while Sentinel did a detailed scan of the system in which they'd just arrived, Tybalt updated their scans of destination systems ahead of them. Even moving a couple of light-years closer to them meant they were seeing them that much more recently in time—and that ignored the current data they could collect through unSpace. While they waited, Dash just stared at the distant point of light that was the magnetar. It looked so innocuous—hard to believe its magnetic pull would rip the Archetype apart if they got just a few hundred million klicks closer.

"I have detected signals suggestive of Verity activity," Tybalt finally said.

Dash looked at the data that Sentinel painted on the heads-up. He winced a bit as the image of a globular cluster lit up the cockpit. This one comprised about ten thousand old, relatively small stars jammed into a volume of space less than twenty light-years across, and seemed to be an intergalactic visitor, originating from somewhere outside the Milky Way and just passing through. Like the magnetar system, stars in a globular cluster were unlikely to have planets, as the perturbations from so many stars so close together quickly knocked them out of orbit, if they were even able to form in the first place.

But it was a great place to hide a fleet.

"The Verity unwisely allowed comms traffic to give away their presence in the cluster," Tybalt went on. "Otherwise, between the broad-spectrum EM emissions, radiation, and dense neutrino flux, there really would have been no way of detecting them."

"Looks like we have a target," Benzel said.

But Dash just frowned at the image. "Yeah, we do, don't we?"

Leira caught Dash's tone. "What are you thinking, Dash?"

"That we have a target. Except it's one that we wouldn't have had, like Tybalt says, if they hadn't screwed up and let some comm traffic leak."

"You think it's a trap," Wei-Ping said.

"I think it's probably a trap, yeah. I mean, they might have gotten careless. We did just kick their butts back near the Aquarian Ring, so they might be in an uproar and got sloppy with their emotions running hot. That's pretty flimsy, since I don't even know if they *have* emotions, and I'm not sure I'd put credits on that."

Dash turned his attention back to the dazzling image of the globular cluster on the heads-up. "Sentinel, what's the safest way for us to approach this? If we wanted to attack whatever force might be lurking in that cluster, what's the surest way to go about it in terms of ingress?"

"Translate our force into the peripheral zone of the cluster, just outside the collective gravitational influence of its stars, and then enter it based on the tactical data we have available at the time."

"Yeah, I figured it might be something like that. How about if we translated directly into the cluster, though?"

"That would be inadvisable. The gravitation of each star impinges on those near it, making for complex, chaotic, and unpredictable effects on translation."

"Such as?"

"Such as considerable error in where or when the translating vessels re-enter real space. In extreme cases, it could result in the loss of the vessels in question."

"Right. In other words, all those good reasons we pilots are taught to not translate too far into a gravity well. But the Dark Between, that's different, right?"

"Gravitation has less effect on vessels that are capable of traveling in the boundary zone between unSpace and real space, yes. However, because the passage of time and distance is closer to what would be experienced in real space, such travel isn't feasible. Traveling through the Dark Between from here to the cluster would still result in seventy-five years elapsing in real space, and several years of subjective time aboard the vessel—you are planning something unconventional, aren't you?"

Dash smiled. "You really *are* getting to know me, aren't you?"

"When you begin to ask questions in this manner, my experience is that you are *up to something*, as you would put it."

His smile grew brilliant. "You got me. What ships do we have that could translate fully into unSpace, make the trip to the cluster, but only come part way back out into the Dark Between?"

"And then maneuver into a favorable tactical position, yes. An admittedly clever, albeit risky plan. The Archetype and Swift are both capable of it. The *Herald* and the other Silent Fleet ships would be as well, although they would require modification to their translation drives. Ironically, in this respect, the *Slipwing* is more capable than they are, thanks to the device that you have named the Fade."

That prompted a satisfied nod from Dash. "I wondered about that. Amy?"

"Amy here, Dash. Go ahead."

"How'd you like to do something crazy and potentially dangerous?"

"I'm in!"

"Wouldn't you like to know what it is?"

Amy laughed. "Sure. Probably isn't going to change my mind, though."

DASH COULDN'T STOP GRITTING his teeth. So much could go wrong with this. Had they bitten off more than they could chew?

"Thirty seconds to transition," Sentinel said.

"How's your link to the *Slipwing*?"

"Still nearly optimal. However, I have bypassed the *Slipwing's* navigation computer and am controlling the ship directly. It simply wasn't capable of performing the necessary calculations fast enough."

"Yeah, well, when I had it installed, I hadn't expected to fight an interstellar war with it, much less one in which we do crazy shit like this. Amy, you ready?"

"Yeah. Kind of bored, actually. Sentinel's doing all the work, I'm just a passenger."

"Fifteen seconds. Standby for transition."

If the plan worked, both the Archetype and the *Slipwing* would slide out of unSpace and into the nether region called the Dark Between, a zone that was both unSpace and real space, and yet neither of those things. From there, they should be able to maneuver into an advantageous position relative to the Verity fleet that Dash was certain awaited them.

The rest of the Cygnus fleet, led by Benzel in the *Herald* and Leira in the Swift, would drop out of space the conventional way, in the safe approach to the globular cluster that the Verity would have expected when setting up their ambush. And *that* should fix the attention of the Verity long enough for Dash and Amy to get the drop on them.

Dash gritted his teeth harder. So many *ifs* and *shoulds* and *woulds*.

"Five seconds," Sentinel said.

The chrono ticked down; at zero, Sentinel transitioned both the mech and the *Slipwing* into the Dark Between.

Very little changed. But they were still in one piece.

"Amy, you still with me?"

"Right here," she said, then added, "Okay, that's weird."

"What?"

"I mean, it might just be all the radiation and stuff from all these stars around us, and the fact we're in the spooky Dark Between zone—but I'm not seeing any Verity activity. Like, none."

Dash's gaze swept across the heads-up and the threat indicator. Indeed, there was nothing.

"Sentinel, are we in the right place?"

"Without returning completely to real space, there is some uncertainty—but, yes, I can determine no significant deviation from our planned transition location."

"Huh. Maybe Tybalt was wrong and those signals weren't from Verity ships at all. Some artifact of all these stars, possibly?"

"It is possible. We would need to return to real space to be certain, however."

Dash nodded and scanned the heads-up for places where the overlapping gravitational fields of the stars were weak enough to allow a safe and complete translation. "Okay, that one, there, is closest. Let's head for it and return to real space to see what's what."

It would have taken many hours in real space, but in the Dark Between, only subjective minutes elapsed for Dash and Amy. They reached the translation point, and Dash began to translate back.

"No! Dash! Don't complete this translation!" Sentinel said. An instant later, she locked out the translation controls.

"Sentinel, what the hell?"

"I have just received a time beacon update from the Forge. They are transmitted at regular intervals through the Dark Between in order to keep the Archetype's chrono synchronized with that of the Forge. This happens autonomously, as a routine background function."

"And?"

"And, check the chrono now."

Dash did. "That's wrong. That says its—what, two days from now?"

"It does. And this is not incorrect."

Dash tapped his screen, a half smile on his face. "What, it's two days from now?"

"Yes."

The smile vanished. "Wait. It's two days from now?"

"I'm afraid that, no matter how many times you ask the question, the answer will be the same—yes."

"Dash, what the hell's going on?" Amy asked. "The *Slipwing's* chrono just flipped into the future by two days."

Dash just stared.

Sentinel answered for him. "I just updated it, Amy. And it is correct. The Archetype and the *Slipwing* have emerged from unSpace two days in the future."

"Uh…Dash? What's going on?" Amy asked.

"I—" He blinked then tried again. "I don't know. Sentinel, what the hell's going on?"

"As I described, it would appear that an unexpected interaction between the translation drive, the nature of unSpace and the Darkness between, and the complex gravitation of the stars in this cluster has resulted in a time displacement."

"When did you describe *that?*"

"When you asked about translating directly into the cluster, I said there was a possibility of *considerable error in where or* when *the translating vessels re-enter real space.*"

"Shit. You did say that, didn't you." Dash shook his head. They had just traveled through time. Just the idea was—

"Wait, what happened to the fleet? Were the Verity here?"

"Sensor returns from real space into the Dark Between are limited and incorporate considerable uncertainty. However, I do have some partial data that may answer that question."

An image appeared on the heads-up, grainy and out of focus. It was still clear enough to be recognizable…and gut-wrenching.

It was the shattered wreckage of the Swift.

"Oh, no," Dash breathed.

"It would appear that the battle did not go in our favor."

"Dash, does this mean—shit, does this mean we've *lost?*" Amy asked, her voice quiet and tight and utterly out of character for her, which just made it that much more appalling.

"This is why I prevented you from translating fully back to real space," Sentinel said. "It is possible that the Archetype and the *Slipwing*, as well as you and Amy, continue to constitute mass in the universe—that you still exist, in some form. If that is the case, and we returned to it, we would violate fundamental conservation laws. The effects of that are literally impossible to predict."

"You mean that, even though we're here, we might be out there, too?"

"That is correct."

The idea was—it was mind-boggling. There could be another Archetype and *Slipwing*, another Dash and Amy, just the remains of a full translation away. And if they did finish that translation, they'd duplicate them, adding new mass to the universe, which wasn't supposed to be able to happen.

"I'm starting to think this might have been a really bad idea," Dash said, his stomach wrenched down to a tight knot.

He couldn't tear his eyes away from the wreckage of the Swift. Had Leira escaped? What had he *done?*

"Sentinel," Amy asked, her voice suddenly cold and deliberate. "Can we undo this? Can we—I don't know, go back in time? Return to where we should be?"

"It is not possible to return to the precise moment we left, no. The universe has changed in ways that cannot be measured. The movement of bodies of which we are entirely unaware could have effects that we cannot even begin to account for."

"Okay, wait," Dash said. "Just wait. Can we actually—rewind time to the same point, though?"

"It is theoretically possible, yes. I can base a new translation on the data and calculations used for the one that brought us here, essentially calculating a back course through unSpace that should return us to the objective past in real space. But, as I said, it is not possible to do so with any degree of accuracy."

"Can you deliberately overshoot?"

"You are *up to something* again."

"Indeed I am. Can you deliberately overshoot the time we came from, go back to a point before it?"

"I could achieve a margin of days, but nothing less than that. However, we would again be unable to return to real space because of the mass-balance problem."

"Yeah, the Archetype and *Slipwing* and Amy and Dash are still there, a few days ago, I get it. What if we go back and just sit in the Dark Between waiting until we started this whole mess to begin with? Once the other Dash and Amy I guess, enter unSpace."

"Then we would leave it," Sentinel replied. "Yes, the reasoning is sound. However, that also does stand to create an infinite time loop, in which this incident will continue to happen, theoretically forever."

"Maybe it already has," Amy said. "And we've been through this a bazillion times now."

Dash sighed. Now there was a terrifying thought. And yet, it might actually be true. How would they ever know?

"Okay, so one last question, Sentinel," he asked. "Once we're out of this, will we just join the regular flow of time and carry on?"

"To the extent I can answer that question, I would say yes."

"But you don't know for sure."

"I do not."

"What do you think, Amy?" Dash asked.

"This future sucks. Let's go back and see if we can make a better one."

"Works for me. Sentinel, do what you have to do, and then let's go back to where we belong."

THE DOWNSIDE of their foray through not just space, but time—aside from the obviously cataclysmic possibilities it raised—was that they ended up five days *ago*, relative to when they'd first translated to start all of this. So Dash and Amy were still aboard the Forge, not yet having spoken to Al'Bijea, who himself wasn't even yet aware that a Verity force was on its way to attack the Ring. It forced Dash and Amy to wait, hanging in the featureless void of the Darkness Between, passing the time as best they could.

It turned out Dash was better than Amy at poker, but she was by far the better chess player.

Now, they'd almost caught up in time. They'd seen the Verity force arrive and lay its trap; now, they prepared themselves to finally return to real space in their right time—more or less, although according to Sentinel it didn't really matter, as long as they finished their long-delayed translation once the other Dash and Amy had entered unSpace.

And, based on the chrono, they just had.

"Sentinel, if we were to drop back into real space *now*, we'd have the drop on the Verity, right?"

"Given that there is no way, in the normal course of things, for the *Slipwing* and Archetype to be here now, then it is likely that they would be taken completely by surprise, yes."

"Amy, you ready to do this?'

"If it means I don't have to play another hand of poker with you, yes, a thousand times yes. I swear you cheat."

"I never cheat friends," Dash said. "Okay, then, let's do this. Sentinel, let's get the hell out of the Dark Between."

Side-by-side, the Archetype and the *Slipwing* finally popped back into the real universe.

Ahead of them, a Verity flotilla was marshalled around two massive ships—a Verity battlecruiser and, to Dash's grim surprise, a ship that clearly belonged to Clan Shirna. It was the twin of one that he'd destroyed with the Unseen device called a Lens, right after he'd killed the Shirna leader called Nathis.

All of them were blissfully unaware of the Archetype and the *Slipwing*, which Sentinel had managed to bring back into real space only a few thousand klicks away. The wash of EM noise and radiation from the multitude of stars flaring around them gave them a brief window of time to act.

"Amy, rake that big ship on the right, the one that's probably Clan Shirna. I'll take the one on the left. Go!"

Together, the Archetype and the *Slipwing* leapt forward, accelerating hard.

The enemy ships grew in the heads-up. The firing solutions were dead simple, practically shoot that way and watch for the boom.

So Dash did.

Dark-lance shots and missiles erupted from the Archetype, tearing into the hull of the big Verity battlecruiser. Dash fired the distortion cannon, too, yanking a chunk out of its hull and sending two smaller ships, a corvette and a fighter, careening into the debris and one another. He glanced at Amy and saw her pumping pulse-cannon shots and missiles into the Clan Shirna ship. She peeled off as return fire started up, point-defense systems first, as they came to automated life; bigger weapons followed, sporadic, but quickly growing in intensity as the enemy fleet realized it was being hammered by an attack that shouldn't even be happening.

Shots began to slam into the Archetype's shield. Dash kept pulsing out shots from the dark-lance, punching into the battlecruiser's hull, leaving clouds of venting atmosphere and spinning debris in his wake. He brought the Archetype to within a few meters of the big ship, deployed the power sword, and slashed at weapons clusters, sensor arrays, and anything else he could reach. And then he was clear, the big ship receding behind him.

He stowed the power-sword and flicked the heads-up to a rearward view. Chaos gripped the Verity fleet. Ships that had prepared themselves for a common attack vector against the rest of the Cygnus fleet now struggled to break formation and reorganize themselves against this new, unexpected attack.

But reorganizing themselves they were. Dash knew they'd kicked a nest of fangrats, riling them up to a frenzy. The question was, did they go back in, or just break and run until Benzel and the rest of the fleet—

"Look out, assholes, here it comes again!"

Dash saw that Amy had reversed course and now burned hard, driving the *Slipwing* right back into battle.

"Oh. *Amy*," Dash muttered.

There was brave, and there was stupid, and there was stupidly brave—and then there was Amy.

Dash somersaulted and drove the Archetype through a hard turn, then he opened up again with missiles and the dark-lance. The weight of return fire was building up to terrifying levels, though. He saw the *Slipwing* dodging and weaving through a storm of fire, taking a few hits, but mostly throwing off the Verity firing solutions—at least, for the moment. But the *Slipwing* had only a single, weak shield, all that even her upgraded reactor could power. Dash straightened out his course, trying to make himself an easier target, hoping to draw the Verity fire.

Which he did. It seemed like most of the fleet had decided to concentrate their fire on him, and now he was the one desperately evading, trying to preserve the Archetype's shields for as long as he could.

The *Slipwing* slashed through the Verity formation, a streak of incandescent fusion exhaust. Amy landed solid hits on a Verity cruiser, but another had raised a shield of its own and just ignored her incoming fire, targeting her, and catching the *Slipwing* in a tsunami of pulse-cannon shots. The *Slipwing* staggered and her fusion exhaust died, leaving her coasting helplessly in a straight line.

"Dammit!"

Dash flung himself at his ship. Since she was no longer accelerating, he caught up fast.

"Sentinel, priority on that shield! Give it everything you can!"

"Understood."

Dash was able to launch a final salvo of missiles, then the Archetype's weapons dropped offline. He caught the *Slipwing* and grabbed her hull, the mech's mighty hands gripping her point defense battery. He couldn't apply much force—he'd just rip the battery off its mounts—but he wasn't trying to. He just wanted to protect the *Slipwing* as best he could and hope that either the rest of the fleet showed up, or they could lose themselves against the background clutter of the globular cluster. But without being able accelerate—

"Amy, you okay?"

"I'm fine. Your ship's a little broken, though. I'm working on the drive now."

Shots slammed into the Archetype's shield, the volume of fire mounting by the second. Dash gritted his teeth against the growing storm, wincing as the Meld began communicating the damage. The shield faltered; shots starting smashing into the Archetype's armor. But he could do nothing except coast along.

"Amy, get that drive lit!"

"Working on it!"

Dash winced again. He let go of the point-defense array and moved the Archetype back, planting his hands on the *Slipwing's* stern. The heads-up was filled by the gaping blackness of his ship's fusion exhaust ports.

"Change of plans, Amy. Don't light the drive. I'm going to try to push—"

Missiles raced in, a whole salvo of them. The *Slipwing's* point defense opened up, taking down some, but the rest struck home, immersing the Archetype and her charge in searing blasts of raw plasma.

The Archetype's shield flared briefly with scintillating energy, then died. Every incoming shot would now strike armor, which wouldn't last long.

Dash found himself facing another of those awful choices. He could try to restore the shield, but that would preclude him powering up the Archetype's drive. Or he could accelerate but forego the shield.

Or he could leave the *Slipwing* to her fate and just break off to save the Archetype.

Pulse-cannon shots began boiling away the Archetype's armor. More struck the *Slipwing*, tearing glowing chunks out of her own armor. He heard Amy cry out as one bolt hit a soft spot, the base of the *Slipwing's* lower sensor array, where its conduits entered the hull.

Dash groaned as the Archetype staggered under the repeated hits. He was going to lose the mech—and they couldn't lose the mech.

Then he had a thought. He'd assumed that his inadvertent vision of the future, the wrecked Swift, had been something they could simply prevent by doing what they did, effectively rewinding time and trying again. But what if the future was fixed? What if this was inevitable? And if it really was an infinitely repeating loop, was there some way they could warn their past selves?

The Archetype went abruptly dark and silent.

"Sentinel!"

Nothing.

"Shit, Sentinel—"

The heads-up flared back to life. "Emergency power only," Sentinel said. "All major systems offline."

"Is there anything we"—Dash grunted, as yet more shots hit home—"we can do?"

"I have no suggestions."

It was probably the bleakest thing Dash had ever heard from the AI.

"You guys need a hand?"

The massive bulk of the *Herald* slid into view, interposing her bulk between Dash and Amy, and the Verity fleet. The sound of Benzel's voice let Dash just hang in the Archetype's cradle for a moment.

"You would not believe how good it is to see you guys," he said.

"Looked for a while there like you and Amy were going to take out this fleet all by yourselves, leave nothing for us."

"Yeah, it started out good, but kind of went sideways after that."

"Sorry, just a sec—" Benzel stayed silent for a moment, then said, "Sorry about that. Had a salvo of incoming missiles to deal with. Can you two extract yourselves from this mess on your own? All these stars are making this battle crazy complicated, there's gravity everywhere, pulling in every direction."

"Amy, how's that drive?"

"If you'd get your face out of my rear end, I could fire it up right now!"

Benzel chuckled. "Well, I'll leave you two alone, then—"

"Very funny," Dash said, backing the Archetype away on thrusters and moving it out of the *Slipwing's* exhaust plume. "Benzel, in all seriousness, have you got this battle under control? Because the Archetype's in pretty rough shape."

It was Leira who answered. "We've got this, Dash. You and Amy made it a lot easier, those two big ships are pretty much out of commission."

Dash let out a long, slow breath. "Leira, is it ever good to hear your voice."

"Miss me?"

The *Slipwing's* fusion drive lit, and Amy powered away from the battle. Dash followed.

"Yeah, Leira—actually, I did."

"Oh. Um, okay." He could tell she wanted to ask more, but there was a battle to finish winning. "We'll talk later."

"You bet," Dash replied, glad to his core that they'd have the chance, because the future didn't seem to be fixed after all.

"I THINK that's one of the worst beating the Archetype ever took," Dash said, looking out from the docking bay and into space. The mech hung out there, motionless, a half dozen of the Forge's maintenance drones swirling around it, removing wrecked armor and components and installing new ones. Heavy repairs like this were just easier to do in space; even so, Sentinel would still have to bring the mech into a docking bay near the fabrication plant for its final fixes.

"Yeah, I guess that's kind of my fault," Amy said.

Dash looked at her. "Yeah, it was."

She turned to him, surprised and little shocked. Leira mirrored her expression.

"I'm sorry, Dash," Amy said.

He turned on her. Sheer relief at how things worked out wasn't enough to offset the fact he was pissed. "You should be. Benzel and Wei-Ping think I'm aggressive, but you're sometimes over the top, Amy. You've got to rein that in, especially if you're going to be flying a mech, but there's another issue here, too."

"Um…what?" Amy said, her voice small.

He gripped her shoulder, his voice taking on a softer note. "You're not bulletproof. None of us are."

She gave a chastened nod. "You're right. I just get carried away."

"Custodian," Dash said. "Whatever AI you set up for Amy in the Talon, it's got to be one that helps her stay a little more…I don't know, careful, judicious, something like that, anyway."

"Understood."

Dash wanted to stay mad at Amy; she looked like a puppy he'd just kicked. He finally sighed and said, "I don't want to lose you," he finally said.

She gave him a weak smile. "Me, or your ship?"

"Eh, maybe a little of both."

"Dash!"

He turned to see Benzel, who was approaching with Wei-Ping.

"We've got the final casualty count," Benzel said. "We lost sixteen, and two ships. One was one of our new Silent Fleet additions, the *Terror*. She was just too badly damaged to bring home in one piece, so we're retrieving her as scrap. The other was a mine layer, the *Persistence*."

"She took a missile that breached her reactor containment," Wei-Ping said. "At least the people aboard her wouldn't have felt a thing."

Dash crossed his arms. "That's not really comforting."

"Don't expect it to be," Wei-Ping said. "It's just that if there's anything not truly shitty out of it, that would be it."

Dash stared at her for a moment, then nodded. She had a point. But so did he.

"Custodian, we've been putting a lot of emphasis on making more weapons. But how about better ones? Do we have design upgrades we make to these ships? Better shields and armor especially, to protect our people? We're leaving too many souls out in the black, and I won't have it."

"The amount of scrap being retrieved from the most recent

battle—particularly Dark Metal—would allow for a number of upgrades," Custodian replied. "However, it would mean curtailing production in some areas."

Dash nodded in thought. They had managed to salvage a lot of scrap from the battle in the globular cluster—including a Golden observation post of some sort, that had been well-hidden from outside the cluster but pretty evident from inside. They'd towed it back to the Forge along with everything else; after a brief examination, Custodian had suggested that it had enough Dark Metal incorporated into it to actually expand production of some weapons, particularly mines.

But if that same Dark Metal could be used for better protective systems—

"Okay, Custodian, let's you and I meet with Viktor and Conover in, say, an hour to talk about our production priorities. I really want to upgrade our ships' systems and try to keep our people safe—or at least safer than they are now."

"Understood."

He asked Benzel and Wei-Ping to join in the meeting, then wandered off to spend a few precious minutes alone.

Leira, though, apparently had other ideas. He turned when he felt someone following him across the docking bay and found her just a few paces away.

"Am I intruding?" she asked.

He nodded. "Yup. But if anyone has a standing invitation to intrude, it would be you."

She smiled. "So Amy mentioned that you guys did a little time traveling."

"Not by choice, but, yeah."

"What was that like?"

"I don't recommend it. Too much maybe-screwing-up-the-whole-universe to make it really worth it."

"I get that. Conover and the AIs seem to be really intrigued, but I agree that time is one thing we should probably leave alone."

Dash nodded.

"So what did you see?"

He looked at her. "What do you mean?"

"Well, Amy wouldn't tell me anything. She said I should talk to you. I'm just wondering what you saw."

Dash looked out at the Archetype and the maintenance drones darting about it. For a moment, with damaged armor being removed to be taken back to the smelters, she looked derelict, just as the Swift had looked during his brief but horrifying glimpse back into the real space of the future from the Darkness Between.

He shrugged. "I didn't see much, really," Dash said. "Anyway, it doesn't matter now because none of it will ever happen."

Leira said nothing. Dash turned to her and saw she was giving him a searching look. Finally, she spoke.

"Makes me wonder what happened to the people in that future. Did they just cease to exist?"

Dash looked into Leira's eyes and smiled. "Actually, I think they're just fine."

14

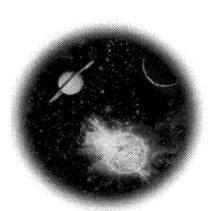

Dash gave the small group of people huddled in the Park a reassuring smile. At least, he hoped it was reassuring. He was still new to this whole diplomatic side to his job as Messenger. It would be easy to fall into the manipulative and somewhat cynical charm that had served him so well as a courier, but these people were genuinely scared, and probably suffering from all sorts of lingering trauma. Benzel and Wei-Ping had found them hidden aboard the derelict Verity ships after the battle, gently taken them off, and brought them back to the Forge for—

That was the question, wasn't it?

"My name's Newton Sawyer," he said. "But everyone calls me Dash. I just wanted to welcome you to the Forge, heart of the Cygnus Realm."

"Never heard of you," one man muttered.

Another said, "Who cares? They got us out of that shit."

"And we're glad we did," Dash said. "And now you're probably wondering what comes next. That's entirely up to you."

"Can't go home," the first man who'd spoken said. "Home's gone."

Dash nodded. "I know. That's why you're free to stay here, as long as you'd like. If you do, though, we're going to ask you to help us out. We're fighting back against the Verity—those are the bastards who attacked you and were holding you. More importantly, we're fighting back against the Golden, the Verity's masters."

"Count me in," a woman said, but others among the crowd didn't look so sure.

"Like I said, it's up to you. If you don't want to stay, then as soon as we can, we'll take you to an inhabited planet or station, and you can go your own way. In the meantime, you've got the run of this part of the Forge, including this park our people have built here. Just don't eat anything without talking to Freya over there." He ended on the most charming smile he could muster, then left the newcomers and joined Leira, Viktor, and Ragsdale.

"We have to screen the hell out of these people before we trust them with anything but their assigned hab space and this park," Dash said.

Ragsdale gave a firm nod. "Already on it. The trouble is that a few of them just have no records. If they did, they were destroyed when the Verity attacked wherever they were from."

"If we can't be entirely confident they're clean, then they can't stay. We just can't risk any more spies or saboteurs."

"That's an advantage the Verity have," Viktor said. "They're not interested in the welfare of these people, so they're not worried about any of them being spies."

"That's true," Dash replied. "And it's going to stay true, because I'd never ask anyone to subject themselves to that as an agent for us."

"Damned right," Leira said.

They left the new refugees with Freya—and several Gentle Friends, armed with concealed pulse-pistols, who'd keep a discreet eye on the situation. They made their way to the main infirmary, which was crowded with more refugees, as well as injured from the battle.

"Let's hope we have no big medical emergencies," Dash said, eyeing the dreary throng of ill and injured. "We're packed to the bulkheads in here."

They were. Every treatment table was occupied, so that some patients were sprawled on gurneys, or even on stretchers on the floor. Had it been a conventional facility, Dash knew, it would have been bedlam, with doctors and nurses bustling about, calling out instructions and orders and questions, people moaning in pain, some probably panicking. But Unseen tech precluded all that. The interconnected treatment bays were quiet and purposeful, with automated systems working away to deliver therapies and treatment.

"There are adequate peripheral facilities to deal with any likely short-term needs," Custodian said. "Moreover, sixty percent of those being treated here are responding well and can soon be discharged."

Dash watched a robotic arm move a device along the arm of

one of the Gentle Friends, which was scorched and blistered with a plasma burn. The woman saw him watching and shrugged.

"Doesn't even hurt," she said.

Dash stepped up to her bedside and examined the burn. Second degree, third in a few places. The pain should be excruciating.

"Really?" Dash asked. "Are you sure you're not just being all stoic about it?"

The woman gazed at her seared arm. "Do I *look* that stoic? I mean it doesn't actually hurt, thanks to whatever Custodian did."

"Your nervous system is a relatively straightforward organo-electrical network," Custodian said. "It is simply a matter of selectively interrupting its electrical impulses."

"Simple for you, maybe," Dash said, then he gave the woman a smile and moved on.

Dash and the others wandered among the injured, visiting everyone, even stopping to spend a moment with those who were unconscious. One such casualty halted him short.

"He's Clan Shirna," Dash said.

"Yeah, he is," Wei-Ping replied. "We pulled him from the wreckage of that Shirna battlecruiser, the one you and Amy attacked first, along with that big Verity battlecruiser. It was called the *Grinding Heel*, by the way."

"What a charming name," Leira said, rolling her eyes.

"Those two ships were awfully damned big and powerful," Benzel put in. "In case I hadn't mentioned it before, you guys doing as much damage to them as you did, right up front, probably made the battle for us."

Dash nodded. Benzel didn't know how right he was. After all, Dash had *seen* what would have happened if they hadn't effectively knocked those two big capital ships mostly out of the fight right at the outset.

"Anyway, as far as we can tell, this was the only survivor," Wei-Ping went on. "Custodian figures that he might literally be the *only* survivor from Clan Shirna, in fact."

"Aside from that woman—what's her name, Sur-natha?" Benzel said. "The one we're holding as a prisoner, anyway."

"And she's human, not actually Clan Shirna, even if she does claim to be Nathis's adopted daughter," Leira added.

Dash narrowed his eyes at the unconscious figure, and the reptilian features he remembered so well from Nathis, their bitter, but now long-gone enemy. "Custodian, what makes you think this is the last survivor of Clan Shirna?"

"An analysis of casualty rates, versus the expected demographics of the Clan Shirna population. There is some uncertainty, of course, but the likelihood of this being the sole surviving member of that faction is approximately eighty percent. If there are other survivors, they no longer constitute a viable population, and will not for a significant number of generations."

"So, except for this guy, Clan Shirna is dead," Dash said.

"That's what it amounts to, yeah," Wei-Ping replied.

"And what are his chances for recovering?"

"He suffered severe trauma. His chances of recovery are approximately fifty percent."

Fifty-fifty. He survives, or he doesn't. Except it wasn't especially funny, this time.

"So could we use this bed for one of our own people, who's more likely to survive?"

"Yes, there are several candidates," Custodian replied.

"So pick the worst of those and give them this bed."

"What do you want to do with this guy?" Wei-Ping asked.

Dash shrugged. "Get him out of the way. Otherwise, I don't care."

Benzel and Wei-Ping just nodded. Leira looked at Dash with concern, but he spoke before she could.

"These bastards allied themselves with the Golden, mainly to grab some power and make some credits, remember?"

She stopped, looked back down at the unconscious figure, then nodded. "Yeah, I do."

And that was that.

They carried on, reaching the other end of the main infirmary, and Dash turned to Benzel. "Okay, this was the easy part. Now for the hard part. Where are our dead?"

Benzel frowned. "Custodian has them in stasis. Why?"

"I want to visit them," Dash said.

"You sure about that?"

"They're not going to be hurt if you give them a pass, you know," Wei-Ping said.

But Dash gave his head a firm shake. "No. I want to see them. I'm always going to want to see them, from now on. To pay my respects."

The others continued to look doubtful but started to turn away. Dash stopped them by carrying on. "Look, over the past while I've started to realize I'm more than just the Messenger. For good or for worse, I'm the leader around here. It's not something I ever especially wanted, certainly nothing I ever asked for—but there it is." He looked back into the crowded infirmary. "I'm *really* starting to realize what that actually means. These people—I'm responsible for them. The decisions I make are going to go a long way in determining if they live, or if they—yeah, if they die. And if they die, I want to—"

Dash stopped, shaking his head. This was *really* hard to put into words.

But Leira smiled and touched his arm. "No, I get it. You want to thank them and say goodbye to them."

Dash nodded. "Yeah. That's it exactly. They've given up everything for what we're trying to do here. I owe them this." He returned Leira's smile. "Sometimes I think I'd be lost without you, you know."

As soon as he said it, an image of the wrecked Swift shoved its way into his mind. He shoved it away just as hard.

Benzel nodded again, this time in a way that said yeah, he got it, too. They left the infirmary and led them to the morgue.

The door was sealed, and they had to ask Custodian explicitly to open it. "This is because there is a low-power stasis field operating in the compartment," the AI said. "It suppresses biological activity. Think of the nerve-impulse blocking I describe earlier, except applied to all life processes."

"So your heart would just stop beating?" Wei-Ping asked.

"Yes. However, the cessation of electrical activity in your brain would be a much more immediate cause of death."

"You know, I realize this is going to sound really inappropriate, considering why we're here, but can we weaponize that?" Benzel said. "It sounds like it could be devastating if you could, say, hit even just part of a ship with some effect like that."

"It is not a practical application of the technology," Custodian replied. "The field generators would require too much power for the effect, which would be restricted to too small an area, and all of it would require considerable miniaturization."

"Well, it was worth a shot," Benzel said.

"Okay, Custodian, open the doors," Dash said.

The door slid smoothly open.

Beyond was a compartment about fifteen meters by ten, empty of anything except racks of shelves. Most of them were empty.

But ten weren't. Dash walked to the first body, enclosed in a black polymer bag. A data chip attached to it lit with a name and other particulars when he touched it.

Dash recognized the name. He'd been one of the Gentle Friends. And that was all Dash knew about him.

He looked at the bag. It concealed a man who had died barely into the beginning of his life, in his early twenties. Dash wondered about him. What had his childhood been like? How had he ended up in the ranks of the Gentle Friends? Did he still have family somewhere? Had he fallen in love with anyone? Kissed anyone? Been easy to get along with? Funny? A miserable asshole? Some of both?

None of that mattered, though, did it? Because it had all died with him.

Dash let go of the data chip and it went dark.

He went from body to body, spending a moment with each one. Leira, Benzel, and Wei-Ping waited a discreet and respectful distance away. As he touched each data chip and it lit up with an identity that had once been a life, Dash found himself growing angrier with each corpse.

By the time he reached the last one, he was seething, a deep, primal rage boiling inside him. He wanted to strap himself into the Archetype, go find some Golden or Verity or Clan Shirna, and destroy them. He imagined not doing with missiles or the dark-lance, but with the mech's power-sword, with its fists. He wanted to slam them repeatedly into the works of the Golden, smash them, break them, tear them down.

"Dash, are you okay?"

He looked up, unaware he'd just been standing motionless and staring intently at the last body. Leira stood beside him, worry etched onto her face.

Dash realized his fists were clenched and relaxed them. It took effort. Finally, he nodded—or meant to, but actually ended up shaking his head.

"Am I okay?" He looked around at the bodies. "No, I'm not." He turned back to Leira. "But I will be. And then we'll get on with the war."

"You know what you need?" Benzel said. "A drink. Freya's got a new batch of plumato wine. Or, if you're really brave, we've got some stuff our folks brewed up on the *Herald*."

He glanced at Wei-Ping, apparently waiting for her take on whatever concoction the Gentle Friends aboard the *Herald* had come up with. She shrugged.

"It's awful," she said. "But it'll get you drunk."

"We call it fusion burn," Benzel said, then nodded at one of the bodies. "Tirel over there was a master at making the stuff. Or at least making it drinkable, anyway."

Dash looked at the body of Tirel. Except he wasn't just a body, was he? He was still a person. He still meant things to people. And that kept him alive, at least in a way.

The thought made Dash feel a little better. He gave Leira a grateful nod, then turned to Benzel and Wei-Ping and said, "You know what? Yeah, I could use a drink."

"I think we all could," Leira said, following Dash and the others back out of the compartment they were using as a morgue. The door slid silently shut and sealed again behind them.

As they walked away, Dash briefly thought about the inside of that compartment, the door now closed, the lights off, plunging it into complete and silent darkness.

FUSION BURN WAS RIGHT, Dash thought. With emphasis on burn. He'd drank some pretty raw stuff in his time, but the Gentle Friends' makeshift liquor was right in the top ranks of harsh, crossing a line from *raw* to *barely drinkable.*

As the hot shower water played over him, sluicing over his skin, he resolved to never actually get drunk on the stuff. One drink made his head tingle and left a slightly bitter dryness in his mouth that he was sure resulted from having lost a layer of skin inside his mouth. Even opening his mouth into the shower stream, letting hot water bubble and gush through his mouth, didn't blunt the feeling.

He watched the last of the soap swirl away down the drain between his bare feet. His shower was done—except he hadn't really decided to take one to get clean, had he? In the shower he had no demands on him except to stand still and let the water rinse away his exhaustion. It was a refuge of sorts, and now, it was over.

"Messenger, if you have a moment," Custodian said.

Dash blew out a sigh. So much for that.

"Yeah, just give me a second here," he said, tapping the control that shut off the water, then stepping out and into a warm-air drier. It took only seconds to waft the water from his body; he slipped on a clean pair of shorts and padded into his private quarters.

"Okay, Custodian, what's up?"

"The *Horse Nebula* and the *Void Stalker* have sent a message to the effect that they are returning to the Forge following an engagement with the enemy."

Dash paused in the middle of pulling on a sock. The two mine layers had been dispatched a couple of days previously, on another of their ongoing missions to mine systems the Forge passed as it advanced. The aim was to deny easy access to the systems by enemy forces, while giving an early warning if they tried, a sign that they might be attempting to outflank the Forge.

"Show me a star chart," Dash said, tugging on his other sock and standing.

A holo image appeared, showing where the *Horse Nebula* and

her consort had been operating, and the current location of the Forge.

"The mine layers were attacked shortly before they translated out of that system," Custodian said. "They had almost completed their mining tasks and confirm that at least two Verity corvettes were attacked by mines, and one was badly damaged or destroyed."

"How are our people?"

"Minor injuries only. No deaths."

"Good."

Dash studied the chart, rotating it with a wave of a hand to get the full, three-dimensional perspective. "So if they ran into enemy forces there," Dash said, pointing at the system in question, "then the Verity, or the Golden, or whoever's behind it, seems to be trying to work around our left flank."

"Yes. The mines are proving quite valuable for securing our flanks."

"Yeah, they are." Dash crossed his arms and frowned at the star chart in thought. "Okay," he finally said. "Let's get more drones patrolling out to our flanks and push them out a little further. If they do try coming at us, I want as much warning as possible. Also, make sure Benzel and Wei-Ping know about this."

"I have already briefed them."

Dash nodded. "Of course you have," he said, and turned to finish getting dressed.

"There is one other matter," Custodian said.

Dash pulled on shirt, paused, and sighed. "Isn't there always. So what is it this time?"

"The injured member of Clan Shirna died just a short time ago."

"Really."

"Yes. I thought you would like to know."

"Okay, then. Just go ahead and space the body."

"Do you wish to be present when that is done?"

"Nope. No one does. Just have one of your maintenance remotes do it."

"If I may make an observation, your lack of concern over the death of what is likely the last member of an entire race stands in marked contrast to your concern for the dead in the morgue."

"Damned right it's markedly different." Dash snapped the waistband closed on his trousers. "Why, does that bother you?"

"Me being *bothered* by any such matters is an irrelevant concept. Rather, I am curious as to why. I assume that it is because this was a dead foe. However, military history—including your own—is replete with accounts of fallen enemies being accorded great respect. For example, in your own history, an individual named Manfred von Richtofen, also known as the *Red Baron*, was the pilot of a crude, heavier-than-air fighter-class vessel in a large, armed conflict. He killed many foes in battle. When he was himself killed, and his body came into the possession of those same foes, he was treated with great reverence. I am curious as to the difference."

"Well, I don't know much about this Manfred—whatever his name was. I guess he was fighting, though, for something he truly believed in, and did it in a way that wasn't all about him being a cruel, opportunistic asshole who was happy to see all life being wiped out." Dash sat on his bed and retrieved his boots. "In any case, he obviously earned his enemy's respect. Clan Shirna, though, no. They made their choice. They aligned themselves with a bunch of xenophobic, genocidal assholes. I won't gloat over the death of this last guy, and the rest of Clan Shirna—I'm not a tyrannical jerk, and I'm not a genocidal maniac myself. But I'm not going to pretend to respect them or treat their dead with any reverence. So space his corpse, and let's move on to deal with the Verity, the Bright, the Golden, or whoever else shows up in our crosshairs."

"Even if it means the destruction of those races as well?"

"Would that bother you? Wasn't that what your Creators were all about?"

"The Creators had a rich and varied culture and society that went far beyond their military prowess. However, circumstances did force them to dedicate themselves to the defeat of the Golden."

Dash pulled on his boots and fastened them. "So if they'd been in my position, and had the life or death decision over the Golden, what do you think they would have done?"

"Exterminated them, of course. It is the only logical course of action."

Dash stood and headed for the door and, from there, the Command Center, where he had yet another meeting. As he exited his quarters, he nodded.

"Damned right it is."

15

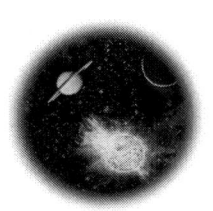

Dash indulged himself in putting his feet up on a console in the Command Center as Custodian spoke. The AI actually oversaw all of the controls and determined whether or not one had been operated deliberately, or accidentally. It meant Dash could put his feet up, and they could lean on the consoles, without inadvertently triggering something that might blow up a planet.

"The construction of the Shroud is nearly complete. It will use about half as much Dark Metal as the inferior version retrieved from the Golden and operate more efficiently. Once it has finally been completed, testing will begin," Custodian said.

Dash looked around. Everyone was assembled here, even Freya, who Dash had decided needed to be included in their planning meetings. Her work was proving to have a huge impact on morale, and Dash was now realizing just how important a factor the morale of their people was in prosecuting this war.

"So we're going to have the *Greenbelt* and the Shroud on permanent station near the Forge?" Wei-Ping asked. "Doesn't that kind of leave them hanging out there, vulnerable?"

"It's a good point," Viktor said. "It would seem to leave them vulnerable. We can't do much about the *Greenbelt*, but can't the Shroud be built inside the Forge?"

"The operation of the Shroud during the fabrication of power cores results in strong emissions of radiation, particularly neutrons. While this can be contained, it means a portion of the Forge will have to be permanently closed as the structure around the Shroud will become heavily contaminated by secondary radiation."

Viktor nodded. "Okay, well, that's a pretty good reason to not build it aboard the Forge, then. But still, isn't it a critical point of vulnerability for us?"

"Yeah, the Golden tried hiding it, and we snatched it from them," Amy said. "Hate to have them turn around and do the same thing to ours."

"That is unlikely," Custodian said. "Even in its current, partially powered-up state, the Forge is more than capable of protecting nearby assets such as the Shroud. Any attack sufficiently strong to overcome that would likely destroy the Forge anyway."

Dash put his feet on the floor. "Okay, so the Shroud sits outside the Forge and makes power cores for us. That's what we should assume we're working with. So the question is, how fast can it make power cores? The technical specs are a—well, a little beyond me."

"I'm an engineer," Viktor said. "And they're beyond me, too."

"It depends on the types of cores being produced. Standard, Level One cores can be manufactured relatively quickly. More powerful Level Two cores require a greater investment of time and resources. Q-cores take even longer, and require significant amounts of Dark Metal."

Dash glanced around, making sure he wasn't the only one who had no idea what a Q-core was. The blank expressions he saw on everyone else's face reassured him he wasn't.

"What's a Q-core?" Amy asked.

"It is a tandem core, with either two or four Level One or Two power cores arranged in a parallel configuration. By taking advantage of certain harmonics, the Creators were able to develop a single power-core unit whose net energy production exceeds that of four individual cores by a significant margin."

"Well, those sound handy," Amy said.

"Is that what we found on Burrow?" Conover asked. "That one core with the brackets that seemed like it was set up for a second core to be added?"

"Yes, it was an incomplete Q-core," Custodian replied.

"So why would we not just make nothing but these Q-cores?" Ragsdale asked. "Assuming they can be substituted for normal ones, that is."

"Each Q-core requires eight hundred kilograms of Dark Metal and will require approximately one week to fabricate," Custodian said. "Those numbers are approximate, admittedly, until the Shroud is finally operational and its actual efficiency can be determined. But they are reasonably close."

Dash whistled. "Eight hundred kilos of Dark Metal? That's a *lot*."

"It means that maybe we should start taking a closer look at that old Dark Metal smelter, or whatever it is, that the Aquarians found inside that comet they turned into a mountain on their Ring," Wei-Ping said. "If we could get something like that running, then hell, we should be able to pump out all the Dark Metal we need."

"That facility is badly degraded by the passage of time, since it wasn't protected or kept in stasis," Custodian replied. "It will take considerable time and effort to reverse engineer anything comparable."

"Still, it's worth a try," Viktor said. "Making our own Dark Metal would be a huge boost to our production."

"It would also mean we wouldn't have to spend half the flight time of our ships trying to find and scavenge the damned stuff," Benzel said.

Dash stood. "Let's put that on the to-do list. Viktor, Conover, I'll leave it to you guys to work with Custodian and the Aquarians to figure out how feasible trying to back engineer it and make our own would be."

"So what advantage would having one of these Q-cores offer besides more power?" Freya asked. Dash glanced at her in surprise; she didn't normally take part in these technical discussions. But she was a skilled botanist with a background in science, and she was highly intelligent.

"Each Q-core would increase the Forge's power levels by approximately six percent," Custodian said. "That includes general power levels, as well as power available for the output of products from the fabrication facilities."

Benzel frowned. "Six percent doesn't sound like a lot for eight hundred kilos of Dark Metal and a week to make, plus whatever else that's needed to make it." He looked at Dash. "Do you really think it's worth it?"

"Custodian," Dash said,. "Can you give us some context to that six percent? Is that a lot?"

"Each increase of one percent in the Forge's capacity offers the opportunity to make a weapon whose raw yield would be sufficient to destroy a capital ship, up to and including battleship and carrier classes."

That made Dash whistle again.

Benzel gave an impressed nod and said, "Okay, then—definitely worth it." He bowed his head but smiled. "I stand corrected."

"Well, let's get the Shroud up and running, and then we can decide our priorities for cores. It sounds, though, that we're going to want some Q-cores for sure," Dash said, then looked around. "And, while we're talking new weapons, I have an idea I want to float. It comes from when Amy and I managed to get the jump on that Verity fleet the way we did by coming at them out of the Darkness Between."

"I thought you said fiddling with time is a bad idea," Leira said.

Dash shook his head. "No, not that. I mean when we literally took them completely by surprise, translating back into real space close to them and attacking before they even knew what was happening. Speed and surprise can be way more effective than raw power, if used effectively. So what if we could do the same thing with missiles? Pop them into the Darkness Between, or even unSpace, then have them pop out again right close to their target?"

"We already do it with the nova cannon on the Swift," Leira said. "It shoots partly through the Darkness Between, so its shots have almost no time-of-flight and can bypass things like shields."

"Yeah, the big blast cannon on the Archetype is the same, but their power requirements are crazy. Hell, just firing the blast cannon risks knocking the Archetype offline, which is why I've only used it once so far. We definitely won't be able to mount a nova cannon, much less a blast cannon, on every ship. But if we had missiles that translated themselves when they fired, well, any ship should be able to carry a battery of those, even our mine layers."

"We'd need to miniaturize translation drives," Viktor said, rubbing his chin and getting the look that was a combination of thoughtful and intrigued which meant he was about to sink his teeth into a problem. "And keep them properly guided while they translate."

"I'm going to leave that with you," Dash said, smiling. "Work with the AIs, and also Conover and Amy. They're going to start practicing simulations of the mechs, soon, I gather, with their new AIs, so they'll be around the Forge a lot more."

"I can't wait to meet mine," Amy said. "I hope he's nice."

"I don't think *nice* is one of the criteria," Leira said flatly. "Right, Tybalt?"

"I have been nothing but pleasant," Tybalt replied. "I take great pride and satisfaction in my charismatic approach to our dealings."

Leira just grinned and rolled her eyes.

Dash made his way across the main fitting bay on the same level as the fabrication plant. The massive bay, even bigger than the ones they used as hangars for the Archetype and the Swift, was where final component assembly was done—or where major components required for something too big for the bay were taken out of the Forge for assembly outside. Right now, it housed the damaged *Slipwing*, which was still being repaired from the battle in the globular cluster, and the *Horse Nebula*, also having her recent battle damage repaired. Mechanical arms swung around the two ships, while maintenance remotes drifted about, welding units flashing.

If this had been a conventional human facility, Dash thought, he'd have to be careful to watch where he walked, to avoid getting clocked by a swinging arm. But everything here just accommodated his presence, moving around him in an intricately choreographed mechanical dance. It struck him how casual he'd become about all this super-advanced tech; it hadn't even occurred to him to watch where he was going, since he just assumed nothing would accidentally slam into him.

He stopped and took a moment to just look at his ship. She seemed so different. She'd changed, like he had. She had upgraded power plant and engines, improved weapons, better armor, new point-defense and sensors, expanded computer capacity. The list went on. In a way, she was the same hull as the old *Slipwing*, but in most other ways, she was a different, completely new ship.

"We've come a long way together, eh old girl?" He touched a hand to the smooth ceramalloy of her armored underside and offered a fond smile. "Don't think either of us saw this coming, did we?"

Commotion rose behind him. A small hauler drifted into the bay, lugging a cargo pod. It landed in a designated spot and two of the Gentle Friends dismounted, giving him a wave. Curious, Dash wandered over to where they were disconnecting the pod.

"Hey, Dash," a woman with a brush cut, said.

Dash nodded. "You guys been out scavenging?"

Her companion, a tall, thin man with a scraggly beard, nodded. "Bits and pieces get away from the ships when they're being scrapped, or even just repaired. Wei-Ping sends us out every day to round them up and bring them back as more scrap."

"Also don't want too much debris around the Forge," the woman added.

Dash nodded and watched as the sailors lowered a ramp from the side of the hauler, then shunted the cargo-pod off the hauler's rack and onto a magnetic trackway running through the bay. Unseen magnetic forces lifted the pod a few centimeters, then it began to slide silently away, following the trackway out of the bay to the lifts that would carry it to the smelters in the fabrication plant.

Watching it sparked an idea.

Dash gave the two Gentle Friends another wave then wandered toward the big portal opening on the starfield beyond. He could see the *Herald* off to his left and, a few klicks beyond her, the *Greenbelt*. The almost-completed Shroud hung a couple of klicks away, to his right.

The idea crystallized a little more. He'd wanted to talk about ideas for new weapons, get people thinking about them; here was one of his own.

"Custodian, what if we copied that oblong design of the Shroud and used it as a missile platform? In other words, construct it like a long magazine with missile launchers at either end? Use magnetic force trackways and the like to move the missiles to the launchers?"

"That would save considerable resources over our current approach to the construction of missile drones. Do you envision this design as being fully robotic?" Custodian asked.

"Um, maybe. Work it up both ways." His mind started to run with the idea as it crystallized more and more. "We could mount one high-volume missile battery on each ship, firing those transluminal missiles we were talking about back in the Command Center, and then link a couple of these platforms to that ship. It would be like a set of triplets working in sync," Dash said, but then snagged on a thought that had actually been bothering him for some time. "Can you make it smarter than a simple drone, though? Those ones are fine at carrying out routine, repetitive tasks, but I'd love to see something that can actually think ahead, plan, and work cooperatively with other ships and platforms."

"That is certainly possible, although the creation of a truly autonomous artificial intelligence would require more Dark Metal that we currently have at our disposal," Custodian replied.

"Huh. Interesting. So it's a part of your matrices, eh? Okay, how about smarter than an average missile avionics package? Can you create something in that range? Smart, but not too smart?"

"It should be possible to create an intermediate level of intelligence that better utilizes our available resources, yes. Shall I begin doing so?" Custodian asked.

"Yes, but don't install them in anything yet. Make...oh, let's say a dozen, with some variation in personality, so to speak, and then keep them powered up and ready in some sort of plug-in module, something that's universal for every ship we build from here on out," Dash said.

"I will begin the construction immediately. Do you have a project designation for this effort?"

Dash smiled. "Yeah, I do. Call them *Red Barons*."

"That is most appropriate," Custodian said, sounding genuinely appreciative. "If I may, I would suggest that there could be another way of employing these new missile platforms—one that would help to optimize the survival rate of our naval personnel in another way. In extreme contingencies, such as when a ship is under severe duress, the platforms could be employed as single-use kinetic-energy weapons after expending their armament."

Dash thought about that. He and Amy had been able to do damage all out of proportion to what they'd actually brought to the battle, when they bounced the Verity and Clan Shirna in the globular cluster. He imagined what they could have done had the Archetype and *Slipwing* each had a pair of intelligent missile platforms accompanying them, loaded with transluminal missiles—and how much more they could have done if those platforms had then become massive missiles themselves. He nodded. "Yeah, I like that even better. Can we give them warheads of their own of some sort? Nuclear weapons, maybe? So that they hit even harder?"

"Certainly. Between velocity and a narrow scanner profile, I can shape the platform so that it becomes itself a ship killer once all of its missiles have been expended. However, we should assume that all of the material, including the Dark Metal used in the construction of the platform, will be lost and unrecoverable. A platform would, therefore, only be allowed to transition into ship-killer mode by direct command of the controlling ship, either as emergency measure, or to exploit a suitable opportunity," Custodian said.

"Can you get them to a decent speed?"

"I can, by bleeding off some of the nuclear yield. Is that acceptable?" Custodian asked.

"It is. Make them go boom."

"Boom it shall be."

16

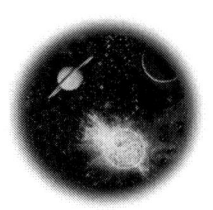

Dash had meant to go spend some time in the park actually taking some quiet time to himself, but it was not to be. No sooner had his feet touched the grass than Custodian announced, "Enemy inbound."

Now, Dash raced for the docking bay and the waiting Archetype. The big mech had been fully repaired, and Sentinel had already powered it up when he arrived.

"Any updates?" Dash asked, climbing into the Archetype's cradle.

"Yes," Custodian said. "The incoming ships are Golden, Harbinger-class mechs, but smaller, lighter, and faster than the versions we have encountered previously. They are operating with the profile of a scouting mission in-force. They are approaching at high velocity and show no signs of decelerating," Custodian said.

"Meaning they plan on a strafing run—or colliding with something. Leira, you online yet?"

"Just got comfy in the Swift's cradle," she replied. "Launching in about twenty seconds."

"Good. As soon as you're clear of the Forge, fire a salvo of missiles at our visitors."

"That's an awfully long-ranged attack, Dash, with lots of time for countermeasures and evasion. Won't they just miss?"

Dash spun the Archetype around and flung it into space. "Probably. But evasion is good. I want them to alter course, maneuver ,and bleed off some speed, see if we can get them playing defense. Benzel?"

"Boss?" Benzel answered instantly.

"Get your people in motion. I want flash mines deployed. Pushed out of the bays by hand if necessary. Any velocity is better than none. I'll upload a scheme to the general channel in just a second. Conform as closely to it as you can."

"Will do," Benzel said.

Dash saw Leira's missiles launch as Sentinel began tracking them. He fired his own salvo then conversed quickly with Sentinel, outlining the plan he'd roughed out in his mind while running to board the Archetype. It was still all about new weapons, and the fact that these were Harbingers only solidified it for him.

"You wish to take these enemy vessels intact?" Sentinel asked.

"Damned right I do. I'd like to see if we can retrofit them with pilots, or at least replace their AI with our own. Either way, I want to make them into *our* mechs."

"There is considerable uncertainty regarding whether that is even possible."

"Yeah, well, you don't try, you don't get. I mean, worse comes to worst and we just use them as scrap anyway. But if we could pull this off—" He gave the threat indicator a feral grin. "Yeah. I'm inspired by the Shroud. We took it from the Golden for ourselves. That's like having *two* Shrouds, right? The one the Golden don't have anymore, and the one we do. I'd love to keep doing that, and these Harbingers are a great place to start."

"Understood. The mine layer *Void Stalker* has several flash and scrambler mines already onboard and was on station with A Squadron of the fleet. Benzel is deploying her now, escorted by the *Herald*."

Dash nodded. "Perfect."

"Two of the approaching enemy craft have begun decelerating," Sentinel said a moment later. "The other three are continuing to approach at high speed."

Dash narrowed his eyes at the heads-up. "Wonder what *that's* about. Keep an eye on them, Sentinel, and let me know what they're doing. Meantime, our missiles should be just about on target."

Sure enough, the three approaching Harbingers accelerated laterally, veering to one side then abruptly shifting thrust and veering again. At the same time, they opened up with insanely rapid-fire pulse-cannons. Each shot was weaker than those from the standard pulse weapons aboard, say, the *Herald*; Dash knew the strength of their shots was somehow a function of the length of the weapon's reaction chamber, so these ones must just be smaller. But they made up for it with an incredible rate of fire. In a few seconds, they'd avoided or destroyed all of the missiles except one, which managed to land a lucky hit on one of the Harbingers. The enemy mech's shield held, but it did slow some, falling behind its comrades.

For the new few minutes, Dash just intently watched the tactical display. Sometimes space battles were like this: periods of doing nothing but flying, sometimes long ones, closing with the enemy. But at their combined closing rate, the Harbingers on the one side and the Archetype and Swift on the other, this *doing nothing but flying* part wouldn't last long at all.

Dash shifted his attention a fraction and saw the *Herald* and the *Void Stalker* closing up behind them. "Benzel, you'd better get those mines deployed. Those Harbingers are coming in *hot*."

"The *Void Stalker's* already started laying them. We figure she'll get twelve to fifteen of them deployed, and then she's going to get the hell out of the way."

"Sounds good." Benzel's caution for the mine layer was commendable; she might be armed, but she was no match even for a light version of a Harbinger. Speaking of which—

Sentinel spoke up, answering the question he was about to ask. "The two Harbingers that decelerated are now on an outbound trajectory. If they intend to translate, they will be able to do so in approximately five minutes."

"They're getaways."

"I don't understand the reference."

Dash allowed himself a smile. "When you're doing a job, something that might get you into trouble, say, you're breaking into a secure compound to steal a shipment of power couplings then you leave a getaway or two."

"That is an unusually specific example."

"Just plucked it out of thin air, honestly. Anyway, you leave one or two people back, watching over the job as it happens. That way, if anything goes wrong, they can break off and report back to the gangster—er, whoever set the job up in the first place. That way, they know what happened and can plan what to do next."

"You believe these two Harbingers intend to observe what happens then withdraw with that information."

Dash nodded. "Yeah. It's a way of testing our capabilities. We might have spooked them when the Archetype and the *Slipwing* were able to suddenly appear right on top of them, without them detecting us until it was too late. They didn't know it happened accidentally after some unplanned time travel."

"A good point. The Golden may now believe we have capabilities of which they were unaware and now they want to understand."

"Exactly. I mean, I don't *know* that's the case, but it would make sense."

"We will be in dark-lance range in fifteen seconds."

"Leira," Dash said. "I don't want to stop these guys. I want them to keep heading for the Forge and hopefully run into those flash mines. So let's just keep accelerating past them, a high-speed pass, and snap out a few shots that mostly miss."

"In other words, not fight very well or smart?" Leira replied. "Yeah, I can definitely do that."

Dash chuckled and watched the range close. He fired the dark-lance a few times, landing a couple of hits that splashed off shields and Dark Metal armor, but mostly missing. Leira did the same with the nova-cannon, deliberately not targeting it to bypass the Harbingers' shields. The enemy mechs returned fire as soon they were close enough to employ their shorter-ranged, rapid-fire pulse-cannons, then launching missiles. They weren't, of course, trying to miss, and both the Archetype and Swift took hits.

The extreme rate of fire of the pulse cannons was actually worrisome; they quickly saturated the Archetype's shield with energy, pumping it in faster than it could radiated away. As they flashed past, the shield failed, and pulse-shots actually slammed into the mech's armor.

Dash decelerated hard. Leira did the same. The Harbingers made no attempt to maneuver after them, instead just boring straight in at the Forge.

"Custodian," Dash said as he flipped the Archetype around. "Just in case those mines don't stop them, you're going to be dealing with three of them coming in really, really fast."

"Understood. I am conferring with Benzel regarding the disposition of the fleet. However, the Forge is more than capable of taking care of itself."

"I'm sure it is. Just don't get cocky about it, okay?"

"Cocky?"

"Yeah, you know, full of yourself, thinking you can do anything without help, that you'll always get away with it, that sort of thing."

"So like you, you mean."

Dash heard Leira's laugh.

He meant to shoot back a scathing retort of some sort, but instead he just shrugged. "Yeah, I guess I did just kind of describe myself, didn't I?"

Sentinel cut in. "Almost perfectly."

"Yeah, well, you all can just get down and—"

"The Harbingers are about to enter the blast radius of the mines," Custodian said.

Dash focused his attention on the tactical display on the heads-up. He expected the Harbingers to destroy the mines before they could detonate; catching even one of them and disabling it was a faint hope, at best.

"Wait. Benzel, what's the *Void Stalker* doing? Get her the hell out of there!"

"Stand by, Dash," Benzel replied.

Dash leaned hard into the acceleration, trying to drive the Archetype back along the Harbingers' trajectory even faster, but it wouldn't matter; he and Leira were both far too distant to influence the next few moments of the battle in any meaningful way.

Which meant it was far too late for the Void Stalker. The Harbingers raced in, pouring out streams of pulse-cannon shots that destroyed mines and also pummeled the Herald. The latter's shields held, but she limited her return fire per Dash's orders, to try to avoid destroying any of the enemy mechs.

Dash opened his mouth, but any sound died in the futility of the moment. The Void Stalker remained far too close to the live battlespace, somehow having been disabled. As the Harbingers raced on, destroying the last of the mines that threatened them, one of them switched briefly, almost contemptuously, to target the mine layer. A stream of pulse-cannon shots ripped into her hull; an instant later, a rippling chain of explosions tore the Void Stalker apart.

Dash slowly blinked as the bleak reality of loss swept over him. He tried to remember which of the Gentle Friends he'd just seen die. He failed, and the moment stretched, punishing in its silence.

Two of the Harbingers abruptly stopped accelerating, their power curves going flat. They were completely offline, dead.

"Okay, we've got two of them, Dash," Benzel said. "We're going to seize them now so Custodian can hack them before they reboot and come back to life."

"Benzel—" Dash started, then shook his head. The man sounded not just completely unfazed, but actually kind of smug. "I mean, damn, how many people did you just lose?"

"None."

"You—what? None?"

Benzel laughed. "That's right. Zero. Nada. The crew of the Void Stalker only sowed about half their mines. They set the rest to explode when the Harbingers made their closest pass. And then they jumped in the escape pod and ran. I'm afraid we lost our mine layer, but we can rebuild her easily enough. Hell, you can take her out of my pay. And we did get two of those damned mechs intact. That's what you wanted, right?

"Well, yeah. That was—" Dash smiled. "That was brilliant!"

His smile became a wry grin. "But I can't very well take the Void Stalker out of your pay, because I don't pay you anything."

"Not yet you don't." Dash could hear the corresponding grin in Benzel's voice.

There was still one Harbinger inbound to the Forge, though, and the fleet was still avoiding engagement. Dash turned his attention to it—his full attention.

"If we've got two of the bastards, we don't really need a third. Not in operating condition, anyway. All units, feel free to take out that last Harbinger."

The fleet didn't need to be told twice. A firestorm engulfed the remaining Harbinger as the Cygnus ships poured fire at it. It flew on, enveloped in a halo of energy discharge, doggedly determined to strike at the Forge.

Dash began to think it might actually make it. The Harbinger's shield seemed to be holding, at least long enough to let it do a single, probably suicidal attack run on the Forge. That was, until the Forge itself joined in the battle, seeming to open fire with every point-defense battery with a line-of-fire all at once.

The Forge seemed to vanish behind a rippling wall of blue-white.

The Harbinger likewise vanished in a hurricane of fire. It only lasted a second or two, then ceased as abruptly as it started. What emerged from the focal point of all that violence was just wreckage, barely recognizable as the mech it had been an instant ago.

The whole fleet had stopped firing. Dash just stared, blinking at the after image left on his retinas by the orgy of fire that had spewed from the Forge.

"Dash," Leira said. "That was just the point-defense stuff. Custodian didn't even warm up the main batteries or the missiles. Tell me why we're not fighting this war drinking plumato wine in a hot tub aboard the Forge?"

Dash rotated the Archetype so it was facing the Swift and made the mech shrug.

"That's a damned good question."

DASH STOOD with his hands on his hips, which kept one of them close to his pulse-pistol. Of course, the weapon would be of absolutely no use if things went bad here.

"That is one scary looking piece of machinery," Leira said.

Dash nodded. "Yup, it is."

Even in this smaller, lighter version, the Harbinger still towered over Dash and his companions. Custodian had brought both of the captured mechs aboard the Forge, but in widely separated docking bays. He maintained that the risk was low; he had thoroughly insinuated carefully crafted strands of control into their systems, and now commanded all functions for both mechs.

There were, nonetheless, logical parts of them still walled off by strong encryption and other countermeasures, so he'd taken the extra precaution of installing explosive charges inside them that could be triggered both remotely and by redundant, physical cables that kept them hardwired into the Forge's systems. At the first hint of uncontrollable rebellion, the mech would be destroyed. It would damage the Forge, yes, but in nowhere near as profound a way as an unrestrained Harbinger could.

Of course, if that happened in, say, the next few seconds, Dash would die with the satisfied knowledge that the Forge would probably still be fine.

"Are you really sure it was wise to bring them aboard in the first place?" Viktor asked. "We had a Golden drone aboard once, and it managed to cripple a huge chunk of the Forge."

"These things are a lot bigger and meaner," Ragsdale added, his arms crossed, a frown creasing his face.

"They are, and I know that," Dash said. "But the risk is worth it. Imagine if we can get these things running on our side—especially if we can figure out how to make them piloted. Two new, powerful mechs, for nothing."

"Plus that's two mechs the Golden have lost," Leira said, echoing Dash's thoughts about how much greater the "force swing" was when they took things from their enemies and repurposed them for their own use.

"All of this said, I would caution against counting on these Harbingers being available for use any time soon," Custodian cut in. "Until we can be sure that any dormant Golden countermeasures that may still be contained with them are neutralized, they are unsafe to even study in any detail. I am planning to both physically and electronically isolate the bays in which they are located from the rest of the Forge before attempting any further, deeper intrusions into their systems."

"Do what you've got to do, Custodian," Dash said, staring at the Harbingers. "But whether we end up using these things or scrapping them for feedstock, all I know is that we've screwed over the Golden a little bit more. And that makes me happy because I know that they don't have unlimited resources."

Even Ragsdale nodded at that.

17

Dash pulled off his boots and stretched out his legs. He had probably walked twenty kilometers today, from one part of the Forge to another, checking out what was going on.

He sighed and stared at the wall of his quarters for a few minutes. A few days ago, he'd asked Custodian to fire up a holo-image of a starfield to cover up a blank wall. Yes, he could just turn around and look out the viewports, but the starfield out there was boring—mostly featureless blackness, shot through with a smattering of brighter stars. If he killed the lights, he could see many more stars but, still, stars weren't very interesting by themselves.

The holo-image, though, switched through scenes of nebulae, miscellaneous clouds of starlit dust and gas, globular clusters, the glory of the galactic core, and even a glowing accretion ring around a distant black hole. The stately progress of the images was calming, soothing even, probably because they removed the creeping sense of dread and danger he'd come to associate with space and rendered it all down to beautiful pictures.

Dash let his eyes drift close, then he cast his thoughts back through the day, sifting memories for anything he might have missed that could be useful. In a war of extinction, every advantage mattered.

No matter how small.

Dash had never seen the fabrication plant so busy. Every system, smelter, and machine was running flat out, components being cast, moved, assembled, ingots being shunted around and melted, glowing metal being poured, machine tools grinding away, cutting and drilling.

"We've reached capacity, at least for now," Viktor had said, standing by his side at the railing of one of the galleries overlooking the fabrication plan. "Custodian tells me that once the Shroud is producing new power cores, and they're installed in the Forge, we'll be able to ramp up production even more."

Dash nodded. "More is good. Overwhelming would be better."

"I agree. And as we gain power and materials, our ability will grow exponentially," Viktor said.

"If there's an empty storage closet, I want it fitted with a smelter the size of a console. I want—I want us to be relentless. Like they are," Dash said.

"We will be. There's apparently even a dormant fabrication plant not much smaller than this one, in that section of Forge near the docking bay we use for the Swift—you know, that whole area that's still powered down."

Dash had nodded again. Mines, mine layers—including a new, upgraded Void Stalker, because how could they not reuse the name?—missiles, weapons, armor, components for new ships, all of it was being manufactured and shipped out to the fleet as fast as it could be.

It was all very impressive, and Dash gave Viktor an appreciative nod. But as he'd walked away, he'd reflected that no matter how much they produced and put into service, they'd no doubt always need more.

HE'D DRIFTED ALONGSIDE BENZEL, the two of them hanging a few hundred meters away from the Forge, watching as a massive section of new armor for the Herald was slowly moved out of one of the fabrication bays. The Gentle Friends, along with maintenance remotes from the Forge, would ease it into place, work it up against the ship's hull, and get it fastened, giving Benzel's flagship another full layer of protection against incoming fire.

Looking past the Herald, Dash saw the captured Verity battlecruiser, which they'd renamed the Retribution. Custodian, Sentinel, and Tybalt had worked long and hard at ensuring there were no sinister Golden back-door programs lurking in its electronic guts, ready to pounce and cause some catastrophe at the worst possible time. They had declared the ship clean just the day before, and now the Gentle Friends were moving in. At the same time, new components and weapons were being ferried out to her to repair her damage and bring her back online. She'd be a powerful addition to the fleet, which raised a question.

"What do you intend to do with her?" Dash asked Benzel.

"Eh? Oh, the Retribution? Yeah, she's a damned fine ship. Think she's going to be made flagship of B Squadron."

"So Wei-Ping's new flagship?"

"Yeah. Girl's earned it. Which is saying something, actually."

"How so?"

Benzel puffed a suit thruster and turned to face Dash. Through his helmet's faceplate, he grinned. "Didn't I ever tell you? She tried to kill me."

"What?"

"Three times, in fact. Last time was the closest she came to success. She learns fast, that's for sure."

"What hell was she trying to kill you for?"

"That's how you become leader of the Gentle Friends. You kill the current one."

"Seriously?"

"Yeah. Makes sure whoever takes the job really wants it."

"So you killed someone to take over?"

"Yup. Damned good guy, too. Hated to see him go."

Dash just stared at the panorama of the Herald and the Retribution beyond her.

"Just so we're clear, we're not introducing that as our succession planning, got it?" Dash finally said.

"You sure? Beats out running some long, drawn-out hiring process."

"Yeah, I'm sure."

"Okay. But if you ever change your mind, let me know. Maybe I'd like to try a spin at being Messenger." Benzel's grin was now positively wicked—and obviously teasing.

Dash smiled broadly. "Tell you what—you ever want to take over as Messenger, just let me know. I'll hand the job to you. If you can handle the probe, of course."

"The…probe?" Benzel said, his smile fading.

"Custodian, tell him about the probe," Dash said.

Custodian didn't miss a beat. "Part of becoming the Messenger involves a probe, charged with moderate electrical current to carry vital information between subject and mainframe. Insertion occurs only after the removal of the candidate's pants; at which time they are spread—"

"Enough! Okay, to hell with being Messenger," Benzel said in horror, then gave Dash a searching look. "You walk normally. How? I mean, with a probe—"

Dash dissolved into laughter, waving his hands helplessly. When he recovered, his eyes were filled with tears of laughter. "Nicely done, Custodian."

"It was my pleasure. Please note that Benzel's heart rate spiked when he thought—"

"Okay, I get it. Hah. The pirate fell for it," Benzel said, but a sly smile spread across his face. "Guess Custodian is becoming more human after all."

Dash shook his head. "Not human. Just more like a pirate."

HE'D WATCHED as mechanical arms worked around the Archetype, which Sentinel had brought to another fabrication bay. Custodian and Sentinel were installing another upgrade, a lattice of Dark Metal alloy, that would allow the mech to cause a localized spatial disruption around itself, not unlike the distortion-cannon. However, it could be sustained longer, and it could also be polarized, so that the gravitational burst could either be a well, causing things to fall toward it, or a peak, making things fall away from it.

"Can we get this installed on the Swift as well?" Dash asked.

"We can," Sentinel said. "However, the geometry of the lattice must be correct to very low margins of error, so Tybalt is redesigning it to accommodate the Swift's particular configuration."

"The intent is to install it in the Pulsar, the mech intended for use by Conover," Custodian added. "However, it may not be possible to include it in the Talon, the mech intended for Amy, as it is considerably smaller and lighter."

"That's fine," Dash said, walking around the Archetype. Much of its armor had been removed, giving him a plain view of parts of the mech he'd never actually seen in detail: actuators, joints, and massive magnetic rams that worked like hydraulic pistons but were far more powerful, efficient, and durable. Dash found himself flexing his arm slightly, imagining the movements transferred to the powerful machinery gleaming under the bay lights.

Crazy, he thought. Absolutely crazy. If anyone had ever told me...

He was still smiling and shaking his head, utterly bemused, as he left the fabrication bay for the Command Center.

WEI-PING HAD RHYMED off a long list of updates, sitreps, miscellaneous notes—and a few complaints. Dash, his feet propped on a console in the Command Center, nodded along. The complaints were minor, he thought—more bitching, really, than anything of substance. And he'd always heard, and believed, the conventional wisdom about bitching from your subordinates; if they were doing it, things were fine. It was when they stopped bitching and went silent that you needed to start looking for trouble.

So Dash made his nods as sympathetic as he could over the minor complaints—the crew of the Snow Leopard were sure their comrades aboard the Herald were getting a better grade of plumato wine than they were, really?—then turned his attention back to weightier matters.

"So the fleet is ready for action when, exactly?" he asked.

"We figure another two days. Maybe three, depending on how long it takes to get the last repairs done to the Retribution."

Dash stood and eyed the big holo-image that was once more depicting the galactic arm and the broad trend of Verity activity along its axis. "Okay. Well, as soon as we're ready"—he glanced at Wei-Ping—"and I mean literally as soon as we're ready, I want to resume the offensive." He walked up to the big image and pointed. "We're there, and that's the bulk of remaining Verity space, there. As far as we know, anyway. I want to make this a major push, maybe even the final one. If we can take the Verity out of the war the way we have Clan Shirna, that'll go a long way toward something I'd really like to accomplish."

"What's that?" Wei-Ping asked.

"Getting the Golden involved in this war in person." He looked back at the star map. "It's something that's been bugging me more and more. We're seeing Clan Shirna, the Bright, the Verity, but not a lot of the Golden themselves."

Wei-Ping gave a fierce nod. "Yeah, that'd be sweet, kicking in a few Golden faces for a change."

Dash crossed his arms and nodded. "Couldn't agree more."

Dash sat in his quarters, stretching out his legs and wiggling his toes, ready to finally enjoy a bit of his scant down time when a chime sounded, indicating someone was at his door.

"Crap."

Dash levered himself out of his chair and padded to the door. It opened on Harolyn, her finger just reaching for the door chime again.

"Sorry, Dash," she said. "Did I come at a bad time?"

"No, it's fine. What's up?"

"I've been told some things I think you should hear."

He frowned, but nodded and invited her in. She sat, extracted a data-pad from a satchel slung over her shoulder, and tapped at it.

"I've finally finished interviewing all of the refugees we've had come aboard so far. I haven't found anything that makes me think security concern. In fact, everyone that hasn't revealed themselves as a spy so far seems clean. We've been able to confirm identities on all but three of them, and Ragsdale's working on those through his contacts."

Dash gave an impressed nod. "Good work. So do we have any that are interested in staying around to help us?"

"Yeah. All of them."

"Really?"

"I guess when you flee a genocidal alien race that's attacking your home, with nothing but the clothes on your back, you develop a certain—let's call it a desire to strike back at them."

"Hey, there's a reason we've renamed that Verity battlecruiser the Retribution." Dash gave Harolyn a sidelong look. "But I don't think you came here just to tell me that."

"Nope. Like I said, I talked to all of the refugees. Some of them had a lot to say. That includes rumors."

"Such as?"

"Such as, some of them claim to have overheard people talking about joining the Verity, instead of trying to keep fighting them. Word is, apparently, that the Verity will spare people, even open up beneficial trade and mutual-protection agreements with them, in exchange for not helping their enemies."

"That would be us."

Harolyn nodded. "There's more, though. A few of them mentioned that they'd heard of the Forge sometime before they even got here or had any idea what it was."

Dash leaned forward. "Really."

"Yeah. Seems word's getting around that this place is designed for wiping out planets, and everyone and everything living on them, and that eventually humanity's going to have to band together to stop us."

"Which is bullshit, of course," Dash said, leaning back. "But that won't matter."

"Not at all. Perception is reality, and all that." Harolyn's brow creased with worry. "It looks like the Verity are starting up an information war, Dash."

"More like a new information front in our current war."

"Either way, we're not currently really fighting back against it, are we?"

Dash sighed. "No, we're not. But we're going to have to."

"Yeah, we are," Harolyn said. "Because if we don't, and the Verity misinformation starts to take hold, starts to contaminate public opinion—"

"Then we might find people starting to support—hell, even start to do stupid things. Things that actually run right against their own interests." He shook his head. "We can't let that happen."

"No, we can't."

"And you believe these people?"

"I do. There's too much commonality between what people from widely separated places are saying. And I can't find even a hint of a conspiracy among them. These are people who've never even had anything to do with one another before, all saying very similar things."

"Okay, leave this one with me for a bit so I can think about it. We're going to have to come up with a way of keeping the Golden from making new allies—and that's not the first time I've thought that today."

"What do you mean?"

"When I was talking to Wei-Ping earlier in the Command Center, it really started to come home to me that the Golden really haven't been in this war much so far. If they can keep making allies, then that's going to keep being true. I want to start forcing them to come to battle themselves... fight us directly."

An alarm cut him off. A moment later, Custodian said, "Medical emergency in docking bay 9-A."

"Custodian, what's going on?" Dash said, an urgent apprehension tightening his voice. Docking bay 9-A held one of the captured Golden Harbingers.

"It is Conover. He is badly injured."

Dash leapt to his feet. He realized he wasn't wearing boots and grabbed them. Harolyn followed closely behind.

DASH RACED up to the last corner before the corridor turned into bay 9-A. Custodian had been updating him and Harolyn along the way; the Harbinger had not, as Dash feared, come to life and attacked, hurting Conover. Instead, Conover had done something —Custodian was still trying to determine exactly what—and been injured in the process.

Dash wheeled around the corner. He'd already had his feet slide out from under him once, so he'd hopped along, jamming his boots on. As he rushed along the corridor, figures appeared in the entry to the docking bay. Dash saw Leira, who'd apparently also been caught out in her down-time clothes since she was wearing what looked like trousers pulled over pajamas with sandals.

"What is it?" Dash asked. "What's going on? Custodian said it wasn't the Harbinger, but—"

"It kind of was the Harbinger, it looks like," Leira cut in, then nudged Dash back as Ragsdale and another middle-aged man— one of the refugees—pushed along a mag-lev gurney with Conover sprawled on it.

Shortly after he'd first met him and brought him aboard the Slipwing, Conover had used his eye implants to interface with some Unseen tech, the star-destroying device known as the Lens. The resulting backlash had left Conover comatose, to the point he'd seemed dead.

He looked worse than that now. Dash saw a pale, bloodless face framing eyes barely open, glassy and blank.

"Coming through!" Ragsdale shouted, then turned to Dash as he passed. "Main infirmary!"

Then they shoved past and hurried away.

Dash took a step after the gurney but stopped himself. He desperately wanted to know how Conover was doing, but he had a more important duty first—making sure the Harbinger wasn't a greater threat.

Setting his mouth in a thin, hard line, he strode into the docking bay.

The Harbinger hadn't, as far as he could tell, moved a centimeter. It still towered over them, implacably and blankly menacing. Dash saw Viktor and Kai standing near the mech, examining something on a workbench set up near its massive right foot.

"What the hell happened?" Dash asked. "Custodian doesn't seem to know, which really bothers me all on its own."

Viktor leaned on the workbench. "We're not too sure. Custodian says that Conover was doing something here, at the workbench, and then his internal scanners went offline in here. It left him blind to what happened over the next twenty seconds or so, until he was able to bring them back online."

"I happened to be nearby, so Custodian alerted me to the situation," Kai said. "I got here as fast I could."

Dash looked at the monk who, like him and Leira, was dressed down—in the monk's case, in what looked like a martial arts workout outfit of some sort. "Wait, you mean Custodian suddenly went blind to something going on in a docking bay with a captured freaking Harbinger in it, and you came running in here anyway?"

Kai returned a look that said he didn't actually get the question. "Of course. Why?"

Despite the awful tension, Dash smiled and clapped the monk on the shoulder. "I'm glad you're on our side, Kai." But his flash of good feelings faded and he looked at the workbench. "Who set this up here? Conover?"

"He and I both did," Viktor replied. "We were starting some external examinations of this Harbinger. External examinations only, though, which is why I can't explain this."

He pointed at an optical interface laying on the bench. "The transceiver is over there, attached to the Harbinger."

"Conover was wearing this interface when I found him," Kai added. "I removed it from him immediately, but in retrospect, perhaps I shouldn't have. Maybe it only made matters worse."

Dash shook his head right back, emphatically. "No. Conover not being interfaced with this damned thing is way better than still being hooked up to it." He turned back to Viktor. "So you had no plans to do this? Interface like this?"

"No. Not any time soon, at least. The AIs are still working at making sure it's safe to start poking around the Harbinger's internal systems to begin with." Viktor scowled at the interface. "Conover decided to do this himself. What I don't get is why."

"Same reason he did much the same thing right after we met him, with the Lens. Remember that?"

"I do. I guess I assumed he'd have learned a lesson from that."

Kai sniffed. "He is young. The young sometimes need to make a mistake more than once to learn anything from it."

"Tell me about it," Dash said, glaring at the interface. "Hell, I'm still like that myself sometimes. Custodian, can you add anything to this? Like why your internal scanners went out?"

"Conover apparently triggered a security sub-system in the Harbinger, activating a damping field similar to the one the Golden drone that crashed into the Forge used to conceal its activities. Since I had already gained access to the Harbinger's systems, however, I was able to activate a countermeasures program that shut it back down. In the time that took, Conover must have initiated the interface."

"Why the hell didn't you sound the alarm or something as soon as you saw what Conover was doing?"

"Because, on your instructions, Conover was given explicit access to virtually all Forge functions, and full latitude to study and evaluate enemy technology."

Dash, who'd been about to keep protesting, just closed his mouth. "Good point. You're right. I did do that." He glanced at Viktor. "I guess I figured Conover wouldn't, you know, stick his brain into an enemy mech."

Viktor sighed. "Especially all by himself."

"If he had asked to do this, would you have allowed it?" Kai asked.

"No way in hell."

"And there you go. That's another thing about the young: they often tend to believe it is better to ask for forgiveness rather than permission."

Dash gave a grim nod and started for the infirmary. "Let's hope I just have a chance to actually forgive the dumb little bastard."

Unlike the last time he'd been here, the infirmary tonight was deathly quiet. Aside from Conover, the only other patient was a woman, one of the Gentle Friends, who'd been shocked by a plasma discharge aboard the Snow Leopard. She rested quietly, watching what was happening with Conover with a grave discretion.

"How is he?" Dash asked, crowding up to the bedside.

"Not good." The speaker was the same middle-aged man who'd helped Ragsdale evacuate Conover from the docking bay. "When I arrived on the scene, he'd gone into cardiac arrest." The man pointed at a prominent burn down the side of Conover's neck. "This is evidence of some sort of electrical discharge that he must have taken across his heart."

Ragsdale, standing nearby, broke in. "Cyrus here got his heart started again. Used nothing but his fist."

Dash gave the man, who was apparently named Cyrus, a look that was surprised, impressed, and grateful all at once. "You're a doctor, right?"

Cyrus nodded. "I am. Or was, anyway, until our settlement got attacked by those bastards."

He'd been laying his fingers against Conover's neck on the unburned side; now he broke off and straightened. "His pulse is weak and thready. I'd do more, but"—he gestured at the infirmary around them—"I think this tech will be able to do a lot more for him than I can." He gave a tired shrug. "This place kind of puts me out of a job."

Dash shook his head. "Don't be so sure. And don't go anywhere. Custodian, what's Conover's condition?"

"The nerve impulses that would normally trigger his heart to beat have been disrupted. Although the emergency intervention in the docking bay restarted them, they remain unstable and erratic. The infirmary medical systems are now maintaining his heartbeat in a regular rhythm."

"So does that mean he's stuck here?"

"For the time being, anyway, this is the best place for him to be"—Cyrus looked around again—"of, well, probably anywhere in known space."

Dash relaxed a fraction and watched Conover, still pale and waxy, lying motionless, the rise and fall of his chest his only movements. "Bloody idiot," Dash snapped. "What the hell was he thinking?"

"He appears to have been attempting to interface with the Harbinger in order to learn more about its operations," Custodian said.

Dash bit off a curse. "Yeah, I kind of figured that. What I meant was—"

"Where is he?"

The voice was Amy's, and it preceded her only by a few seconds as she shoved her way up to the bedside. "Conover? Dammit—" She stopped, swallowing hard. "How is he?"

The grave silence around the bed answered her question. Amy stared for a moment, then blinked her eyes fast and muttered, "Shit. Conover."

Dash exchanged a look with Viktor and Leira. Conover's

puppy-like attraction to Amy was now the stuff of legend among them. None of them had raised it with her, though, and just assumed she was indulgently okay with it.

What a horrible time to find out she might actually have some of the same feelings toward him.

Dash scrubbed a hand through his hair. "Well, we should probably just let him rest."

Conover's eyes opened. As they stared, stunned, he blinked and looked around.

"Where am—oh. Infirmary." His voice sounded like a sticky hatch grinding open. "Guess things didn't go quite as I'd hoped."

Dash gaped for a moment, then shook his head in disbelief. "Custodian, what did you do?"

"Nothing specific. Conover's nervous system has stabilized and re-established a regular heart rhythm. I have discontinued further medical intervention."

"Okay, good." Dash swung a hard glare onto Conover. "Because now I can kill him myself. Dammit, Conover, what the hell were you—"

"I know," he croaked, holding up a hand. Cyrus handed him a cup of water. He sipped at it, then tried to sit up.

Amy pushed him back down. "Not so fast," she snapped. "You stay right there, so that when Dash is done killing you, I can take my turn at it."

"That was damned irresponsible, Conover," Viktor said.

He put the glass of water down. "I know. And I'm sorry. I should have learned my lesson from that time with the Lens."

"Yeah, you should have," Dash said, caught between rage and

relief and not entirely sure which side to come down on. "If you ever do anything like this again, I'm going to tell Custodian to lock you out of any alien tech, pull you off piloting the Pulsar, and send you to apprentice under Freya. Got it? A lifetime shovelling shit to grow plants."

"We don't actually use shit, you know. Or shovels," Viktor said to Dash, grinning.

"I'll find some of both. You mark me?" Dash asked Conover, who'd been watching the exchange.

Conover's eyes widened, but he nodded again. "Got it, Dash." He hesitated a moment, then added, "I did learn some things, though. Once I have time to sort them out in my own mind, I'll give everyone a full briefing on it."

"Can you give us a summary?" Dash asked.

"I—" Conover began, then shrugged. "There's a lot to work through. What I can say is that it'll probably take our research, and how we use the Forge, in a different direction."

"Meantime, you just rest," Amy said. She touched the scar on his neck. "And I know you just promised Dash this, but I want you to promise me, too." She looked into his eyes. "Don't you ever do anything that stupid again."

Conover nodded. "I promise."

Amy finally favored Conover with a smile. Dash gave everyone else a look, and they quietly withdrew, leaving the two of them alone.

18

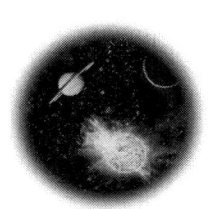

"Hard to believe they're going to be able to fit that thing inside the Rockhound," Dash said, and Leira nodded.

"Much less power needed for it," she added.

They were standing in one of the big installation and assembly bays adjacent to the fabrication level, watching as the components of a new weapon system were installed in the Rockhound. It was a railgun, a weapon that magnetically accelerated a projectile to phenomenal velocities. Custodian, working with Viktor and a still-recovering Conover, had determined their conventional ships—the Rockhound, the Snow Leopard, and the Slipwing most prominent among them—could be outfitted with a dark-lance or a railgun, but not both.

The issue was power; without entirely replacing the ships' power plants, and all related systems like power distribution and even drives, it simply wasn't possible to operate more than one of these systems. And, as Custodian pointed out, it would probably be easier to just build entirely new ships at that point.

Still, a railgun was a fearsome weapon at close range; it gave the Rockhound a punch she'd been lacking. Even then, it required banks of capacitors, accumulating a charge, and releasing it in a stupendous burst of kinetic impulse. Using Unseen tech, Viktor estimated they could pump a projectile up to nearly five percent of light-speed, with the recoil energy being fed back into the capacitors, allowing for a decent rate of fire.

Dash glanced at Leira as the maintenance remotes worked a bulky bank of capacitors into the Rockhound through an open cargo hatch.

"This is great," he said. "It gives us more capability, and damned if it isn't just the smallest bit dangerous. Those velocities are unnatural."

She nodded, but just watched the ongoing work, the maintenance remotes engaged in an intricate series of precisely choreographed moves.

"We need more people, too," Dash went on.

Again, Leira nodded but said nothing.

Dash decided to voice his thoughts anyway, even if she wasn't going to immediately reply. "And we need both of them soon. Now, in fact, despite not being able to trust—well, not everyone is going to be onboard with our concept of a free galaxy. Each different group means a new security concern, but I believe in taking the longer view. We're not going to discount entire ships filled with people due to a potential threat. So for every intake of humanity, we trust, but verify. Until I have reason to believe otherwise, we're going to bring people inside, vet them as best we can, and then find where they'll thrive in this war effort."

She finally turned to him, her eyes bright with determination. "I agree on every point. We're too few to fight those bastards while looking over our shoulder all the time. So let's go get them."

"Which? Ships? Or people? Or both?"

"Ships we probably have to build ourselves, at least for now. People, though, we can get."

"You seem to have someone in particular in mind."

"Most of the refugees we've offered a place on the Forge say yes. They hate the Golden, and the Verity, and all their other minions. Sounds like a ready-made force to me."

Dash cocked his head. "You mean the Verity slaves? The people they've taken and are holding? I—well, then yes. I'd considered most of our new forces coming from free people, but if you're okay with recruiting among the enslaved, then I am."

"Then let's do this," Leira replied. "The Verity are scum, after all, and probably have a lot more slaves somewhere."

Dash nodded, then turned away from the bustle of activity around the Rockhound. "Custodian, have the most informed people we freed from the Verity brought to the War Room. It's time to add a new target to the plan."

"Instructions have been sent. They're on their way and should be gathered within the next twenty minutes," Custodian said.

Dash glanced at Leira, who nodded in thanks. "We're on our way."

A half dozen refugees—no, Dash reminded himself, former refugees, and now citizens of the Cygnus Realm, for the moment at least—sat in the War Room, looking variously awkward, uncomfortable, and curious. And worried, Dash noted, which prompted him to offer a charming smile.

"You guys look like you think we're about to bite your heads off." He turned to Leira, who also flashed a smile. "We're not. We're hoping you can help us out with something, so we just want to ask some questions."

He'd been looking at Cyrus, the doctor, who had been one of those asked here by Custodian, but it wasn't Cyrus who answered.

"Help you with what?" a young girl asked. Dash figured she couldn't be more than sixteen or seventeen, with olive skin, short brown hair, and remarkably wide, grey eyes. She also probably looked the least uncomfortable of the bunch, and maybe even a little defiant.

Dash found himself immediately liking her.

"What's your name?" Dash asked her.

"Roxandra."

"Well, Roxandra—and everyone else here—we're hoping that you might know something, anything, about people like yourselves. People who are being held by the Verity."

"We want to rescue them," Leira added.

"And, honestly, we'd then like to see if we can recruit them to our cause."

Cyrus gave a fierce nod. "That shouldn't be a problem. Anyone who's seen what those...those bastards are capable of, they'd be more than happy to help you defeat them."

"Damned right," someone muttered.

"The only trouble is that I was taken on board that ship you guys captured, and that's all I know," Cyrus said. "I don't know where anyone else might be being held."

The others nodded—except for Roxandra, who leaned forward, a fierce, hard light burning in her eyes.

"I know where they're holding people. A lot of them. I was held with them for a while."

"Custodian," Dash said. "Give us a star chart." The holo-image appeared, and Dash turned to Roxandra. "Okay, if you could—"

She stood and pointed at a specific system. "There. Right there. They're being held there."

Leira narrowed her eyes. "Are you sure?" She glanced at Dash, and he got her meaning. The system Roxandra had identified was well removed from the broad trend of Verity activity that had been quite neatly paralleling the long axis of the galactic arm.

But Roxandra nodded her head firmly. "Absolutely. I was held there and...and..."

She stopped, swallowing.

Dash waited for her to go on.

Roxandra finally found her voice again. "And that's where my brother, Mircea, is. Or was, anyway. It's where I saw him last, before they took me away."

Dash stepped up to the opposite side of the holo-image and studied the system she'd pointed out. An unremarkable yellow-orange star, with two major planets, both gas giants, and more than a hundred moons between them. That made it not greatly different from thousands, maybe millions of other systems in this arm of the galaxy alone. But Roxandra had immediately identified this one.

"Custodian, put that trend of Verity activity on this map," Dash said.

The broad, curving line describing everything from hard data to rumors about Verity actions appeared. Sure enough, the system Roxandra had pointed out fell well off the trend.

"This is our best and most complete picture of what the Verity have been doing," Dash said, now studying Roxandra through the holo-image. "This star system you've pointed us at isn't on it."

"You think I'm lying?"

"No, it's not that," Dash quickly replied. "I'm just wondering if there's more you might know about what the Verity are doing there. Maybe you even know things without knowing you know them."

Roxandra shrugged. "All I know is there are a lot of people there, on an orbiting station of some sort. These Verity seem to have something big going on they want a lot of people for."

Dash glanced at Leira, who'd also been studying Roxandra. She returned a nod.

I believe her.

He looked back at the girl. "Okay. It looks like we're going to this system. When we do, we're going to rescue everyone there. That includes your brother, if he's still"—Dash was going to say alive but switched it to—"there."

Roxandra managed to push a weak smile through her otherwise hard demeanor. "Thank you. He's...he's all the family I have left."

Dash nodded. "If he's still there, we'll bring him home to you."

She nodded back and smiled a little more.

That smile, Dash thought, suddenly made being the Messenger worth it—at least for now. He only hoped they actually found her brother there, and alive, so that smile didn't just vanish again, and for good.

THEY LEFT Roxandra and the others with Custodian, who continued debriefing them. In the meantime, Dash called his commanders together in the Command Center and outlined for them what Roxandra had said.

"And you believe her?" Benzel asked.

"Yeah, Leira and I both do."

"She also checks out," Ragsdale said. "We can trace her identity back along with the claims she's made, right to a birth certificate on a settlement called Torrence's Landing."

"I've been there," Wei-Ping said. "An orbiting platform in an asteroid belt. Mining, mostly." She looked at Benzel. "It's where I got the idea, in fact, of setting up those nav buoys the way I did. Remember?"

"That's fine, I believe you guys, too," Dash cut in. "Anyway, assuming she's not a spy and this isn't a trap—"

"Which is still a possibility," Ragsdale said. "We can be reasonably sure she's not, but we can't be a hundred percent certain."

"Understood," Dash replied. "So, assuming that, we're going to attack here. I want to free these people. That's job number one. Number two, though, is trying to recruit them to help us."

"How many people are we talking about?" Benzel asked.

"Based on Roxandra's observations, I would estimate approximately two hundred."

"So we've got to get two hundred people back here to the Forge," Leira said.

"Yeah, the Herald won't hold that sort of crowd," Benzel said, and turned to Wei-Ping. "You've been wanting to take the Retribution out for a shakedown cruise. Here's your chance."

Wei-Ping nodded. "Works for me."

"Me too," Dash said. "And it's appropriate, too."

"How so?" Leira asked.

"Because," Dash replied, giving her a feral grin. "Retribution is a theme I'm quite happy with when it comes to the Verity."

19

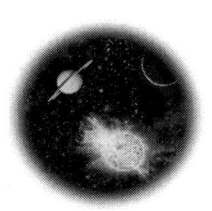

THE SYSTEM CONTAINING QUARANTINE STATION—ROXANDRA had eventually remembered that was the name of the Verity holding station here—was quiet. Dash couldn't help feeling it might very well be deceptively so. Benzel, Wei-Ping, Leira, even Viktor and Ragsdale had all urged caution regarding how they approached this. They'd been burned before by Verity traps, and even Dash couldn't stop a nagging little voice that said Roxandra might be a spy.

Dash studied the heads-up, on which he'd called up the telemetry from the stealth drone they'd launched into the system. It was yet another new design, a drone with a Dark Metal-alloy armor configured to bend incoming energy around it. The physics were far beyond Dash, but it meant that x-rays, radio waves, and even light would refract around the drone, with nothing reflecting off it and making it effectively invisible. The problem was that the system required a huge amount of Dark Metal just to stealth up this single drone; it just wasn't practical even for small ships, much less something the size of the Herald. This also meant it would register on a Dark Metal detector, but that was another advantage of the drone's small size—from more than a few thousand klicks away, it would be virtually impossible to see as a neutrino shadow.

"Sentinel, I am seeing absolutely nothing in this telemetry," Dash said.

"Dash, are you well? There is clearly data being transmitted."

"Yeah, you're right, and no, that's not what I mean. I see what we would expect to see, all the natural background stuff, plus emissions from that Quarantine Station, and not much more. I don't see anything to indicate there's a large fleet lying in wait around here somewhere."

"I concur. Unless the Verity are themselves employing an inordinately effective stealth technology, there appear to be no hidden forces in or near this system."

Tybalt chimed in. "I would point out that that does not preclude Verity forces located outside the system that are close enough to intervene relatively quickly."

"Yeah, I hear you, Tybalt," Dash replied. "But we can only control so much. I mean, yeah, there are definitely Verity forces out there somewhere, but they're not here. At least, not right now. So—Leira, Benzel, Wei-Ping, we're a go on this. Let's move."

When the chorus of agreement died down, Dash powered up the Archetype's drive and started in from where they'd been lurking among the comets and other debris in the system's Oort

Cloud. Wei-Ping, commanding the Retribution, fell into formation with him, while the Herald took station with the Swift.

Dash glanced at the Retribution, now fully repaired, upgraded, and emblazoned with the Cygnus logo. He hoped the Verity saw her and recognized her for what had once been their own ship—and that now she was coming to earn her new name.

Four Verity ships raced away from Quarantine Station to challenge them. They weren't a surprise; their emissions had shown up in the stealth drone's telemetry, even if their Dark Metal signatures had been too small to resolve without a much bigger detector. They were pretty unimpressive craft, essentially just a frigate and three corvettes. Still, Dash was reluctantly impressed by their dogged insistence in not just confronting the Cygnus flotilla, but doing it with a surprisingly aggressive panache.

"These guys aren't going to take no for an answer, are they?" Leira said, echoing Dash's thought.

"Nope, they sure aren't," Dash replied. "That's good for them—well, right up until they die."

"I wonder why the Verity have such a small force here protecting what seems to be a pretty important installation," Benzel said. "We're starting to see a bunch of resource-extraction stuff going on in this system—remote miners on some of the asteroids, helium-3 collectors near the gas giants, all sorts of stuff."

"I don't know," Dash replied. "I'd actually been starting to wonder the same thing. Maybe the losses we've inflicted on the Verity are forcing them to spread out pretty thinly."

"It is more probable that this system, being located so far off the main trend of Verity activity in the galactic arm, was considered relatively safe from attack," Sentinel put in.

Dash gave a slow nod of agreement. "Good point. Seems they missed the part about how some of their slaves might end up being rescued, including a teenage girl who happened to have just the info we needed." Then the threat indicator changed, and Dash felt his attention sharpen yet again as multiple launches from the Verity ships crowded the scans.

"Missiles. And a lot of them," Dash said.

The ensuing battle was chaotic and brutal. The Verity ships landed a few hits, including one missile that managed to slip through the Herald's point defense and punch a nasty gash in her hull. But it didn't last long. The Verity ships faltered under the weight of fire from the Cygnus flotilla and then, one by one, died, shredded by missiles, pulse cannons, dark-lances, and nova guns.

Dash watched the shattered carcass of the Verity frigate spin away from the battle, trailing a dissipating wake of vented atmosphere and drive plasma, and bits and pieces of debris. Ahead, Quarantine Station now hung alone against the starfield, orbiting the nearer gas giant.

Point defense systems opened up at them as they approached. Dash cursed and raced forward with the Archetype, deployed the power-sword, and hacked the station's point-defense batteries in scrap. The mech absorbed the pounding from the small, rapid-fire weapons, even taking some armor damage, but the fire from

Quarantine Station fell silent. By the time he'd managed to maneuver the Archetype close to a docking port on the station, Benzel, Wei-Ping, and boarding parties from each of their ships had already breached and entered.

Dash entered the airlock, which was secured by a pair of suited figures—one of the Gentle Friends, and a woman he recognized as one of the refugees. She stopped Dash as soon as he arrived.

"Benzel told me to wait here for you," she said. "I was held here for a while, so I know the layout—at least, most of it."

"What's your name?" Dash asked.

"Sera," the woman replied.

"Well, Sera, let's go free these people."

Through her helmet's faceplate, she gave a hard nod and a look that Dash figured could only be erased by Verity blood. Fitting, he thought, that she bore the logo for the Retribution on her vac suit.

Sera led Dash along a series of corridors, pausing at each corner to peer around it before proceeding. After the fourth time she did this, Dash stopped her.

"You have military experience, don't you?"

"I was trained up for our settlement's militia, yeah. Didn't do a damned bit of good against these Verity scum, though." She said it with a vehemence that made Dash blink.

"When we get back to the Forge, come and see me," he said to her. "I think we can give you another shot at them on way more even terms."

She hefted a pulse-gun. "You're giving me a shot at them

now. And I intend to take it. Hope you weren't planning on trying to take any of them alive."

"Nope, just the prisoners. They live at all costs, so if you're going to kill Verity, make sure you only kill Verity."

"Don't worry. I was top shot in our militia outfit. If I want to hit something, I'll hit it."

Dash nodded and Sera carried on.

They passed Verity corpses, dead with pulse-gun and snap-gun wounds, or deep gashes from blades, boarding axes, and cutlasses. They also passed wounded Gentle Friends being evacuated back to the Herald or Retribution. Only one of them seemed serious, fortunately.

So far, what they hadn't passed was any of the prisoners. An uncomfortable feeling began gnawing at Dash. Were there prisoners even here, or had they been moved?

Or had something worse happened to them?

Swallowing his dread, he carried on with Sera, following her to the station's bridge. There, they found Benzel and Wei-Ping at the head of three squads of Cygnus attackers that were assembled outside a sealed blast door.

"Believe it or not, the commander of this station is inside there, demanding to negotiate," Benzel said.

Dash stared at Benzel through his faceplate. "Negotiate about what?"

"Surviving, I guess," Wei-Ping said.

Dash opened the channel the Verity commander had been using. "This is the Messenger. I'm in charge of the force that just kicked your ass. You want to negotiate? Fine. Surrender unconditionally, and I might let you live. There, negotiating done."

The voice that came back was so flat and mechanical it made even Custodian sound bubbly. "Unacceptable. If you do not negotiate in good faith, then I will blow the airlocks on this station and kill every single one of those you came here to save."

Dash muted the channel. "Sentinel, is that a real threat?"

"It was, but no longer. The crews of the Herald and Retribution have secured portable docking adapters to the airlocks in the station's hab section to facilitate the evacuation of prisoners."

"So even if he does blow the locks, he'll just be opening them up on—well, more airlocks."

"Correct."

Dash turned to Benzel. "You ready to breach that door?"

"As soon as you give the word."

"Consider it given."

Benzel grinned then turned to a nearby Gentle Friend holding a detonator module.

Dash switched back to the Verity commander's channel. "Yeah, I've thought it over and, well, here's my counteroffer."

A heavy blast shuddered the bulkheads and deck as the shaped charges cut the locking hardware on the blast door. Vac suited figures raced forward and wedged the door open with oversized pry bars, while others threw in dazzle charges.

"Let's go!" Benzel said, rising and running toward the opening. Inside, the dazzle charges flashed; at the same time, static crashed across the comm as the broad-spectrum pulses ripped through the bridge. The first squad through, from the Herald, went left through the door; Dash followed Benzel to the right, with Wei-Ping and one of her squads from the Retribution following.

The resulting firefight was brief and bloody. By the time Dash was in a firing position, the only Verity left was the commander himself, screened behind a console.

"You were warned," Dash heard him say, and saw him operate a control on the console before anyone could get a shot lined up.

Nothing seemed to happen.

"Sentinel, did those airlocks blow?"

"No. The command function failed, perhaps due to damage."

"Yeah, that would probably be me," Leira suddenly cut in over the comm. "The squads I'm with seized engineering a few minutes ago and shut down every system they could find that wasn't life support."

"Good work," Dash said, then lifted his head and looked at the Verity commander. "Okay, you've got no—"

The Verity raised a pulse-gun and fired. The shot missed Dash's head by centimeters. Before he could fire again, though, a pulse-gun bolt flashed back at the commander, blowing his weapon out of his hands. He staggered back and slumped against a bulkhead.

As crew from the Retribution dashed forward to secure the Verity commander as a prisoner, Dash turned to the vac-suited figure that had shot the pulse gun out of his hands. It was Sera.

She shrugged. "Told you I was a good shot."

"I'm kind of surprised you didn't just kill him."

"I thought you wanted him alive."

Benzel and Wei-Ping dragged the Verity commander before Dash. "You want to talk to this jerk before we throw him into custody?" Benzel asked.

Dash glanced at Sera, then back to the commander. "Not really. And we're not taking him into custody."

The Verity commander's face switched from contempt to panic like a thrown switch. "What do you intend for me?"

Dash answered by gesturing to a nearby airlock, one that hadn't been rigged with a docking adapter. Benzel nodded, yanked out a combat blade, and sliced a gash into the commander's suit.

As he was dragged to the airlock, the commander began kicking and flailing. "No! No, you cannot do this! You claim to be civilized, but you're—"

"Just like you?" Dash said, then shook his head. "No, wait, we're not like you at all. We don't harvest innocent people like livestock for the bits we want to use to extend our own, miserable lives. We just kill our enemies and move on."

"I am a prisoner!"

"Not for long, you're not," Benzel said, then he and Wei-Ping flung the commander into the airlock and sealed it. The Verity pounded on the inner door, terror twisting his face.

Dash turned to Sera. "Benzel asked if I had anything I wanted to say to this guy. I don't, but you might."

She stepped up to the viewport in the airlock. "Yeah, I do. That look on your face? You know, the pain, and fear, and panic?

That's exactly the same look I saw on the faces of my friends when you attacked us and took us prisoner." She reached for the airlock cycle control. "The same look I saw on my mother's face. So, yes, I have something to say to you."

Her eyes locked on those of the Verity, she said, "Screw you," and hit the control.

Sera didn't look away, not even for an instant, as the Verity commander was blown into space, a trail of freezing blood and air trailing from the gash in his suit.

They rounded up the throng of prisoners aboard Quarantine Station, Dash going from person to person, shaking hands, letting himself be seen, and quietly looking for Mircea.

He pulled aside a tech, her tunic spattered in fluids of all colors, describing Mircea as a note of unease began to grow in his senses.

"Haven't seen anyone like him. Grey eyes? I'd remember that. Sorry," the tech said, then moved off in a tired shamble toward a wounded man with most of his head wrapped in a stained bandage.

When he was done searching the survivors, he combed the bodies.

No Mircea.

Standing, hands on hips, Dash let his eyes play over the scene, watching for what was there and what wasn't. A pair of wounded people were strapped to the blast door of an escape pod, their suits torn into so much chaff, but they were alive—if unconscious. The blast doors made good stretchers, so Dash began to count—

—And every door for the fifteen pods was accounted for, except number three.

"Where's pod three?" Dash bellowed, taking everyone near him by surprise. He got confused looks and the odd motion to keep his voice down, but an engineer named Hawley came over, pointing out of the ship.

"It's not in here, which means…it's out there. We couldn't get everyone, and I think the crews are all in," Hawley said. He was a small, neat man, with a cropped beard and flash burns on one side of his face.

"Sentinel. Meet me at the bay. I need to find something," Dash said, his boots ringing on the floor as he pelted away.

"What do you wish to find?" Sentinel asked.

"Life pod. Beacon number three. It will be—"

"I have it."

"Where?"

"Cradle in, and we will depart. The pod is in a tumble and will strike debris in two minutes, nineteen seconds," Sentinel said.

Dash was gasping as he linked in, and the archetype sped away in a blur.

"Let's clear the field. I want a direct line to that pod," he said, and the archetype became a blaze of fire as it shattered debris, asteroids, and the remains of a small comet. In seconds, they reached the tiny, silver speck as it spun ever closer to a mass of slag—the remains of an unfortunate enemy craft, stretched into a web-like shape from centrifugal forces.

"Got him," Dash said, clasping a massive mechanical hand around the pod, its surface a pitted, scorched mass of divots.

"Scan indicates it is Mircea inside. He is wounded, but alive."

Dash opened up the comms as he kicked the engines hard, streaking back to the Quarantine Station. "All craft—get the hell out of my way. I want a med team inside the doors. Blow the outer lock early to let me in and stand down for ten seconds. Pressurize immediately. I'm cracking this pod open by force, and I don't want anyone hurt when I do it."

There was a crackle of assent over the comms, and then the station loomed ahead. Dash got the pod inside one of the makeshift locks, then twisted the damaged door with a touch that was oddly delicate given the power of the Archetype.

"Don't want to let hard vacuum in. I'll press the door into its seal. It'll hold for a few seconds while the atmo rises," Dash said.

When he withdrew the massive arm from the airlock, the door closed behind him and medical staff swarmed out into the space. From outside, Dash saw Mircea pulled out, a smear of blood on his pale skin.

"Alive?" Dash heard himself say.

Sentinel answered. "Alive."

With a rush of relief, Dash let himself collapse in the cradle, adrenaline draining away in a sickening flurry. "Good. I hate breaking promises."

Moments later, inside the hab, Leira brought Dash to Mircea as he was being loaded onto a pallet for evacuation to the Herald.

He was younger than Roxandra, a lean, wiry kid with the same olive skin and grey eyes as his sister. He looked up at Dash and nodded gratefully as he was carried away.

"Broken bones," Leira said. "An arm, a leg, at least a couple of ribs."

"Not from falling down, I assume."

"Well, he probably did fall down, yeah, as he was being beaten."

"How did he get in the pod?" Dash asked.

"He's young, and strong, and quick-thinking. He's a tough one," Leira said.

"Good." Dash felt relief flood his veins all over again.

A sudden cheer went up around them, echoing from through the dreary hab level of the station. Someone had put up an image of the Verity commander being blown into space onto view screens that were probably normally filled with menacing warnings and Verity propaganda.

"I hope it took him a long time to die," Mircea snapped.

Dash clicked his tongue. "Now what would your sister say, hearing you say something like that?"

"She'd probably say, yeah, that's Mircea for you." The young man winced as he shifted on the pallet. "She got all the smarts, and I got all the mouth."

Dash grinned and gestured for Mircea to be taken away and made comfortable on the Herald.

He grinned even more when Sentinel recounted the spoils from the battle; between the wrecked Verity ships, this station, an even older and apparently disused station still orbiting the other gas giant, and the various smaller Verity resource-extraction operations in the system, they'd just scored one of their biggest hauls of Dark Metal and rare alloys yet. But the grin didn't last. Benzel came to Dash, pulled him aside, and switched to a private comm channel.

"We have a problem, Dash."

"A problem? Only one?"

It was the look Benzel returned that made his grin finally die. "It's a big problem, Dash. A serious one."

"Okay, what is it?"

"Based on what Roxandra told us, we were expecting just over two hundred prisoners here. Based on that, we brought only the Herald and Retribution, which gave us enough room for two-fifty, if we really packed them in. But there are over three hundred here. Three hundred and thirteen, in fact. And that's even taking into account casualties because, unfortunately, we had thirteen killed during the boarding action."

"So, an extra seventy or so? We can't fit them aboard our ships?"

"We can physically pack them in, sure," Benzel replied. "But Wei-Ping ran the numbers—three times, in fact. The air cyclers on both ships just can't handle that many people. We're looking at some serious carbon dioxide buildup by the time we get back to the Forge."

Dash just stared for a moment, his mind racing. What a stupid mistake to have made. His stupid mistake. If they'd brought along one more ship as a contingency, such as the Snow Leopard—

"All due respect to Wei-Ping, who I'm sure knows her stuff, but have you checked this with Sentinel or Tybalt?"

"He has," Sentinel said. "And the calculations are correct. The two ships' life-support systems do not have the capacity to safely transport this many people."

"And you didn't think it was important to say something to me?" Dash snapped at Sentinel, but Benzel held up a hand.

"I asked her not to. This is my screwup, so I wanted to be the one to tell you."

"Your screw up?" Dash said. "More like mine. Like I told that Verity commander, I'm the Messenger, so I'm the one who wears things like this."

"Dash, you can't be expected to think of every—"

Leira, who'd joined them, cut into the conversation. "Tybalt patched me into this because he thought I should be part of it. Honestly, we're all at fault," she said. "Which doesn't really matter, does it? We've learned something for next time. What we need to do now, for this time, is figure out what we're going to do about it."

"She's right," Dash said. "Okay, so—ideas."

"Call back to the Forge and have them send another ship," Leira suggested. "That'd be the easiest way."

"Unwise," Sentinel put in. "Several transmissions were sent from this station before we interrupted them. The risk of a superior Verity or Golden retaliatory force arriving increases with each passing minute."

"Besides, I'm not really keen on trying to fight a battle with a ship jammed to the deck-joists with refugees," Benzel said. "I mean, one hull breach…"

He trailed off, not needing to go on.

Dash took a deep breath then let it out. "Well, we simply can't transport anyone aboard the mechs. And Sentinel's right, we can't hang around here. We should harvest whatever Dark Metal we can while we're here and send a force back to try and grab the rest of the resources. But we need to get these people out of here and back to safety." He bit his lip for a moment. "How about a stop at an intermediate system? Either to refresh our air, or even to drop some refugees off?"

But Wei-Ping, who'd also joined them, interrupted while shaking her head. "Already checked. The only systems a shorter flight time away than the Forge either have no habitable planets or might be controlled by the Verity."

Dash scowled. "Shit."

"Yeah, shit, indeed," Benzel said.

"Well, then we have no choice," Dash finally replied. "We have to pack them in, evacuate them, and hope we can manage to make the air last until we get back to the Forge."

DASH FOUND the return trip to the Forge the most nerve-wracking yet—and he had some pretty scary return trips under his belt.

He felt so helpless. Benzel and Wei-Ping gave steady reports on the air quality aboard the Herald and the Retribution, and they weren't good. Even keeping as many of the crew in vac suits for as long as they could, the air-cyclers simply couldn't keep up with the throngs jammed into their corridors and compartments. Worse, because they had no idea if there were Verity spies or saboteurs among the refugees, large sections of both ships—bridge, weapons, magazines, and engineering—had to be kept off-limits, meaning each ship had more than a hundred and fifty extra people packed into what space remained.

Dash could only imagine the deteriorating conditions aboard the two ships. The rising tension and increasing breathlessness of both Benzel's and Wei-Ping's voices over the comm unfortunately made his imaginings much easier, and more vivid.

What if everyone aboard those ships just died?

He even raised this with Sentinel, asking her if the ships could pilot themselves back to the Forge, or if she and Tybalt could do it.

"Controlling the ships remotely is a relatively simple matter," she replied. "However—"

She stopped.

"However what?" Dash asked.

"However, I am expressing a desire that it not come to that."

That made Dash's eyes widen in surprise, and even sting a bit. "Sentinel, that's so—so human of you."

"There is no need to be insulting."

That actually made Dash laugh. But then he glanced at the Herald, and the Retribution beyond her, and his laughter stopped.

Dash ran into the docking bay. It was one of the biggest, one they didn't normally use; Dash had Custodian power it up so they could use it to unload the Herald directly into the Forge. Her prow and forward ten meters or so now protruded into the bay through the force field maintaining environmental integrity, and people had been stumbling out of her forward airlock, wheezing, coughing, scattered around the bay and sucking in fresh air. The Retribution wouldn't fit in here at the same time, so she'd been eased into another docking bay on the fabrication level, enough that she could poke an emergency airlock in through the force field and disgorge her gasping occupants.

Dash found Benzel snapping out orders amid the chaos—or trying to, between deep, hoarse breaths.

"Benzel! You okay?"

Benzel turned to him, his face nearly the same pale, neutral grey as the deck plates. However, a little flush had started back into his cheeks, which Dash took as a good sign.

"No," Benzel gasped. "Let's not…do that again…okay?"

Dash gave him a relieved clap on the shoulder. "Next time, we bring at least one more ship than we think we need, I promise." He looked around at the throng still pouring out of the Herald. "Any casualties?"

Benzel nodded. "Yeah. Two. One guy—really old. And another—some respiratory thing."

"Shit."

"Could've been worse."

"Yeah, true enough."

It was. Sentinel had estimated the Herald had about two

hours of breathable air left, the Retribution only one. If either had been delayed by—any number of things, really—a tense and dangerous situation could have become a disaster.

Dash moved to help a woman and her young child, who were wobbly and on the edge of collapse. As he did, it struck him he'd assumed that their worst casualties would come at the hands of the Golden, and not because he and his fellow leaders of the Cygnus Realm had simply screwed up.

20

Dash offered Benzel a smile. "You're looking better than the last time I saw you."

Benzel, Wei-Ping close behind, nodded back as they entered the Command Center. "Yeah, it's amazing what a shower, a meal, and clean clothes can do. Oh yeah, and breathable freakin' air."

"For me, it wasn't even so much the air," Wei-Ping said. "It was the smell. Ugh. I think I still catch hints of it aboard the Retribution. Going to have to change all those scrubber filters."

They found places among the others already assembled. Again, everyone was here. Even Conover had come, still hobbling a little, helped by Amy. The burn on his neck had mostly healed, thanks to the Forge's med tech, but would leave a striking white scar like an intricately branching tree.

"You're also looking better," Dash said, passing Conover on his way to the front of the Command Center. "Way better."

"Still a little wobbly," Conover replied. "But I can manage. Doc Cyrus says I should be pretty much recovered in a few days."

"Good, because I need you back at work."

Amy shot Dash a frown. "Hey, give the guy a break."

"Why? Because he was a damned fool who almost got himself killed doing something stupid?"

Amy looked ready to fire back a retort but didn't. She just looked at Conover and shrugged. "He's right, you know. I tried to stick up for you, but sorry, you're on your own for this."

Dash grinned as he turned away. The way she'd said it, the way she'd looked at Conover as she did—yeah, this was no longer a one-way relationship.

"Okay, everyone, we've got decisions to make," Dash said, stepping up in front of the big star chart. "First, though, let's hear everyone's report."

One by one, they each stood and gave a quick rundown of their particular area. Overall, it was pretty much as Dash had expected. They were in reasonably good shape, but it could definitely be better.

"So it sounds like our production is going well," Dash said. "But we're still waiting on the Shroud, aren't we?"

"We are," Custodian said. "Final calibrations will be complete within a day, and then we will do the first test fabrication of a basic power core. That will take another two days."

Viktor chimed in. "And if that all works out, and we end up with a working power core, we'll ramp up into full production."

"Well that's good news," Dash said. "It means those pieces

we've started fabricating for the Talon and the Pulsar aren't going to end up just sitting in storage."

"We also now have two ship killers operational," Custodian said. Dash had seen them, two sleek and sinister shapes hanging against the stars. Each vaguely resembled the Shroud, upon which they were based, but had been outfitted with rapid fire missile launchers and a full load of trans-luminal missiles. Between them, Custodian and Viktor had even come up with a way to swap out warheads as the missiles were about to be loaded into the launchers; they could select simple plasma-blast warheads, scrambler warheads to knock ships out of translation, or even flash warheads to disrupt their systems. They had to use the latter two sparingly, though, because they required Dark Metal and were complex to manufacture in such miniaturized forms.

"And then there's ships," Dash said, turning and looking at a window Custodian had popped open on the big display that showed the status of the fleet. "We're in pretty good shape, and it gets a little better every day. I'd really like to get a few more bigger capital ships in play, though, along the lines of the Herald."

"That is feasible if power cores constructed by the Shroud are used to energize more of the Forge's fabrication systems," Custodian said.

"I can see those power cores are going to become a bottleneck," Leira said. "We're going to have to make some decisions about priorities."

"That we are," Dash agreed, nodding. "But that's not our

biggest bottleneck. We could have a huge fleet, but it won't do much good without anyone to crew it. And AIs only go so far—with all due respect to Custodian, Sentinel, and Tybalt, of course."

"You are correct," Sentinel said. "As you have amply demonstrated, humans and similar species have a capacity for spontaneity and creativity that artificial intelligences lack."

"Well, you're looking for people," Harolyn said. "You just rescued three hundred from the Verity."

"Yeah, sure, and I'm glad we did, but really, how many of those people can crew a ship? Even fight?"

"More than you might think," Harolyn replied, looking at a data-pad. "We've done our first screening and have identified one hundred and"—she brushed a finger across the screen—"twenty-seven who have military experience or are trained in skills we could use. That includes four doctors, seven nurses, and five engineers of various types. Almost two hundred of them have experience crewing a ship of some description, too."

"But we've only done a first pass," Ragsdale put in. "We need to dig into their backgrounds and do a much more thorough screening before I'd be happy calling them safe and reliable."

"Of course," Dash said. "But let's give priority to screening anyone with military experience, and then anyone with valuable skills."

Ragsdale and Harolyn nodded.

"In the meantime, get them all assembled," Dash went on. "I want to talk to them, start getting them used to us—and me, and how we're going to fight this war." He gestured around him.

"We'll have them gathered in the big docking bay in an hour," Harolyn said.

"Sounds good." Dash turned to the star chart. "Now, on to strategy. What's our next move?"

DASH MOVED among the freed captives, chatting, shaking hands, hugging, and generally uttering variations of "No problem, glad we could help you," over and over again in response to effusive and often tearful thanks. When he finally made his way through the crowd, he climbed up onto a scrambler mine waiting to be loaded into the Horse Nebula and waited for everyone to fall silent.

"I know you've all heard this already, but I want to say it formally—welcome to the Cygnus Realm, the Forge, and freedom."

It was trite and even a little corny, but it worked. A cheer went up, along with applause that didn't stop until he raised his hands.

"That's the feel-good part," he said. "Now for the reality check, which isn't anywhere near as rosy. I'd love to say you can relax here as long as you'd like, and recover from what you've been through—including us almost asphyxiating the whole lot of you."

That actually prompted more laughter than Dash had expected, driving home just how glad these people were simply to not be in the hands of the Verity any longer. He raised his hands again, and again waited for silence.

"The grimmer truth is, we can't do that. The Cygnus Realm really doesn't have civilians, at least not yet. We're at war, and whether you're aboard a ship in battle, or back here helping us do all the things we need to do to make those battles ones we can win, our people are all at war, too. If you want to stay and help us, we'd be glad of it. That's especially true if you have skills we need, such as military experience, or you're a doctor or engineer or something like that. Even if you don't, we'll definitely find useful things for you to do. But you will be part of fighting that war if you stay with us."

Dash gave a moment for it all to sink in, then went on. "And if you don't want to be part of that, it's entirely up to you. We'll make arrangements to transport you to a nearby inhabited world, somewhere with a spaceport, and from there you can go wherever you want."

Dash saw the reaction ripple through the crowd. Some stepped forward, eager to get to work. Others withdrew into themselves, or into small groups, speaking in hushed tones. And some, unsurprisingly, just stood and stared, their minds obviously still not in a place to truly understand what was going on, other than the horror of their captivity had ended.

"We're not asking you to make your decision this instant," Dash said. "Think about it for a day or so. But it can't be much more than that, because the Golden won't wait. Neither can we, and the sooner we take the fight to them, the sooner we can build something lasting. Something more than just endless fear and fighting. I promise you that."

Dash clambered down off the mine, only to have someone step in front of him. It was Sera, the woman who'd guided him through Quarantine Station.

"I don't need to think about it," she said. "I'm ready to assume whatever duties you want me to, right now."

Dash gave her a grateful smile. "Okay, and thank you. Go talk to Ragsdale—he's the guy over there who's scowling and looks like he has no sense of humor. He'll get you sorted out."

More people moved toward Dash, but Leira appeared, snagging his attention. He excused himself.

"What's up?"

"Custodian's finished putting together an intelligence picture from all of our data—drones, Dark Metal signals, that sort of thing—and the survivor accounts we've gathered so far," Leira said, leading Dash away from the crowd. "The Verity are building a fleet. That's why they were stripping resources out of that system where they were holding all these people. They're doing the same in a whole bunch of other systems, too."

"Doesn't that just say they're gathering resources, though? How do we know it's for a fleet?"

Leira allowed herself a triumphant smile. "Because Custodian has figured out where they're building it. It's a whole shipyard, Dash, with a partly completed fleet."

Dash just stared for a moment, letting it sink in. The opportunity—holy shit. But the risk would also be enormous, because nothing the Verity had was likely to be as well-protected as a fleet under construction. It probably explained why Verity forces seemed so thin everywhere else.

"Dash?"

He felt a slow smile grow. "Finally. This is—it's what we've been looking for. This is the piece. Does Custodian have a firm location?" His smile remained, more predatory than ever.

"He does. It's a red giant, about forty light-years from here. Three rocky planets, one ice giant, and a lot of asteroids. The asteroids are being mined, and the shipyard is kind of hidden away among the moons of the ice giant."

"Okay. We need to make this a top priority." He looked at Leira. "I want that fleet. But if we can't have it, then I want to destroy it. Have Custodian assemble everything into a planning map, and—"

"Messenger," Custodian said. "We have an inbound ship."

"Speak of the devil," Dash said. "What is it?"

"A Golden drone. It is approaching at a high velocity, nearly point-two-five light speed."

"No rest for the utterly exhausted," Dash said to Leira as they both headed for their mechs.

As the Forge dwindled behind the Archetype, Dash studied the threat indicator. There was one drone, moving at a quarter of the speed of light. It was only minutes away.

But—one drone? Why only one?

"What the hell are you up to?" Dash asked as the image of

the approaching drone shifted toward blue from the Doppler effect. "There's got to be more to it than—"

Sure enough, even as he watched, a swarm of smaller objects detached from the drone, like escape pods jetting away from a stricken mother ship. The smaller drones raced onward toward the Forge, while the main drone altered its trajectory, veering to rise back up and out of the plane of the nearby star's ecliptic. It was making a run for it.

"Can we catch that thing?" Dash asked.

"Unlikely, at least before it is able to translate," Sentinel replied. "Even overcharging the Archetype's drive will not allow for sufficient acceleration to ensure an intercept."

"Custodian, will you be able to handle all of those little, incoming whatever-they-are?"

"The swarm of smaller vehicles are likely intended only to trigger our defenses. Because they have retained the velocity of their parent craft, it is further likely this is a test of the Forge's close-range weapon systems."

"Mapping out our defenses, yeah. Which means that bigger drone is going to stick around long enough to watch, receive a bunch of telemetry, and then scoot."

"Agreed," Sentinel said. "Unfortunately, it will still be possible for the drone to do that, and then escape."

Dash frowned at the imagery. It was too bad they didn't have scrambler mines deployed—

"Wait. Custodian, here's a chance to test out our ship-killer systems in live combat. A trans-luminal missile with a scrambler warhead should be able to stop that drone, right?"

"In theory, based on simulations, yes."

"Do it. Load a scrambler missile and fire."

"Complying."

Dash powered up the Archetype's drive to emergency combat power and zoomed after the fleeing drone. "Leira, you hang back near the Forge in case something nasty comes up that we just haven't seen yet."

"Will do."

Dash watched as the battle unfolded. The ship-killer missile launched just before the Forge's point-defense batteries opened up. The swarm of smaller drones immediately began to weave through complex evasive patterns; Dash noted that they seemed to be anticipating the firing patterns of the Forge weapons, dodging the incoming fire. It still ended up being in vain; the last of them was swatted into debris long before even getting close to the Forge.

Still, Dash narrowed his eyes over it.

The ship-killer missile translated, just as the main drone did the same. An instant later, it reappeared and detonated on the drone's predicted path. Sure enough, the Golden drone dropped back into real space and stayed there, the missile's effect lingering through a large volume of space. It was just enough to give Dash time to catch up to it.

The Golden drone spun on its axis and fired a searing beam of energy that punched through the Archetype's shield and scoured a gouge in its armor. It was superficial damage, but the weapon itself, which they'd never encountered before, was worrisome; a bigger, more powerful version, mounted on a ship, could be a serious threat.

Dash dodged the next shot, or tried to, but the drone anticipated his next move. Wincing at the hit, Dash dodged again and fired the dark-lance. The drone anticipated that, too, and darted hard aside, the flickering beam of the dark-lance ripping through space less than a klick away from it.

The drone was about to shoot again; Dash knew it. So he did nothing.

Sure enough, the drone's beam missed just as the dark-lance had, flashing close past the Archetype.

"Huh."

"An observation, Messenger?" Sentinel asked.

"There will be. Just give me a minute."

Dash lined up the dark-lance on where he least expected the drone to go, and fired.

The Golden drone flew right into the beam. The dark-lance punched through it, blasting its components into quantum debris. The drone continued on its trajectory, coasting.

"Power emissions have dropped to zero," Sentinel said. "The Golden drone is dead."

"No it isn't," Dash said.

"Messenger, I can confirm—"

"Watch."

Dash powered the Archetype directly toward the drone, as though to recover it as salvage. When he was only a few tens of klicks away, the drone suddenly came back to life, spun—

—and died, this time for real, as the dark-lance tore through it from bow to stern.

"Now it's dead," Dash said.

"How did you know it was a ruse?"

"Because it's something I would have done."

"You are suggesting that this Golden drone was behaving…differently?"

"I am. Whatever AI was controlling it has come a long way from where they started out, kind of stilted and predictable."

"That is a matter of concern."

"Yeah. It is. If Golden AIs have started to develop real fighting instincts, then it's a matter of great concern, because this war just got a lot harder to win."

21

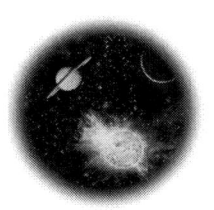

IF THE WAR just got harder to win, Dash thought, then they had to fight it even harder. And that started with attacking the Verity shipyard Custodian had sussed out. They had to keep that fleet from ever deploying against them. Dash wanted to capture it, or as much of it as he could—but if they had to destroy it, so be it.

And that was why Dash now studied the telemetry from the stealth drone they'd sent into the system ahead of the fleet. Not counting the partially built ships in space-dock, of course, or the multitude of tenders and other small vessels involved in their construction, the Verity had seventeen combat vessels in the system. The drone telemetry didn't hint at any more. So seventeen, versus the fourteen of the Cygnus fleet. Two of the Cygnus ships, though, were the Archetype and the Swift, which meant they weren't as outnumbered as it seemed.

Still. Seventeen combat-capable ships. This was going to be a tough fight.

Dash's thoughts grimly trudged on from there. A fight that would probably see a lot of people getting hurt. A lot of people dying.

A fight upon which the course of the war would turn.

"Dash," Benzel said. "The mine layers are ready to deploy. The rest of the fleet is ready, too. All we need is the word from you."

"Got it. Stand by."

But there was no reason to stand by. Dash was just putting off the inevitable: giving the order that would start the battle, that would lead to all those casualties, and that would potentially change the entire course of the war, for better or worse.

"Dash?"

It was Leira, calling him on a private channel.

"Yeah?"

"I know where you are," she said.

"Not exactly a secret. I'm in the Archetype—"

"Not what I mean. I know where your head is right now."

"Staring down the barrel of a battle that could see us lose a lot of people, and maybe the war?"

"None of these people have to be here, Dash. You've given every one of them ample opportunity to leave. They haven't. You need to respect that choice."

"I do. It's just that—" He stopped, words failing him.

"I know," Leira said.

"I wish I wasn't the Messenger, you know. Don't know if I've ever said that."

"You don't have to. We all know it."

"As do I," Sentinel said. "I believe that's what makes you so good at it."

"You are far from perfect, Messenger," Tybalt added. "But you are the least imperfect human being I have encountered, and are therefore best suited for the role."

"First, that's the closest thing you're going to get to a compliment out of Tybalt," Leira said. "And second, gee, thanks, Tybalt."

"My second preference among available individuals for the role of Messenger would be you, Leira."

"And that's the closest thing to a compliment I'm going to get out of Tybalt," Leira replied.

Despite the awful gravity of the situation, Dash found himself smiling at Sentinel and Tybalt—and Leira.

Especially Leira.

He switched to the fleet channel.

"I think this is the part where I'm supposed to say something inspirational," Dash said. "But you all know me. I'm not an inspirational speech kind of guy. So—let's go spank these Verity clowns, take their shit, and go home."

Someone laughed over the comm. Dash thought it might be Benzel. But it was Wei-Ping who spoke up.

"That sounded pretty inspirational to me!"

THE PLAN WAS SIMPLE. The main body of the fleet would drive directly in at the shipyard, its two squadrons attacking along two different vectors far enough apart to encourage the Verity to split their own forces. But if they didn't, and instead chose to concentrate everything on one squadron, then the second would be close enough to take the Verity in the flank or rear. In the meantime, two squadrons of mine layers would arrive in-system above and below the plane of the ecliptic, one led by the Horse Nebula, the other by the Void Stalker, and begin sowing scrambler and flash mines in two fields that would converge just beyond the shipyard. The hope was to hem the Verity in and catch anything that tried to escape, while inhibiting any relief forces that might arrive during the battle.

Thinking back on the Golden drone he'd recently fought, Dash and the other Cygnus leaders had tried to leave as much flexibility in the plan as possible to account for their enemies doing unexpected and spontaneous things. Speed and surprise were, as always, key, and that might win them the day. But that's where the mines came in—speed and surprise and minefields were even better, because they could leave a fleet dead in space, ripe for capture.

"We will be in dark-lance range in fifteen—" Sentinel began, then paused as the threat indicator lit up. "The Verity have just launched a large and coordinated salvo of missiles. Ninety seconds until impact at our current closing speed."

"I see it. Holy shit that's a lot of missiles." There were at least a hundred in one massive wave. Dash could tell these were smart missiles, too, from the way they constantly shifted their formation, first maximizing their threat posture against the Herald and A Squadron, then the Retribution and B Squadron, and back again.

"Okay, let's return the favor," Dash said. "Fire the ship killers, and then brace for all that incoming ordnance."

Acknowledgements came in from Benzel and Wei-Ping. A moment later, their two ship killers, one on station with each of the Herald and Retribution, opened fire. Dash saw trans-luminal missiles flash away then vanish into unSpace. He could imagine the rapid reloads going on inside the automated ship-killers, more missiles being unracked, moved, loaded, and fired, over and over, the weapons launching and zipping away at the furious rate of two every three seconds.

Explosions began to ripple through the ranks of the Verity fleet. Every second missile the ship killers launched had a flash warhead; they were programmed to attack different targets than the plasma-blast missiles, so that ideally half the Verity ships would be disabled and half damaged or destroyed. And because they popped out of unSpace so close to the enemy fleet, there was scant time for the Verity countermeasures and point-defense systems to respond. By the time the ship killers had expended the last of their ordnance, five of the seventeen Verity ships were dead in space, coasting along unpowered on whatever trajectory they happened to be following.

Fourteen to twelve, now. Much better odds, at least for however long it took the stricken Verity ships to recuperate and reboot their failed systems and get back in the fight.

"Thirty seconds to impact by incoming Verity missiles," Sentinel said.

"Okay, countermeasures, go!"

This had been Benzel's idea. The Forge had been hard-pressed to build enough of the miniaturized flash warheads to fully load out the ship killers, but the bulkier flash mines were much easier to produce. Now, each ship in the fleet literally lobbed flash mines out of airlocks and cargo bays; at the same time, both squadrons, as one, decelerated hard. A swarm of flash mines, still moving with the velocity imparted to them when they were thrown into space, now began outpacing the fleet, sailing ahead of it, further and faster with each passing second.

The onrushing wall of Verity missiles began a frantic series of maneuvers, trying to adjust for the mines suddenly looming ahead of them. Over the next ten or fifteen seconds, the battle was solely between automated ordnance, missiles versus mines.

Despite their best efforts, the mines began detonating and knocking missiles offline.

"Okay, Leira, we're up!" Dash called. "Let's go!"

The Archetype and Swift hadn't decelerated with the rest of the fleet, instead veering aside, opening the distance between them and the two Cygnus squadrons, then cutting their drives and coasting. Now, both mechs powered up their drives and accelerated hard. Each attracted the attention of some of the surviving missiles, which saw the mechs as priority targets and raced after them, diminishing the threat to the rest of the fleet that much more.

The mines had taken down half the missiles. A quarter of what remained had locked onto the Archetype and Swift. Now the fleet's point defense batteries opened up, spewing shots at the rest. Still, despite their best efforts, some of the missiles made it through, slamming into Cygnus ships and detonating.

One, a recently acquired Silent Fleet frigate they christened the Irresistible, staggered out of line in A Squadron, her drive section a shambles of wreckage and venting plasma. Another, the Forge-built light cruiser named the Blue Sun, reeled under impacts that blew apart her bridge, but she managed to stay in line as auxiliary controls in her engineering section took over. Dash immediately started wondering about the cost, but he shoved his mind back where it belonged: fighting and winning this battle.

"We have four missiles inbound," Sentinel said. "Impact in twenty seconds."

"Okay, stand by with the distortion grid."

"Online and ready."

A Verity cruiser had just entered dark-lance range; he snapped out a shot at it. The weapon had seen further upgrades, increasing its range and power and decreasing its recuperation time, so he was able to fire twice more, landing solid hits on the Verity ship in the time it took the missiles to close.

Seconds before impact, Dash triggered the new distortion grid, another retrofit to the Archetype.

A powerful gravity pulse, similar to the output of the distortion-cannon, erupted from the mech. Dash had reverse-polarized it, so instead of becoming an instantaneous gravitational hole in space, it became a towering peak—one that the approaching missiles suddenly had to climb.

Sentinel fired up the point-defense battery and blasted apart the missiles, now slowed to a relative crawl by the presence of a new and drastic gravity field. One slipped through and detonated close to the Archetype, flash-searing its armor, but doing little else.

Dash aimed the Archetype at the Verity fleet. It had slowed, trying to keep a decent stand-off distance from the Cygnus fleet, but Benzel and Wei-Ping were having none of that. They'd driven their squadrons hard, plunging into a general engagement with the enemy ships. That meant the plan had taken them as far as it could; at this point, the battle was no longer about plans, but about the multitude of small, deadly vignettes playing out as the two fleets tore away at one another.

For a moment, Dash just listened to his fleet's general channel.

"—to your left flank, engage as you pass—"

"—shit, we've lost attitude control—!"

"—veer to starboard, you're getting too close—!"

"—got him, look at that bastard spin—"

"NO—!"

The last was a scream that was suddenly cut off. At the same time Dash saw one of the A Squadron ships blown apart in massive explosion, probably a reactor containment breach. He winced. The heads-up told him it was the Star Wind, another of their newly built frigates. She had been mostly crewed by recent arrivals at the Forge who had naval or shipboard experience.

Shit.

Benzel's voice cut through the chatter, the excited shouts, the screams.

"All units, stay on plan! Wei-Ping, it looks like they're trying to concentrate on us, so execute maneuver Tango! And keep this channel clear!"

Maneuver Tango, a flanking sweep, would bring Wei-Ping's B Squadron boring in from the left. Several ships detached themselves from the main Verity force to block their approach and began pumping out missiles at a terrifying rate. It forced the Retribution to focus her main and secondary batteries, along with her point-defense systems, on the incoming projectiles. That left the Verity free to follow up with rapid-fire pulse-cannons, which began pounding the Retribution and her consorts.

Dash raced in, Leira following. He targeted a missile cruiser firing at the Retribution and fired the dark-lance. The beams punched into the cruiser's hull, but it kept up its ferocious rate of fire, apparently willing to die if it meant the rest of the Verity fleet could decimate the Herald and Benzel's squadron—

A colossal explosion ripped through a second missile cruiser off to the starboard flank of the one Dash had been attacking. Debris whipped past the Archetype at breathtaking velocities.

"What the hell—" Dash started, but Sentinel cut him off.

"That was the result of an impact from one of the ship-killer weapons, fired by Wei-Ping."

"Oh. Well, that worked, didn't it?"

"Exceedingly well, yes."

Dash turned his attention back to the other missile cruiser. He pummeled it with dark-lance shots and loosed a barrage of missiles its battered point-defense systems were unable to stop.

Explosions rippled along the length of its hull, and its drive died, leaving it coasting along, more wreck than ship.

Dash glanced at Leira's progress. She'd slammed shots home into a frigate, then closed in and punched at it with the Swift, the massive fists ripping away hull plates amid spewing gouts of atmosphere. He swooped up and away from the battle to gain a better vantage and see where he could best apply the Archetype's power. On the way, he raced past the Rockhound, which had been pumping shots from her rail-gun at targets of opportunity; the Snow Leopard hung close by her, bolstering the smaller ships close-in defences with her own, even while blazing away with her pulse-cannons.

"Messenger, there are large contacts inbound from above the ecliptic plane"

Dash looked back at the threat indicator. Sure enough, three big ships had just translated into the system, and now stared down the minefield laid by the Horse Nebula and her consorts.

They were battleships. Three of them, and they didn't belong to the Verity.

They belonged to the Bright—and that meant a slew of powerful Golden tech had just entered the battle.

THE BRIGHT OPENED up on the mines, trying to punch a hole through the field so they could enter the battle. That couldn't happen. Each one of the Bright battleships outclassed the Herald or Retribution, albeit not by much—but it wouldn't take much to swing the battle.

Dash flung the Archetype toward the Bright ships. "Leira, on me! We need to stop those damned things, or at least slow them down until the rest of the fleet is done with the Verity and can regroup!"

"I'm right behind you, Dash!"

The two mechs charged headlong, side-by-side, toward the looming Bright ships. On impulse, Dash slowed as they approached their side of the minefield. Leira immediately pulled ahead.

"Dash, what the hell?"

"Leira, grab a flash mine. Take it with you."

"Grab—oh. Right, got it."

Each clutching a flash mine, the Archetype and Swift powered up again, zooming directly toward the Bright squadron. The battleships shifted their fire from the mines to the mechs, heavy pulse-cannon batteries and petawatt lasers lashing out. The mechs' shields immediately stepped up their opacity, blocking the worst of the laser energy; it was another upgrade, one learned from hard experience the last time they'd faced the tremendously powerful light beams. It meant Dash and Leira lost some situational awareness, anything coming in from near-infrared to ultraviolet, but the mechs' scanners still worked through the shields. Dash flicked the heads-up to a schematic display, the battlespace now rendered down to icons moving around 3D axes.

It was like fighting through fog, Dash thought. Despite the fact the Archetype could gather data across the EM spectrum, and through her active scanners, it struck Dash that he'd still relied on what he could see with his eyes for a lot of piloting. It made no sense, but there it was.

He switched to firing solutions taken solely from the scanners then fired the dark-lance and more missiles. Incoming fire buffeted the Archetype; even the upgraded shield began approaching saturation.

"I'll take the one forward left, Leira. You go forward right."

"Got it."

Dash studied the display, veering the Archetype, watching as the relative position of the icons changed—

A heavy blow hammered the Archetype. A missile impact. Then another. Dash cried out at the second impact, one he felt down to his bones. Grimly, he drove on, closing the range, firing the dark-lance as fast as it would recycle.

The enormous bulk of the battleship suddenly appeared, filling the heads-up as the Archetype's shield died.

Close enough.

He flung the flash mine, at the same time accelerating hard the other way. The nearest battleship's point defenses lashed out, streams of shots like searching fingers seeking the mine, trying desperately to destroy it before it could—

Detonate, just like that.

The Archetype was hardened against the effects of the blast; even so, a power surge rippled through the mech, sending some of its systems into reboot mode. But the effect on the battleship was far worse. It was much too large and robust to be taken entirely offline by a single mine, but virtually all of her systems on the side facing the blast went abruptly dead.

Dash saw Leira executing much the same attack on her target, with much the same effect. She jackknifed the Swift and raced in to attack the battleship at close quarters, taking advantage of the sudden dormancy of half of her opponent.

What she didn't realize, though, was that the third battleship had maneuvered to get her full view and was about to open up with a full broadside of fire that could very well hurt the Swift—badly.

"Leira, get clear of there."

"What? Why—oh, shit!"

He saw the Swift suddenly power up, driving up relative to the battleships, trying to get away from the looming threat. Dash threw the Archetype's drive into combat over-power, racing over top of the battleship he'd attacked to help her, but he was too far away and just couldn't maneuver fast enough—

Something flashed by at high speed, swooping beneath the nearest Bright ship, charging on and pulling up beneath the as-yet undamaged one about to open fire on Leira. A torrent of pulse-cannon fire erupted from it as it raced under the enemy ship, raking it from stern to bow.

"Eat that, assholes," he heard someone say in a cheerful tone.

Dash immediately recognized Amy's voice, and his own ship, the Slipwing, now shredding the underside of the third Bright battleship. Explosions flung debris all around her, and for a moment, he thought she'd been lost in a huge, searing blast that must have marked an exploding missile battery. An instant later, though, the Slipwing raced back out of the glowing debris cloud, Amy letting out a fierce whoop of triumph.

"Yes! Dash, I love that I'm getting a mech, but not as much as I love this sweet little ship of yours!"

Dash couldn't help laughing at the absurdity of Amy's ferocious glee amid a raging battle, with the outcome still very much undecided. But they'd kept the three Bright battleships out of the immediate fight, at least for now.

Even damaged, the battleships remained a potent threat; he and Leira—and Amy, now—couldn't let them join the battle still raging near the shipyards. He flung the Archetype through a hard reversal and began another run. Shots flashed past the Archetype, some striking with heavy, jarring impacts, but he gritted his teeth and held course, firing the dark-lance as fast as he could. He wanted to fire the Archetype's big blast-cannon, tapping the raw power that could critically damage one of these battleships, but it took too long to charge up. Things were just happening too fast.

In war, no one ever slows down. Unless they're dead.

"Dash!" Benzel called out. "We've got the Verity on the run here! What's left of their fleet's trying to make a break for it!"

Dash snapped out a dark-lance shot then veered to swoop over his target's hull and slash at it with the power-sword. "Okay," he shot back. "Up to you if you chase them or not. But these three big bastards"—he winced as yet another shot slammed home, blasting another gouge in the Archetype's armor

—"they're still kicking, so you need to be ready for them if they break through."

"I would suggest when they break through is more correct," Sentinel cut in.

"Thanks for the vote of confidence."

"It is not that. I have detected new power signatures from an asteroid bordering the shipyard. They are Harbingers."

"What? Damn it, you've got to be kidding me!"

"I am not. Fortunately, however, they appear to be smaller, modified versions of the Harbinger-pattern mech in Verity service."

Dash scowled at the threat display. He saw the rising power emissions from the asteroid; the Harbingers must have been stored there, and their crews had finally arrived to power them up and get them into action.

He took a deep breath as the Bright battleship receded behind him, sporadic fire reaching after him from it. "Okay, Benzel, let whoever's running away from you keep going—the flash mines will thin them out, I guarantee it. But Leira and I have to take on this new problem, which means these three battleships are going to be coming your way."

"We did beat them up some for you," Leira put in as the Swift fell into formation with the Archetype. "I think one of them is nearly dead in space."

"You guys do what you have to do," Benzel replied. "We'll take care of the rest."

Dash had to smile at the former Gentle Friend's confident tone. He knew that the Cygnus fleet had been beaten up, as Leira put it, as badly as the Bright battleships. The battle was still far from won, and if some other major threat appeared, they probably wouldn't be able to handle it.

"Dash," Sentinel said. "The Verity Harbingers are fully powered up."

Dash glanced at the heads-up. "They haven't launched yet. Looks like we're going to be able to catch them on that rock of theirs. Leira, when was the last time you were in a real knock-down, drag-out brawl?"

"About a month before I met you. Three assholes decided they wanted my table in a bar on Passage—you know, that one near the helium-3 storage plant?"

"I want to hear the whole story. Meantime, though, when we mix it up with these Harbingers, just remember that."

"Where the hell am I going to find a giant bottle of hooch to smash over one of their heads?"

This time, Dash actually laughed out loud.

DASH TACKLED A HARBINGER, slamming into it headlong, driving back against the side of a storage bunker squatting on the asteroid's rocky surface. The recoil sent the Archetype bouncing back into space. The asteroid's gravity was too low to hold onto the mechs, so as the wild melee raged, they'd be flung into space, then power themselves back down into the fight.

Six against two—not good odds. But the Verity apparently piloting the Harbingers had probably never seen a real, down-

and-dirty fight, much less ever been in one. Dash and Leira quickly found their best tactic was to get their opponents embroiled in a close-up fracas on the asteroid's surface, and then try to keep them there—

Something slammed into the Archetype as it touched back down, spinning the mech sideways, knocking it forward at the same time. Dash caught himself, the Archetype's massive hands pulverising rock as he halted his fall; at the same time, he kicked back and got a solid, satisfying slam of contact in return. The Harbinger pitched forward, one leg driven out from under it. Dash rolled aside, striking out with a fist. All of his movements were smoothly turned into an intricate interplay of actuators, joints, thrusters, and even the main drive. It meant he could concentrate on doing what he did best—kicking the shit out of some bad guys.

Another Harbinger appeared, lining up a pulse-cannon shot. Dash grabbed the Harbinger that had almost fallen on top of him and heaved, pulling it up to shield him just as the pulse-cannon opened up. A couple of shots clipped the Archetype, but the rest squarely struck the Harbinger he'd grabbed as a shield. He flung the enemy mech at the one that had just shot; it was an easy dodge for the enemy, but it prevented the Verity pilot from firing again. That gave Dash the few seconds he needed to launch himself at the second Harbinger, while it struggled to stabilize itself about fifty meters above the rocky surface.

The Archetype crashed into the Harbinger, briefly shoving it back, until its drive kicked in. The Verity pilot apparently decided to try and slam Dash back against the asteroid, powering up the mech's drive to combat overpower. Dash responded in kind, and the Archetype quickly won the shoving match—it was just bigger, and more massive and powerful than the slender Harbinger. Reddish light flared around both mechs as they rose from the surface, out of the gloomy shadow of the asteroid and back into the ruddy sunlight.

The Harbinger punched, a solid hit that caused warnings to flare across the heads-up. The Archetype's left hip actuator went offline. Dash cursed as he struck back. Such a loss of mobility could be fatal in a fight like this.

"Sentinel!"

"I am aware and am attempting to bypass a damaged motivator circuit."

Dash left her to it and concentrated on taking this Harbinger out of the fight for good. He drove a fist into its head, and another into its armored torso. The plates buckled under the blow, and one spun off into space. Dash didn't hesitate, ignoring a glancing blow that still took the Archetype's point-defense system offline, and driving his fist into the gap left by the missing plate. It sank deep into the mech's internals.

He began to pull and rip, tearing away at anything he could grab.

The Harbinger desperately shoved at him, trying to get away. A second later, something vital failed, and the enemy mech went dead.

Dash kept digging away at its mechanical guts anyway. He finally wrenched off the Harbinger's entire chest plate, flung it aside, and smashed at the internal workings again and again.

That included the pilot's capsule, which crumpled under the blows.

Dash literally hammered the capsule flat.

He spun away from the wreck and turned back to the battle. The Archetype had lifted a good two klicks off the asteroid's surface, where the Swift still fought a pair of Harbingers. For a few seconds, Dash just watched her. She fought with a style and grace that was stark contrast to his own more brutal, beat-'em-down approach to brawls. Leveraging the Swift's lithe power and natural quickness, she spun, punched, kicked, dodged, and kicked again. The Harbingers were clumsy by comparison, lumbering at her, their attacks uncoordinated; for every blow they managed to land on her, she drove home three or four of her own.

Dash powered up the thrusters and drove the Archetype back toward the surface. As the red sun went behind the asteroid again, there was one more Harbinger still operational, apparently determined to line up a firing solution with its pulse or chest cannon. The Harbinger pilot would have to be desperate indeed to use the chest-cannon, as the close range would destroy everyone nearby—friend and foe.

Dash kicked in the main drive, deployed the power-sword, and came thundering down on the Harbinger like a meteor.

A tremendous shock rattled the Archetype deep to its Dark Metal bones. It spun the mech around, momentarily turning the view on the heads-up into a blur. Dash fought to correct and regain attitude control—and where was the Harbinger he'd just hit, was it about to fire—?

He jammed a foot—actually feet, since it looked like Sentinel had just managed to get the balky hip actuator working again—against the asteroid; the momentum of the mech kept it plunging along, gouging rock from the surface with a cascade of sparks that shot off into space. At the same time, the thrusters kicked in. He regained control and reacquired the Harbinger about a hundred meters away, dreadfully certain it was about to fire and kill them all.

But it toppled back instead, the power-sword having severed it through the waist. He jetted the Archetype back to it, the power-sword raised—found himself looking straight down the muzzle of its chest-cannon—and slashed across chest and cannon, ripping both open.

"Dash!"

He glanced up from the fallen Harbinger. It was Leira.

The Swift hovered over two broken Harbingers, debris and pulverized rock drifting around it. Dash saw the mech had been battered so badly entire armor plates were gone, as was one foot, and one entire forearm.

"You look like hell," Dash said.

"You don't look so good yourself."

Dash opened his mouth to shoot something back but recoiled as something drifted into the heads-up imagery.

It was a Verity, her face contorted in stunned horror, globules of fluid leaking from her broken body. He glanced down and saw that he'd cut the pilot's capsule of the Harbinger open, letting her corpse drift free.

"Dash, look out!"

He turned at Leira's warning. The first Harbinger they'd

taken out of the battle had partly risen, its power output soaring to a spike—either some sort of overcharged shot from its chest cannon, or its reactor was about to blow. Dash didn't hesitate. He lunged and drove the power-sword out, then slammed it straight through the mech's head.

A hissing shriek briefly flooded the comm, a howling burst of Golden machine-language. It went on for a second or two, pierce Dash's senses like a storm, then stopped.

"The Verity pilot of that Harbinger was clearly dead," Sentinel said. "That final attempt at an attack must have been an onboard Golden AI."

"Yeah. The Verity should have let them fight," Dash replied, once more thinking of the unpredictable tactics of the Golden drone he'd recently fought near the Forge.

"Arrogant jerks," Leira said. "They must have figured they could do a better job."

Taking in the scattered remains of the Harbingers, and the debris-strewn battlespace around the asteroid, Dash shook his head. "Well, they were wrong. But if there are AIs on board these Harbingers, they might still be kicking like this one was. Let's make sure they're all really dead."

Far above the asteroid, searing flashes continued to ripple through space as the battle between the battered Cygnus fleet and the two Bright battleships raged on. Dash saw plumes of glowing gas, heard desperate shouts across the comm, and launched himself back toward the battle, Leira falling in alongside him. Before they even got anywhere near weapons range, though, the flashes and cries died, and the space ahead went dark and silent once more.

A long moment passed. Dash wanted to call for Benzel, but he also didn't, in case he never got an answer.

Silence.

Okay, Dash thought, this might be bad. Better get ready for it. It might be very, very bad.

"Hey, Dash, you guys done playing around down there yet?" Benzel said, his voice booming across the comm. "We might've won this battle, but we've got lots of work to do yet!"

22

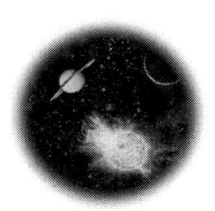

"—AND we can now run two, simultaneous fabrication lines for mechs," Custodian said. "So, in summary, with the increased capacity given to the Forge by the new Q-core, manufacturing output will be increased at least fifteen percent."

Dash nodded and looked around the Command Center where everyone was gathered. They'd already done their initial post-battle briefing, immediately upon arrival back at the Forge and even before showering or eating. Dash wanted to capture as much information as they could, while it was still fresh in all their minds. Now, after cleaning up, eating, and getting some rest, they'd taken time to do a more thorough analysis of what had happened.

"So Sentinel tells me it's going to be awhile before we can really appreciate what we accomplished. There's so much scrap and salvage from the battle—not to mention a bunch of half-built

Verity ships—that we're going to be working to recover it all for at least a couple of weeks," he said.

"How many of those partly built Verity ships do you think we'll be able to get into service?" Leira asked.

Viktor scrubbed a hand through his hair. "We're not sure yet. There seem to be enough unassembled components to get at least four or five of them completed. And Custodian says we can probably reverse engineer and make the missing components from most of the rest. But it's going to be a lot of work."

"Yeah, it's not like we've got a whole shipyard crew to put to work," Wei-Ping said. "And I don't know how much use the Verity construction drones and the like are going to be. Getting them cleaned up of countermeasures and pressed into service might be more trouble than it's worth."

"We might be better off just making our own drones and using them," Leira offered.

That was a popular idea at first—but then Benzel crossed his arms in a sign of contemplation. "No matter what we do, it's going to be dangerous work. If there's anything left of the Verity, they're going to want blood."

"And the Golden might have something to say about it, too," Wei-Ping said.

Dash nodded. "That's why we're moving the Forge into that system. We just gave our enemies a bloody nose, and you're right, they're going to want to hit back. But we hurt them badly, so they might think twice about taking on our fleet and the Forge."

Viktor stepped forward. "By the time we get there, we should have all the new Forge weapons online. We're giving priority to the rail-guns." The big holo-image changed to a schematic of the Forge, with twelve stations, spaced equidistant around its equator, highlighted. "Rail-guns are pretty good on ships, but fired from the Forge—well, we've got almost unlimited power for them, and we don't have to worry much about recoil. Custodian and I figure they'll probably be the Forge's deadliest weapon system, at least at closer ranges."

"Good," Dash said. "I like it. Let's work up some tactics and procedures to try and lure enemy ships into range. If we can disable them by punching holes through their armor, but otherwise keeping them or less intact, we might have more ships to add to the fleet."

Wei-Ping nodded and made notes on a data-pad.

"Okay, I think that just about covers everything," Dash said. "The fleet should be mostly back online." He glanced at Benzel. "You figure another couple of days?"

"For the Herald, Retribution, and four other ships, yeah. For the rest—well, we took some serious damage, so the rest of the fleet, the ships that survived, anyway, is going to take at least a week."

Dash gave a somber nod. The ships that survived. There were more of those than he'd feared going into the battle, but not as many as he'd have liked. They lost five, either completely destroyed, or so damaged they were useful only as scrap now.

But ships could be replaced, and would be. Soon, too, thanks to the Forge's growing fabrication capacity. For the people they'd lost, it was a different story.

On impulse, Dash called up a list of names on the big display.

Their dead. One hundred and fourteen of them.

Everyone assembled just stared at the list. Nobody said anything.

There was nothing to say.

"I'm always surprised it's not a lot hotter this close to the molds," Leira said.

Dash nodded. "Yeah. Something about Dark Metal actually having a low melting point—which seems really weird to me, considering how we use it—and a bunch of heat-shielding around the molds. Custodian told me all about it once, but it got pretty technical."

"And you're just not a very technical guy."

"Actually, for a guy who lives in space and flies ships for a living, I'm really not. I prefer to fight."

Leira smiled, and for a moment they just watched streams of glowing metal being poured into molds, a mesmerizing display of automated purpose.

Dash found his gaze caught on the glowing metal, but his thoughts started to roam.

"Hey," Leira hissed. "Look."

Dash did. Off to one side of the fabrication plant, he saw Amy and Conover walking together and talking. He exchanged a smile with Leira.

"That's kind of adorable, actually," he said.

Leira nodded. "Yeah, it is," she said, her gaze lingering on him for just a brief moment—one that he felt.

Another of those impulses. Dash put his arm around Leira, hugged her against him for a moment, then let her go.

Hard on the heels of that came an, oh shit, what did I just do? moment. He braced himself for a backlash, outrage, Leira to storm off—

But she didn't. He glanced at her sidelong and just saw her smiling at the pouring metal.

They wandered away from the fabrication plant and into one of the big, adjacent docking bays. The Slipwing was here, with yet more battle damage being repaired, more upgrades installed. Beyond her, outside the Forge, he saw the Herald, surrounded by vac suited figures, sparks of welding glare flaring and dying as her own wounds were healed.

"Why did you do it?" Leira suddenly asked, looking up at Dash with a cryptic smile.

"Do what?"

She put her arm around him, held it there, then let it drop. Her smile didn't fade. "That."

He thought about it for a minute, this time choosing his words with care. He might be naturally impulsive, a do-something-now, worry-about-consequences-later kind of guy, but he really was careful about the truly important things. And this was a truly important thing.

"Someday, we're going to win this war," he finally said.

"And?" Leira's brow lifted in a challenging way.

He shrugged. "And, who knows? I mean, when the war is done and over, we'll still have lives to live, right? That even goes for the Messenger." He meant to go on, but decided that was enough, and just ended on a shrug and a turn toward Leira.

She said nothing and just looked back into space, toward the Herald. He could sense her breathing suddenly change, but that was all.

Damn his mouth. Had he just gone somewhere he'd never been meant to go?

Something touched his hand. It was hers.

Outside, in space, it was utterly cold and dark. That suddenly contrasted with where they stood, each in the presence of the other, their hands finally touching. Here, it was very warm.

For a few minutes, at least.

DASH, SENTINEL, LEIRA, VIKTOR, and CONOVER will return in RAGE OF NIGHT, coming April 2020!

For more updates on this series, be sure to join the Facebook Group, "J.N. Chaney's Renegade Readers."

STAY UP TO DATE

Join the conversation and get updates on new and upcoming releases in the Facebook group called "JN Chaney's Renegade Readers." This is a hotspot where readers come together and share their lives and interests, discuss the series, and speak directly to J.N. Chaney and his co-authors.

https://www.facebook.com/groups/jnchaneyreaders/

He also post updates, official art, and other awesome stuff on his website and you can also follow him on Instagram, Facebook, and Twitter.

For email updates about new releases, as well as exclusive promotions, visit his website and sign up for the VIP mailing list. Head there now to receive a free copy of *The Other Side of Nowhere*.

Stay Up To Date

https://www.jnchaney.com/the-messenger-subscribe

Enjoying the series? Help others discover *The Messenger* series by leaving a review on Amazon.

ABOUT THE AUTHORS

J. N. Chaney is a USA Today Bestselling author and has a Master's of Fine Arts in Creative Writing. He fancies himself quite the Super Mario Bros. fan. When he isn't writing or gaming, you can find him online at **www.jnchaney.com**.

He migrates often, but was last seen in Las Vegas, NV. Any sightings should be reported, as they are rare.

Terry Maggert is left-handed, likes dragons, coffee, waffles, running, and giraffes; order unimportant. He's also half of author Daniel Pierce, and half of the humor team at Cledus du Drizzle.

With thirty-one titles, he has something to thrill, entertain, or make you cringe in horror. Guaranteed.

Note: He doesn't sleep. But you sort of guessed that already.

Made in the USA
Middletown, DE
22 April 2020